NADINE LITTLE

Better the Devil You Know

LITTLE PUBLISHING

Sign up to my mailing list to get an exclusive bonus scene by scanning the QR code at the back of the book. Members of my mailing list get other free stuff and behind-the-scenes material.

Members are always the first to hear about my new books and discounts.

Join now!

'We are all searching for someone
whose demons play well with ours.'
Heidi R. Kling

'The devil doesn't come dressed
in a red cape and pointy horns.
He comes as everything you've ever wished for.'
Tucker Max, *Assholes Finish First*

1

Cabaret Voltaire in Edinburgh's Old Town is great for when I want to feel like an attractive woman instead of a blob of knitted cardigan hunched over a keyboard. Hot sex in the club's bathroom, then back home alone to unwind in bed with a mug of hot chocolate.

Not a bad night.

Real relationships are for normal people who live normal lives and see normal things. What's the point if I can never tell the truth? Better to scratch the itch and move on. No need for names. And while I fancy a bit of vanilla every now and again, most men aren't into what I'm into. Which is a shame.

I scan the darkened crowd, my hip propped on a pillar of rough stone. Coloured beams flicker through smoke and dance on the brick ceiling. People crowd around the bright lights and glass of the bar to my left. I sip my unicorn juice cocktail. The Buckfast bubbles tickle my nose and slip, syrupy-sweet, down my throat with the raspberry gin and the tartness of lime.

I usually drink tap water, but my book sales finally picked up and my royalties arrived today. I deserve a little celebration.

A woman in the corner booth tosses her head, her sharp laugh cutting through the thud of bass and the shout of voices.

Other women in tiny dresses perch on the stools and cram onto the brown-leather couch, all of them with tasteful make-up, sparkly eyes and enough jewellery to pay my heating bill for the next decade. The ones not lucky enough to be sitting pretty on the furniture mill around in a forest of long, long legs.

Not that I'm jealous.

I glance at my much shorter legs and longer skirt. The green silk matches my eyes and swishes around my calf-high boots when I move. Charity shop bargains. My black lace top clings invitingly, though not as inviting as the flesh on show in the corner booth.

Bet none of them have to wear a push-up bra to appear larger than an A-cup.

I tug at the offending garment, the underwire digging into my ribs, then gulp my cocktail. I strain to see past the posse of ladies to the person lavished by their attention.

Some rich but blandly handsome investment banker? A local rock star? Anyone can pop up in the historic basement vaults of the North Bridge.

Goosebumps prickle my arms at the familiar caress of heat tracing my body. The burn of its attention. I choke on bubbles, and meet the gaze of the creature watching me, my vision blurred by tears.

It's been almost a year. I was starting to hope they'd all returned to whatever hole they crawled out of.

The women part like branches in the wind to expose the back wall of the club. A thing that looks like a man sprawls on the sofa, legs spread wide, flanked by his twittering and bejewelled fan club. High cheekbones, blond hair swept to the side and flopping over one eyebrow, slim hips in tight-fitting jeans.

Dangerous.

His shirt shows a triangle of smooth skin and frames the hollow of his throat. A woman with hair the same crimson as her dress slides her fingers between his buttons to stroke his stomach. He captures her hand and kisses her palm, never taking his focus off me. She swoons in her seat, her face flushed. He stands and glides through his gaggle of ladies, who pet him as he passes, but let him go, their expressions hungry.

I find myself half-way across the floor before I stop, my forgotten drink slopping across my knuckles. The man smirks at me, and my stomach flips.

"That's far enough," I say when he's a metre away.

I wouldn't usually let one get this close, but the packed club offers safety. For now.

"Reiley MacEwen, author and Diviner," he says, the weight of his stare brushing me from top to toe with its intrusive sizzle of warmth. "I knew the latter, of course, from the content of your books."

Diviner? Why does he think I'm a fortune-teller, or someone who finds water with a stick?

But wait…

I goggle at him, then herd my face into an intelligent expression. "You've read my books?"

His smile widens, flashing perfect, white teeth and glinting in eyes as blue as a husky's.

That's what the normals will see. Granted, he is the most human-looking of his species, just like my aunt's book described. The other kinds I've met had lots to hide—wings and tails and lumps and such—but he's only shielding his eyes and his mouth. If I stare too long, the illusion wavers, makes me dizzy, but I can never penetrate it.

Even I can't see the truth unless he shows me.

"I don't read trash," he says, the smile flowing into another smirk.

Tension sings across my shoulders. I bristle but force myself to relax. I squeeze the drink in my hand and think about throwing it in his face.

He laughs. "Oh, you didn't like that. Are you going to go for your little knife? Where is it—strapped to your thigh or tucked in your boot?"

"What are you talking about? Why would I have a knife?"

He takes a step and I retreat, my back hitting the rough stone pillar where my night started so pleasantly. Ice cubes clink on glass.

"I could search for it." His eyes trace a path of heat and return to mine. "Slowly and in private."

His lips curve. A promise of sin and pleasure. Darkness and lust. Hot mouths, slick skin, silken muscle—

"Stop that," I say, and my breath wobbles out.

"I'm not doing anything."

"The hell you aren't."

"It's not my fault you're attracted to me."

"I'm not attracted to a—" My teeth snap shut. "Why are you here?"

His smile splits into a grin. "You're untrained."

"Untrained in what?"

He performs another body scan, lingering on places he has no business lingering. I tell myself it's irritation flushing my cheeks and squirming in my belly.

"How intriguing," he says, finally back at my face.

He's a head taller than me, my gaze level with that glimpse of chest and collarbone. Muscled but sleek. He watches me with interest, his lashes so thick and dark, it's like he's wearing eyeliner.

Dammit, is he closer?

I sidle around the pillar and lean my shoulder on it, the picture of nonchalance while my heart bounces along my ribs.

"Look, mate," I say, and carefully sip my drink, the sherbet and egg white curdling in my stomach, "either answer a damn question or leave me—"

"Kade, why are you wasting time wiv her?" a voice purrs. An arm loops around his neck and a tall woman with straight blonde hair longer than her dress drapes herself against his side. "Come back to ze party."

The woman is all limbs and cheekbones, her plump lips the only fat on her. Not counting her massive tits, but I'm guessing they're mostly plastic.

A second woman cuddles into Kade's other side, poured into a maroon dress that looks great with her dark skin and hair. Delicate bruises bloom on the women's necks like the ghost of kisses.

I shiver, and my fingers flutter to my throat. Kade smirks, pulling the women tighter to him with a hand on their waists. I stare at his mouth, but frown at the floor when vertigo swoops from my head to my stomach.

I hate the wavering. How they hide what they are, but no one else can see it.

"You shouldn't hang around with him," I say to the women's expensive, strappy shoes. "It's not safe."

The blonde laughs—the same laugh I heard earlier. Sharp

enough to pierce to the bone.

"You are jealous, yes?" She slips her hand in Kade's open collar. "For you are safe. Too plain for his taste."

"And she's got no tits," brays the second woman. "I've seen bigger midge bites."

Kade sucks on his full bottom lip, his eyes glittering. My shoulders hunch, but I force them back and stare him down.

"You don't know what he is," I say.

He cocks his head. "Are you going to tell them what I am, Reiley MacEwen?"

"Not my place," I mumble. "*Kade.*"

"And they wouldn't believe you."

"No," I sigh.

The two women nuzzle his neck. Their hands slide down his long, lean torso to meet—perfectly choreographed—at his crotch, their fingers framing the bulge in his jeans.

I whip my eyes up to his smirking face.

"Only a coward preys on sleeping women," I say through gritted teeth.

"That's an old wives' tale. My women are very much awake when I prey on them." His grin flashes in the smoke and lights. "But maybe you shouldn't fall asleep."

"Is that a threat?"

"Perhaps I'll visit you in your dreams."

He can't do that… can he? The book never mentioned it.

"I think you'll dream of me tonight," he says to my silence.

"I'd rather eat my own eyeballs."

His lips twist. "While my brethren would help you do that, I'm built for the gentler tortures."

He tips his head back, his eyes half-lidded. His breath shudders out.

Oh, Christ. The women are massaging him through his jeans.

Time to go.

I force myself to look at the two ladies kissing his neck, and try again. "If you ever lose weight, feel lethargic or become anaemic, get as far away from him as you can. Please."

They ignore me, intent on their ministrations.

Kade purrs low in his throat. "It's been a pleasure talking to you, Reiley MacEwen. I hope we meet again."

"I don't," I snap. "Leave me alone and I'll leave you alone."

His laughter chases me from the humid club into the chilly streets of the Old Town. Leaves scuttle along the cobblestones. I huddle inside my jacket, my hands buried in my pockets.

Edinburgh in October—biting wind and frost.

I flag a taxi. An expense I shouldn't indulge, but I can't face the forty-minute walk to Duddingston around Arthur's Seat. Especially not tonight. I settle into the back of the black cab, the driver content to leave me in quiet contemplation. Every few minutes, I glance out the rear window.

Kade is the first of his kind I've ever bumped into, but if he's anything like the rest of his 'brethren' I've had the misfortune of meeting, it won't be long before he tries to kill me.

I twist my upper body to peer through the glass. No vehicles follow for longer than a few streets. By the time we turn onto Duddingston Low Road, the night behind us is empty. I relax into the seat, replaying our conversation.

What did Kade mean by author *and* Diviner? Why did he expect me to have a knife? A knife has never helped me before.

And, perhaps most importantly, what the hell is an incubus demon doing in my city?

2

I sob a name. His name—Kade.

Soft lips brand my neck and trail to my breast. Muscles glisten in candlelight. Shadows cloak his body, giving glimpses of a wicked, smirking mouth, his flat stomach, the line of a hip. Scorching breath brushes my belly then lower to my thighs, spread wide. A chuckle drifts from the blackness as I writhe for him. Clever fingers stroke and tease, so close to where I ache. Not close enough. He arches above me, his face hidden. Only his eyes glint in the dark. I tilt my pelvis, a begging noise in my throat. The heat of his gaze throbs between my legs.

"Is this what you want?" he purrs.

"Yes! Yes… *No!*" I shout, and claw myself awake.

Damp sheets twist around my waist and I thud onto the carpet, narrowly missing the bedside cabinet. My heart pounds in the hollow of my throat and pulses to my fingers and toes, swelling in some places more than others. Chill air dries the sweat beneath my flannel pyjamas. I scrape my hair from my eyes and throw myself back on the bed with a huff, the metal bars of the headboard thumping the wall.

It's been the same for the last bloody week—Kade in every dream. Touching me. Whispering naughty things in my ear. The feel and scent of him confusing my senses. Then, just as he's about to seal the deal, I wake up alone, horny and unsatisfied.

Goddamn incubus demon.

If I shag him in my sleep, will he have a hold over me? If he has the power to manipulate my dreams, who knows what he can do. Or am I only dreaming of him because he planted the idea in my head?

It was easier when demons were just trying to kill me.

The book my aunt found said nothing about dream manipulation for incubus demons, and I remember every word, though I've not read it since her death. It's packed away in the attic, the sight of it too painful a reminder.

I slide out of bed and change into my favourite, pea-soup-coloured jumper that hits mid-thigh, pairing it with thick socks and leggings. My bones slowly warm as I click the kettle on and potter around the kitchen. I inhale the steam from my cardamom-flavoured coffee, the mug cuddled in my hands, a hot water bottle tucked in my armpit. Bright sunlight turns the leaves outside to gold and bronze and slants across my writing desk squeezed in the breakfast nook. The boiler in the corner coughs and rattles to life, liquid gurgling in the ancient pipes.

I'll treat myself to an hour of heat. I'm not made of money. My royalties barely cover the bills despite my strict budgeting. Maybe if I have another good month or two, save up a bit, I can replace it. Fix the roof. Plaster the crack that lets the damp seep in. I love my little cottage, but I'd love it a lot more if it were warm and dry.

My wooden writing chair creaks under my bum, the pillow almost flat. I rest my feet on the hot water bottle and open my laptop, clicking on Scrivener, my writing programme of choice, instead of my book sales dashboard.

I've limited myself to checking my figures once a week and only after I've done some writing. Nothing like increasing sales to give you inspiration.

I start a new character sheet, an idea whirling in my brain for the next book in my *Demon* series. Working title *Demon Lover*, where the antagonist is also the love interest and the protagonist hates that she's fallen for him, fights it as long as she can before succumbing in a spectacular sex scene. I type the distinguishing characteristics—blue eyes, blond hair, gorgeous but arrogant, full lips, perfect body. Not based on a real guy, of course. Purely my imagination. I draft a quick outline, then return to editing my fifth novel, *Demon Fire*.

The books keep me sane. They contain the truth masked as fiction. My life and soul poured into the words. When I'm writing, I don't feel so alone. I'm not a freak. I'm just an author with a vivid imagination.

Write what you know, they say.

I was ten when I saw my first demon. It looked like a hunched man shuffling down the street. I tugged on my mum's hand and asked what was wrong with his face. She shushed me, hustling us along the pavement, but the man's eyes stayed on me. I asked my mum why he was blurry. She shot him an apologetic glance before we disappeared around the corner.

He tried to drown me in my paddling pool.

I Google 'Diviner', but get nothing except articles on occult rituals and searching for water. It's not like they're going to have a website. Are they like me? Kade said I was untrained, implying there are people out there who train people like me. Who *are* trained. I always assumed there were others, stumbling around, desperate for someone to believe them, frantic to avoid being detained or sectioned. But I never thought they'd be organised. Or maybe Diviner is just a demonic term for people who can see what demons are in the wavering they hide behind. I definitely know what's going to happen in my future whenever I see it.

Pain.

God, I'd love it if Diviner turned out to be the name for a shadowy organisation of demon hunters, especially if Kade becomes a nuisance. He knows who I am. He doesn't know where I live, but no doubt he's searching for me.

I was thirteen when the second demon found me. By that point, I'd forgotten the old man. The second demon was young. Good-looking. The wavering covered its face, hands and back. I stared so long, I almost threw up.

He showed me exactly what the wavering hid.

The police thought someone had assaulted me with a garden rake. They dismissed my description of a monster with claws and wings and black horns sprouting from a ridged brow as the babble of a trauma victim.

At fifteen, I ignored the third, thinking that would save me. It didn't.

I worried I was schizophrenic. Even my parents thought I was nuts. My aunt rescued me in more ways than one when she took me in. She couldn't see demons, but she took my word for it. Her support was life-changing after I'd spent my formative years being attacked and disbelieved.

Pity I couldn't save her, when it mattered.

The doorbell rings and I leap off my seat, slamming my knee on the underside of my desk and spilling my cardamom coffee in a brown wash across the battered wood. Liquid patters on the tile floor.

"Tits!" I gasp, clutching my throbbing knee and hopping around the kitchen.

Someone hammers on the front door.

Kade. It's Kade. He's found me. He'll sink black talons into my flesh like the rest of his species and—

Shut up, you fool, and answer the bloody door. Demons aren't polite enough to knock.

Instead of a smirking monster, a rosy-cheeked man greets me with a smile and a, "Hullo hen, how you keepin' the day?" A green Asda delivery van sits in my short, leaf-strewn drive.

I coax my heart rate to normal limits and return the man's smile, accepting my crate of cheap, own-brand groceries. I scrawl my signature on his tablet.

"See you next week then, lass," he says and, whistling, hops into his van.

I never remember his name even though he's delivered my food shopping for months. Same with the postie or the Amazon driver, and it's not because I don't see them regularly—I order everything in.

Even men.

I might need to get some sex delivered since I won't be returning to the clubs anytime soon. Stupid demons. Stupid Kade.

I start to shut my door, but catch a glimpse of fluorescent-pink leggings spiriting their owner up my driveway as the Asda van disappears onto Old Church Lane in a puff of exhaust.

Shit. Maybe she hasn't seen me. I can pretend I'm not in.

Crap, she's waving.

"Coo-ee, Reiley," she says, wiggling her fingers and blinding me with the sunlight reflecting off her diamond ring. "I hoped you were home."

I paste on a smile that feels like a grimace, and push the door wider. "Hello, Mrs Dounray. Can I help you with something?"

A pink headband circles her perfect, blonde bob, matching the leggings and a belt cinching her tiny waist beneath her daffodil-yellow top. Her puff of a chihuahua trots at her feet. He curls his lip, and barks.

"Shush, Chesington," Mrs Dounray says absently, failing to hide her own lip curl as her gaze travels from the ragged hem of my jumper to the hole in my sock. "Reiley, dear, I wondered if you'd noticed the missing tiles on your roof. You really should get them fixed."

"Yes, Mrs Dounray," I say through my teeth. "I'm saving up."

"Not to mention the state of your garden. I see it when I'm doing my morning ablutions. It's really not in keeping with the rest of the neighbourhood."

"I'll get right on it, Mrs Dounray."

"I can't imagine why you want to rattle around this draughty old cottage. You really should sell, dear. It must be a burden for one such as yourself."

For someone poor, she means.

I swallow a growl. "The cottage belonged to my aunt."

"But, dear, she's been gone five years now. My husband and I will give you a fair price. Goodness, we'd take it off your hands tomorrow. We've always wanted to build an extension. That would free you up to move somewhere more in your price range"—she coughs delicately into her hand—"like Sighthill."

The damn neighbours have been itching to bulldoze my cottage since my aunt died.

"No, thank you, Mrs Dounray," I say minus any hint of snarl. "I need to get back to work now."

She sniffs. "Writing isn't a real job, dear. Clearly, it doesn't pay the bills."

Her chihuahua fixes his black, beady eyes on me, cocks his leg and pisses on my flagstones.

"Come along now, Chesington," she says, tugging on his lead.

They both flounce off with their noses in the air. I shut my door a little harder than necessary.

Condescending old bat.

After unpacking my shopping, I reclaim my seat at my writing desk and finally allow myself to check my book sales. A fizz of excitement bubbles in my chest.

This could be it. My books finally taking off, gaining traction. A following of eager fans who'll buy everything I publish until the end of time.

I frown at the graph on the screen. That can't be right. I refresh the browser. No change. My fizz of excitement sizzles to a clod of ash.

Refresh. Refresh.

The bar graph, showing a healthy twenty to thirty sales a day through September, has dropped to nothing. Zero sales for the last week.

My heart stutters and my hand clenches in my jumper. I click through to my bookshelf where my four published novels are listed for sale. Next to each one, a word in black capital letters stares back at me.

"Blocked," I pant. "What the fuck is blocked?"

I pull up my emails, though I check them regularly and there was nothing to say 'sorry Reiley, we've cut your only source of income. Have a lovely day.'

There must be some mistake. They can't block me without

justification.

No new messages.

My shaking fingers stab the keys to take me to the retailer's contact page. I slap my forehead and skip back to my emails, expanding the drop-down list.

One message in the spam folder, sent a week ago by the self-publishing platform. My heart drops. The terms 'copyright infringement notice' and 'removed availability of your books' swim in front of my eyes.

Copyright? I own the damn copyright. I've never infringed on anyone. They're my original work. This has to be some kind of admin error.

Or I'm ruined.

3

The polite response to my semi-hysterical email the next day confirms it's not a mistake. A third party has raised copyright concerns on all of my books. *All* of my books. The self-publishing platform was happy to inform me that they don't involve themselves in these disputes, but they do remove the books until the matter is resolved. They suggested I contact my solicitor. They helpfully included the details of the claimant.

"But I've never even heard of her," I sob into the phone to the poor man who's been listening to me blubber for the last half hour. "I mean, who the hell is Lilith Rakshasa? I searched her name and her email, littledevilbooks@zmail.com, but got nothing."

"I understand this is distressing, Ms MacEwen, but we're here to support you," says the very nice and calm Spencer Cunningham, an independent lawyer from IP For Free.

No way could I have afforded a solicitor otherwise. Not with all my books in copyright jail because of some little witch with her panties in a twist.

I sniffle into my tissue, curled in bed beneath a mound of blankets to combat the chill. My stomach churns from stress and too much caffeine, the only thing I can swallow.

Who needs food and heat? Maybe I can nibble leaves from my back garden, like a slug.

"Are you absolutely certain there could be no infringement?" Spencer says gently. "Nothing you may have inadvertently used from your research or as a quote?"

"No," I say, forcing myself to sit up straighter in my heap of pillows when it comes out as a whine. "I haven't copied anyone. It's all my original work. I didn't need to do research because it's all true"—I clear my throat—"truly from my imagination."

Good job, Reiley. Let the lawyer think you're crazy.

"I'll have a look through the files you sent me, see if I can come up with anything that may be classed as an infringement," Spencer says, the sound of his pen scratching on paper filtering into my ear. "In the meantime, I suggest you contact the claimant directly—be professional—and ask for clarification of their concerns. I take it the retailer didn't provide any evidence from the third party?"

I sniff. "No, they didn't send me anything but the woman's information. What if she doesn't respond? The email says they need permission from both parties for the books to become available. What if she doesn't give her permission? Will my books never be put up for sale again?"

I rub my belly, a fresh burst of tears slipping down my cheeks.

What the hell will I do? Starting from scratch would take so long and feel like a failure. I love my demon books. They are me, the real me no one gets to see. My real life that people wouldn't understand beyond fiction. I'm unlikely to get a job beyond minimum wage. I have no qualifications. My planned degree in English died before it started after my parents had me detained in a psychiatric ward.

"Try not to worry, Ms MacEwen. There are several avenues we can pursue at this stage." Fabric rustles as Spencer shifts. "I should mention it's not uncommon for a takedown notice to be filed maliciously in order to damage an author's reputation. Is there any reason why this person could be targeting you?"

"But I don't even know her! I don't have enemies—"

My teeth snap shut.

Kade. *The sneaky arsehole.* Could he have provided false details? Little devil books—what a smug prick he is. Did no one verify the identity of the third party before they banished my books from the storefronts? How easy it would be for Kade to file a complaint. Seems he got bored searching for me and decided to destroy my livelihood, if not my life.

"It may not be personal, I'm afraid," Spencer continues. "Self-published authors are often victims of scammers because they're easy targets and don't have the protection of a large publishing house. In other cases, false claims are filed because the person was offended by the book's content or the author's political or religious views."

I have no political or religious views. I'm a hermit, for god's sake. And, okay, the contents of the books can get a little steamy, but that doesn't seem cause enough to inspire a stranger to file notice against me.

It must be Kade. Isn't Lilith some kind of female demon?

"How do I stop hi—her from blocking my books permanently?" I say, gripping my phone hard.

My tears dry in a wave of heat. Indignant fury tightens my shoulders and creaks through my jaw.

"Contact them in the first instance," Spencer says. "I'll start drafting a counter notice, which we can send to the retailer, depending on the claimant's response and if there is no response. Unfortunately, retailers aren't bound by the counter notice like internet service providers. They can, on rare occasions, ignore it. However, in my experience, they still tend to restore the content within ten days of filing the counter notice."

Ten days! Ten more days of no sales means an abysmal income for October, assuming people start buying my books again immediately. I already live frugally. What if they cut off my heat and electricity? No internet means no business.

Oh god, this is bad.

I slump into my pillows, my knees a blunt mound beneath the many blankets. "What if they ignore it? Or the person continues to accuse me of copyright infringement?"

"It's likely we would have to resolve the matter in court."

My gut flips. "How long would that take? Would my books stay blocked the whole time?"

"It could be a few months, I'm afraid. And the books would remain blocked if the retailer discards the counter notice."

I can't survive a few months of no sales. There's no mortgage on the cottage, but what am I supposed to eat—my notebook? Maybe I'll freeze to death first.

"But let's not get bogged down in what might happen," Spencer soothes while I spiral into a panic attack. "Message the claimant and send me your contact details—full name, email, mailing address—and I'll draft the counter notice while we wait for a response. Then we'll take it from there."

"So all my details will be on the notice? Does the claimant get a copy of that?"

"They usually do, yes."

Oh, hell no. What if this whole thing is a ploy for Kade to get my home address? Ruin my reputation, then leave me drowning in my own blood. Double whammy.

"Would a PO box be okay to use?" I say. "I don't want to give out my actual address."

"It's not ideal but, yes, that should be acceptable."

"Great. I'll have to get that set up, then I'll send you the details."

"Perfect. I have every hope this will be resolved to your satisfaction if no copyright infringement has actually occurred."

"Thank you," I say, getting teary again. "Thank you so much."

"It's my pleasure, Ms MacEwen."

The smile in his voice warms my frigid toes. I imagine him with a kind face—fifty something—in a tasteful, expensive suit, grey in his hair and more laugh lines than frown lines. A father figure who believes what I tell him instead of lobbing me into hospital care faster than I can say, "That demon winked at me."

I hang up and blow my nose into an already sopping tissue, feeling a little more positive about my chances.

This could all be over in a day or two.

4

It takes seven days for my books to be reinstated on my online store. Seven days of making myself sick from worry, not eating, cursing Kade and pacing in my house, as if that will help speed things along. I'm too distracted to write or reach out to any of my fans who might be wondering what's going on.

The 'claimant' didn't respond to my polite but inquisitive email on their copyright concerns, so Spencer Cunningham sent the counter notice. Now, if the claimant wants to take the matter further, they'll have to sue me, which means appearing in court and producing actual evidence for their accusation of copyright infringement. If it's Kade, the claim is bullshit. And no way will he want to appear in court. Spencer Cunningham says we could sue for fraud, but I doubt the claimant's details are genuine and I can't face the hassle.

I just want Kade to leave me alone.

I breathe a little easier after my books go live again, with not a peep from the so-called claimant. I manage to sell twenty copies on the first day from posting about my ordeal on social media and contacting my mailing list. Spencer bought some, too. He said he got caught up in the story instead of just scanning for possible copyright infringements.

They're good books. I may not make enough to support myself beyond the basics but it's from discoverability, not quality. I just need more readers to find me, but marketing is difficult on my budget. The only way to make money is to keep writing and publishing books. It will all pay off when I get enough traction.

Staring at my bank account depresses me. I shut the browser window and open my work in progress, struggling to type a paragraph of *Demon Lover*.

Why is this so hard today?

My phone buzzes. Forgot to put the damn thing on silent, not that I have any friends calling to chat. Comments from fans I've never met are about all I get.

My screen flashes the envelope symbol for a direct message on Twitter. I click on the notification. Dread swoops into my stomach to join the single slice of cheap, cardboard toast I had for breakfast.

This guy keeps bad-mouthing you in his tweets, the text reads. *Just thought you should know.*

An image shows a tweet sent yesterday. And right next to a little blue tick is the name Kade McKade.

The rat-fucking little bastard. Who the hell is he?

The tweet tells his followers my books are trash—without tagging me, the coward—and he recommends they avoid them. The words 'trite' and 'derivative' are bandied about. I swallow a squirt of bile. The message has two hundred and fifty thousand likes.

If I had an audience of two hundred and fifty thousand, I'd never have to worry about money again. I could rebuild my damn cottage if I wanted to.

Kade's Twitter profile has a headshot of him in a pair of red devil horns. Gag. I lean close to the laptop, my nose almost pressed to the screen. His biography is blank. His location says 'from the netherworld' and his account has over a million followers.

A million.

My hand clenches on my mouse, opening an enlarged image of his profile photo by accident, filling my laptop screen with his smug smile and cheekbones. The photo is blurry over his eyes and mouth, as if it captured the wavering he hides behind.

I have six thousand followers. I thought I was doing all right.

Today, Kade has tweeted to say I copy other authors and can't come up with my own material. Three hundred thousand retweets. More tweets about how my books are boring and unoriginal all the way up to the day after we met in Cabaret Voltaire. Before that, there are screeds of photos with beautiful women hanging on his arm, staring at him adoringly. Some have faint bruises on their necks.

He seems to be some kind of It boy. Do you get It boys? Maybe fuckboi is more accurate. He travels a lot—Paris, Milan, New York. Why the hell is he in Edinburgh? It's hardly the celebrity capital of the world. London would have been a better choice and not just because it's hundreds of miles away from me.

Okay. No need to panic. So he's got a large following and is talking shite about me. So what? I doubt anyone who follows him is my ideal reader anyway. His fans will be vapid narcissists and wannabes. People obsessed with looks and money. Women panting over him.

I report his tweets as harassment and block his profile. He

may not have found my Twitter account, but if he has, he can no longer spy on me, though I can still check in on whatever hate-filled drivel he's spewing next. I sit on my hands and pretend they're not shaking.

This isn't a disaster, not like the takedown notice. I bet none of his followers even read. Hopefully, he'll get bored soon. Everything's going to be fine.

I peek at my book figures, unease curdling the bitter coffee in my stomach. No more fancy cardamom coffee for me, only tasteless, value crap. I haven't checked my sales for the last four days as it was becoming an obsession. One in total. My breath wheezes in and out.

No. Oh, no.

I navigate to the sales page of my first book, *Demon Hunter*. A blaze of fire surrounds the silhouette of a woman on the front cover. I relax a little.

When my book was blocked, the website didn't appear at all, showing nothing but a 'Page Not Found' message.

It's there. It's fine. It's working. My book description is killer. My reviews are—

What the fuck.

I rub my eyes. The little row of stars stays the same, the number of reviews showing as over two hundred and eighty.

Normally, I'd dance around the house if I got two hundred plus reviews. The last time I looked, I had seventy. My average rating was four point eight stars.

Three stars wink back at me.

No need for heart palpitations. There must be a clerical error. How could I have got over two hundred reviews in the past four days?

I nearly break my finger scrolling to the bottom of the screen where the reviews are listed. Three star, two star, one star. Pages and pages of them. 'Mediocre' they say. 'Not worth the money' they say. 'The author needs to learn to write' they say.

I whimper, and stuff my fist in my mouth.

None of the reviews have the Verified Purchase tag, meaning none of them bought the fucking book. This is a troll attack by Kade's slavering minions. All of my verified five-star reviews still appear at the top, but it's cold comfort. My second book in the series, *Demon Sworn*, has an average two-star rating instead of five. The gist of the reviews is the second book is the same rubbish as the first. But worse.

My gut in knots, I send an email to the retailer, explaining how the low reviews in the last few days have come from trolls wanting to damage my career, not actual readers. I write to my fans. I post on forums, asking for help.

Then I curl under my desk in my ratty woollen jumper, and sob.

5

A week later, the cold forces me to leave my house. I pull my hood tighter around my face and lock up my bike—an old Raleigh, the black frame mottled bronze and flaking. Rain patters on my jacket. I clutch my precious laptop bag tighter to my chest.

Edinburgh in November—freezing, grey and wet.

Let's hope it gets too cold for a certain twat-faced demon. He can bugger off to the Bahamas for all I care. Though he can still wage online war from the comfort of his hammock while sipping a cocktail and shagging innumerable women.

I push open a glass door and hustle into the warmth. The scent of ground coffee soothes my nostrils. The milk frother hisses, and steam curls to the ceiling. A short queue lines the display counter, most of the tables empty at this early hour. I order a pot of tea and a shortbread biscuit—the cheapest things on the menu—and claim the couch in the corner at the window, looking onto a sodden South Clerk Street. Water streaks the glass and blurs the figures rushing by, heads bent, umbrellas bobbing in packs.

I need to save more money somehow. The end of this month will see the last of my decent royalty payments from September, two months in arrears. When life was looking good, my hard work paying off.

Then I met Kade.

October sales were dismal and November seems to be going the same way. My payment in December won't even buy me a sandwich. If it doesn't let up, I'll have to get a job. But at least I'll always have a house, even if it's as cold and damp as the streets outside.

I inhale the steam from my mug of tea, warming my fingers against the ceramic. Water drips from my coat draped over the arm of the couch and forms a puddle on the wooden floor. I open my laptop, and nibble a corner of biscuit. My stomach rumbles at the aroma of pastries and bacon. A woman at the next table tucks into a hefty slice of black forest gateaux topped with cherries, though it's barely eight o'clock. Saliva floods my mouth, but I force my gaze away.

The tea and shortbread are enough with the free heat and electricity. I can stay all day while the baristas give me the side-eye.

I open *Demon Fire*, my fifth novel and the next in line to publish. My goal is to finish the edits today and put it up for pre-order. The cover is my best yet—another woman, more fire and a black shape with wings and horns behind her.

I taught myself how to create professional-looking book covers from necessity rather than desire since I don't have hundreds of pounds to spend. Same for editing. I rely heavily on my own skills and a small army of advanced readers to catch any glaring typos or plot holes.

I start to polish my words, lulled by the clink of crockery and murmur of voices, a familiar tingle in my stomach.

The novel is good. No—*great*. Fuck Kade and his bile and his puppets. As soon as I find a large enough tribe who loves my stories as much as I do, the bastard won't be able to stop me. He can bleat all he wants to his followers. Mine will destroy them. And I'll have enough money to smother any false takedown notices before they have a chance to sprout.

I'll show *you* trash, you little demon wankstain.

Smirking to myself, I edit a chapter and move on to the next, slipping into the flow, the sounds of the coffee shop fading. I sip my tea, finish my biscuit and tap out the words that will save me.

Write, publish, repeat, as my favourite trio of authors likes to say.

I chew on a fingernail and stare into space, searching my brain for a better word than 'conjugate'. A word that means together. Paired. But good. When you're part of a whole, but opposite. Complementary.

The bell over the door tinkles. I focus on my keyboard. A wash of heat prickles my arms under my maroon hoodie. My head snaps up.

Kade grins at me from the front of the coffee shop, his blond hair wet and sticking to his cheekbones in spikes. Some kind of black, designer jacket emphasises his broad shoulders and slim waist, the collar turned up at his throat. Two unfamiliar women strut around him, both brunettes, and thin. One is wearing a cropped, fur-lined jacket, flashing her concave belly and jutting hipbones. Her skin looks a little blue. The other woman has jeans that probably cost more than my house and a short, deep-purple coat.

"It's so pretentious when people come here to write, isn't it?" she says loudly.

The woman in fur nods. "No one wants to read that crap."

They giggle and follow Kade to the barista at the counter.

Kade's predatory gaze stays on me. I duck my head and frown at my keyboard, my heart suddenly in my mouth.

Don't let him know he's got to you. He's nothing. His pathetic campaign of terror means *nothing*. Act nonchalant. I am fucking nonchalant.

Half of the reviews left by Kade's attack were removed—the ones that were clearly copied and pasted from other reviews. My star rating has gone back to four, which isn't a disaster, but it rankles.

I pretend to concentrate on my laptop, tracking Kade in my periphery. He orders a coconut latte—my favourite coffee—two skinny lattes and a salad.

How can he order a freaking salad with all those cakes tempting him? And what are they going to do—share?

I slurp the last of my cold tea. The mug clatters on the tabletop.

Damn shaky hands.

Kade and his entourage drape themselves artfully in seats a table's length from me. My shoulders hunch. The heat of his gaze strokes my face, my neck. A shudder travels down my spine.

Christ, I'm just a walking cliche—heart in mouth, shuddering spine. I'd never put that rubbish in my novels.

I glare at my laptop screen until the words blur.

I will not engage. I won't give him the satisfaction. And it's too risky. The last time I spoke to him, he invaded my dreams for a week.

"Hello, Reiley," he says in his nowhere-and-anywhere accent. "You look… fetching."

I scroll through my document and ignore him.

He is an amoeba. Slime on my shoe.

"Did you find that hoodie in a charity shop?" Purple-coat sniggers. "I wouldn't be seen dead in that."

Fur-coat stabs a forkful of salad. "And your *hair*. Who's your stylist, Fred Flintstone?"

Kade smirks at the patter of his companions and sips his latte, the coconut drifting across to tease my nose. Sweat gathers in the small of my back, the air stifling. I reread the same sentence ten times. The two women feed each other clumps of leaves, and titter at Kade.

Gross.

He watches me with interest, his long legs stretched out, one arm hooked over the chair back. The picture of easy wealth and relaxation. Of never having to work for a living.

Was he even born or do demons just spring up, fully formed, like mushrooms after rain? They seem to age, but I've never seen a demon child. Or a female. The book never mentions them, either.

"Working on the next bestseller?" Kade says, his mouth quirked.

Slim, deft fingers unfasten an ebony button on his jacket. He moves to the next, playing the stone through his fingertips. My teeth grind on a retort.

The smarmy, infuriating arsepiece.

"I look forward to reading it," he says, minus any hint of sarcasm.

"Oh, fuck off," I snap, then kick myself.

I frown harder at my laptop, and he chuckles. I start to reword a crucial bit of dialogue between my protagonist and her quarry. My mind goes blank. I huff out a breath and grab my coat, punching my arms into the sleeves and jerking the zip closed, nearly decapitating myself. I pack my laptop away and shove to my feet. My thighs hit the table, and it screeches on the floor.

"Leaving so soon?" Kade says.

He sips his coffee with a satisfied sigh. My tastebuds ache for a hit of coconut and syrup.

"I thought you'd have enough to keep yourself occupied," I growl, sweeping a disdainful glance over his companions. "Or are you getting bored of your fluff?"

"At least the fluff is getting laid," sneers Fur-coat, her skin finally turning a normal shade. "You look like a jakey."

"I bet she smells like one, too," sings her friend.

I leave them to their mocking laughter, and step into the blustery rain. The padlock of my bike sticks, and I jar my fingers prying it open. I swipe at the water on the seat, but wetness instantly seeps into my bum when I sit and kick up the pedal. The coffee shop door tinkles open.

Fantastic. Round two of make Reiley feel like shit.

"Look at the state of her!" Purple-coat guffaws. "Poor, ugly *and* pathetic. What a catch."

Fur-coat is too intent on shivering to offer her two-pence worth. She cuddles under Kade's arm. He tosses me a salute and steers her towards a black Porsche with red wheel trims. I pedal past, my gaze fixed on the slick road. An engine rumbles and revs louder, vibrating in my chest. The wicked curves of the car creep level to me at the traffic lights onto Newington Road. I keep my eyes forward. The Porsche growls like a coiled jaguar. The light turns green. Tyres squeal. A splash of water drenches me as the car roars past, spray splattering my face. The brake lights flash red and the Porsche turns right onto West Preston Street.

I sigh and turn left, pedalling for the safety of home.

And the comfort of wine.

6

The wine bottle thunks on the floor of my bedroom. Straight Buckfast this time. Cheap and cheerful. No more fancy unicorn juice cocktails for me. No more clubbing or nights of fun. Just poverty and demons.

I screw up my face and slurp from my refilled glass. The foot of my bed digs into my back, my arse on the carpet. I turn a page of the book open across my lap, careful not to spill my drink. The thick tome is filled with hand-drawn images and two styles of text, one neat and printed, the other cursive. The blank pages at the back wait to be completed. The vellum smells of ink and leather and ancient secrets.

When my aunt got me out of the psychiatric ward, we went on a shopping spree for demon books. She said if I saw demons, then they must be real and someone will have written about it.

I may have sobbed a little amongst the shelves when she wasn't looking. Her faith in me was all I'd ever wanted from my parents. It made me feel less alone, for once.

It's surprising what you can unearth in the indie bookstores in Edinburgh's backstreets and wynds. We found demon dictionaries, devil encyclopedias, satanic field guides and all the demonology and devil-lore you could want.

Most of it was complete bollocks, of course. Nothing about a wavering invisible to normal humans. Nothing about the prickling heat of their attention or their apparent indestructibility. In retrospect, some of the incubus stuff was bang on, as were the descriptions of horns and cloven hooves and wings and whatnot. The religious texts were useless.

Still, we made an event of it. Normal humans had wine and cheese nights. My aunt and I had wine and demons.

I turn another page of the book. Gulp another mouthful of sweet and fruity wine to drown the sadness swirling in my stomach.

I miss her so much.

There's a theological section that struggles to link Christian demons with the monsters roaming our world. Lucifer, Beelzebub, Asmodeus. The latter isn't far off Kade since it's a demon of lust and anger. Ugly, though. The rest of the book splits demons into two main sections—those that feed on life energy and those that feed on other energy, like sex.

Turns out, Kade is quite rare.

These pages have a series of labelled drawings and descriptive paragraphs—how to identify demons instead of something innocuous, like plants. Or mushrooms. Each one that feeds on life energy has a different manifestation of lumps, bumps, scales and tails. Their true forms would never be mistaken for human, if only people could see them.

How did the authors witness so many demons and live to tell the tale? Are they the mysterious Diviners?

I flick to the front end, but I already know there's no title page or claim of ownership. No 'this book belongs to…' and 'you can find me at…'. Too easy. There's nothing on the cover except cracked leather.

My aunt found it in a bookstore on West Nicholson Street after our initial foray. I remember my excitement when she surprised me with it at home. All the other books had been fascinating duds, but this was the real thing. Evidence that I wasn't out of my mind. Some of the pictures were demons I'd actually *seen*.

My aunt transformed my life. I was hopeless and lost, torturing myself with uncertainty, convinced I was mentally ill. She fought for me, rescued me from psychiatric care, and produced evidence that I wasn't alone. I wasn't the only one who saw demons.

I swipe a tear from my cheek before it drips on a pristine page and blurs the ink. A mouthful of Buckfast clogs the back of my throat.

I flip to the section on incubus demons. A few sentences, no drawing. They show demon characteristics only around the mouth and eyes, though there's no explanation for what that means. They feed on sexual energy and cause lust in unwilling victims—usually sleeping women, though Kade refuted that.

Course he would, the rapey man-whore.

If my aunt were here, she'd get us to batten the hatches for a few weeks. Pretend like we were living in the apocalypse and couldn't go outside. Make it fun with movies and books and snacks. And wine.

More tears spill. I shut the book and nudge it away from me, raising my blurred gaze so I don't have to look at it anymore.

A glass display case on the wall opposite the bed reflects the lamplight, obscuring the knife inside.

I discovered it when I packed away the demon books after my aunt's death. It was buried in the attic alongside a box of crystals and notepads containing strange symbols. The knife was too pretty to abandon to rust, so I mounted it on the bedroom wall. There's a tiny keyhole beneath the lid, but I've never been able to find the key.

She was a kook, my aunt, and she had her own demons. I'd often find her staring at nothing, sorrow etched on her face. I wish I could have helped her as much as she helped me. But I couldn't see her demons, either.

I sniffle, and slurp some wine.

She wouldn't talk about whatever was bothering her, even when I pressed. Instead, she'd go on long walks by herself.

And, five years ago, she went on one of those long walks and never came back.

7

"Reiley, Boss says no breaks tonight. Sheena and Dave have called in sick."

I blink at the six-foot-eight wall of muscle tucking his shirt into his black dress trousers.

"Both of them? But we're fully booked!" I drop my bag on the floor and fix my ponytail. "I've only been here a week. I can't cover the whole place myself."

Colin shrugs. "Don't blame me, I'm just the bartender."

"You can help though, right?"

"Probably not."

He leaves the staff room, whistling. I throw up my hands, then shimmy into my own white shirt and trousers, my jeans and hoodie damp from the cycle over.

I was surprised to get the offer from The Spark House, Edinburgh's poshest restaurant in a prime location on Princes Street, but that should have been a clue. The Boss is a money-grabbing, slave-driving bampot. The clientele pay hundreds of pounds for avocado purée and artisanal donkey foam while we get minimum wage to serve them until our feet bleed. I only took the job as I figured the tips from the rich folk would supplement the dross. Shame most of them are tighter than a badger's arse.

I kick out of my mucky trainers and pull on black flats. Another charity shop purchase. They're a little chunky, but at least they're comfortable. I need all the help I can get to survive the night.

Please god, give me some big tippers.

I tie my black apron around my waist, take a deep breath and head out into the restaurant to prepare for opening.

The last few weeks have been a writing and promoting nightmare, hence the pressure to get a job. Kade and his motley crew hounded me from coffee shop to coffee shop. No matter what obscure place I hid in, they always found me. I got so paranoid, I searched my clothes for a tracking device. My cycle home became an elaborate journey of over an hour, using side streets, footpaths and parks to stop Kade from stalking and torturing me—literally—in my only refuge.

Waiting for him to find me in the restaurant is giving me stomach ulcers.

I check the tables are set to the Boss's exacting standards, the linen crisp and white, the silver cutlery equally spaced in reverse order. Lighting all the floating candles in the centrepieces takes five years off my life. Their yellow glow joins the sconces on the burgundy walls, and the chandeliers dripping with crystal. Ravenous patrons arrive and a queue of tutting, sniffing people forms while I show other parties to their seats. I apologise to everyone and explain we're short-staffed until my smile cracks from the strain. Colin hides behind the bar and ignores my frantic signals.

This is going to be impossible. When do the rich wait politely for anything?

The hours pass in a haze of waving hands and snapping fingers. Thankfully, most of the patrons are reasonable human beings, for once, but there are still a few snobs irate at even the slightest delay. My legs ache. Pain sizzles up my spine from being on my feet for so long. I haven't been drinking to avoid using the bathroom, but my tongue is so dry, it sticks to the roof of my mouth. Swallowing hurts. Sweat slicks my hair to my forehead and my shirt to the small of my back. My fantasies consist of ice water and stretching out in bed.

In a brief lull, I rest my feet and scan the bookings. One more to come for the night, thank you, Jesus. I'm so tired, my vision alternates between sparkly specks and blurriness. The booking reads 'McKade, party of three.'

Oh fuck, please no. There has to be more than one McKade. Has to be. I'm too exhausted to deal with his shit tonight.

But at precisely half past eight, Kade McKade glides through the door, sexy and unruffled in black. I blow a damp clump of hair out of my eyes. His smile widens at the sight of me hovering behind the greeter's desk. Identical twins trail behind him, arm in arm, both tall, blonde and blue-eyed.

I bare my teeth. "Welcome to The Spark House. May I take your coats?"

"So nice to keep bumping into you, Reiley," Kade says. "I like spending time with you."

Condescending prick.

He removes his jacket like he's stripping to less than his shirt, and drapes it over my waiting arm. I twitch away to avoid touching him. The twins lob their coats at my face, and a button slaps me in the eye.

"Bitch," I mutter from beneath the material.

I fight free, struggling to breathe with the amount of perfume leached into the lining, and show them to their seats—the best table at the back, furthest from the kitchen.

"How demeaning it must be to work here," Twin-one says, flouncing past.

Their dresses are identical scraps of silver that strain over perfectly pert (and perfectly fake) boobs, the hems barely reaching the curve of their arses. Eyes follow their progress, others intent on Kade's tall figure. Twin-one waits with her sister, brow raised, until I pull their seats out. Kade settles into his chair like a bird of prey, his gaze on me.

"Different women again?" I say with my own eyebrow arch, ignoring my heart slamming against my ribs.

He smirks. "Maybe I get bored."

The twins seem unfazed that he could drop them faster than they can bleat, "But I thought we were special." They don't appear to have bruises on their swan-like necks or anywhere else on the acres of skin on show. I guess there are other areas where blood runs close to the surface. Areas not shown in polite company.

An image of Kade, his head buried between a pair of legs, flashes behind my eyeballs. His mouth pressed to the pulse of an inner thigh. Maybe higher.

I jerk my gaze from the dizzying mouth in question and slap menus on the tabletop, scuttling away to ping-pong between the demands of five other groups. I return out of breath and dishevelled to the three beautiful faces regarding me with varying expressions. The twins sneer. Kade seems thoughtful.

I stare at his cheekbone instead of his vertigo-inducing eyes. Or mouth. "What would you like to drink?"

"What do you recommend?"

He places his chin on his clasped hands, his full attention goosepimpling my arms and squirming in my stomach.

"The Krug," I say, naming our most expensive champagne,

my eyes sparking a challenge.

"Bring the bottle," he says without so much as a blink.

Arrogant bastard.

I deliver the champagne in an ice bucket and pop the cork, trying not to wince at the bang. The soles of my feet throb in time to my pulse. I pour the fizz, bubbles coating the inside of the glasses. Twin-one guzzles half and holds her flute out for more.

"Writing not paying the bills?" she says sweetly.

I glare at Kade. "Are you ready to order?"

The unspoken expletives curdle in my gut, but they must be pasted on my face because Kade smirks at me.

"Are you all right, Reiley?"

"Like you give a fuck," I hiss.

"You can't talk to us like that," Twin-two says, looking smug. "We're paying customers."

"Are you ready to order?" I grind out.

My pen scratches my notepad so hard, I almost tear the paper. I barely register what Kade says. My skin itches to flee. I scuttle to the reprieve of the kitchen, the heat of the burners flushing my cheeks. The chefs take pity on my bedraggled state and ply me with food.

It's the only reason I haven't fainted during my non-stop shift.

Colin is idly scrolling on his phone when I zoom past. If my arms weren't filled with plates, I'd throttle the lazy shite. I ring up three tables. None tip, moaning about the wait. I manage not to growl at them as they leave. The cold air creeping through the door is wonderful on my cheeks. I suck the crispness down and shut my eyes for a second. Even my kneecaps ache.

Too soon, Kade's food is ready. Two orders. I check my notepad. Kade got nothing for himself, only an espresso to pair with his champagne. Thank god his ladies only want a main course, too. I pray they leave before dessert. My tolerance for their bullshit is wafer thin.

I carefully place Twin-two's cauliflower veloute in front of her, a wave of dizziness making my head light.

"Took long enough," Twin-one grumbles, her arms crossed over her sizeable tits.

"As I explained when you arrived, we're short-staffed. I'm going as fast as I can."

"Maybe that's your problem." Twin-two points her fork at my feet. "The nineties called—they want their ugly shoes back."

The twins snort. My leg buckles, and I plant a hand on the tablecloth for balance. A slop of baked hake stew plops onto the crisp linen in front of Twin-one. She leaps to her feet.

"You nearly burned me!" she shrieks.

She slaps my hand holding the bowl, upending the scalding contents on my chest. Bits of fish and vegetable bounce off my shoes. The ceramic shatters on the floor. I peel my shirt off my skin, the white stained a lovely beige, like I've vomited on myself. My stinging flesh turns pink.

"You goddamn cow—"

"Reiley!" barks a voice behind me, loud in the silence filling the restaurant.

The Boss trundles towards us, short and stocky in his grey suit. Colin deigns to look up from his phone at the excitement.

"What is going on here?" the Boss says, his beady eyes on me. "Mr McKade is our best customer."

He tells everyone that. Anyone rich enough to grace our

establishment is his best customer.

I fan my chest, hot liquid soaked into my bra. "I accidentally—"

"She deliberately spilled food on me," Twin-one says breathlessly. "She's been rude and unprofessional from the beginning. I mean, look at her—she's sweating in the food. It's disgusting."

"I'm *wearing* the food, you dozy boot," I snarl.

The Boss's face turns puce. "Miss MacEwen, that behaviour is not acceptable on my premises."

"It's Ms. And these people have been harassing me for months."

"You're fired, Miss MacEwen. You're no longer welcome in The Spark House." The Boss pivots to the twins. "I am so sorry for the inconvenience. Please, let me get you a fresh dish and a round of drinks, on the house."

Humiliation burns hotter than the fish stew. My fists clench at the smugness radiating from the twins. Tears prickle my eyes, and I force myself not to look at Kade.

"Do not make me call the police, Miss MacEwen," the Boss says, his back to me while he fawns over the twins.

I grab my bag from the staff room, not bothering to change. I stalk back into the restaurant proper, chin in the air, and empty the contents of the tip jar into my purse. Every eye in the room stays on me.

"What do you think you're doing?" the Boss splutters, tearing his lips from Kade's arse.

I aim for the door. "Since I was the only one working tonight, the tips are mine. And I expect to get my week's wages or you'll be hearing from my lawyer."

The pretentious entrance of curlicued metal shuts on his

grunt of protest. My last glimpse is of Kade, his gorgeous face split in a grin.

8

Christmas day dawns frosty and clear. I huddle under my duvet, shivering and staring at the wall.

It's too much effort to get up. Too cold. What's the point? I have nothing to celebrate.

Hunger forces me out of bed an hour or so later. I pad through the living room, the Christmas tree in the corner old and balding, the gold tinsel the sole colour since I won't turn the lights on. No presents sit underneath.

There could be presents under the tree, but that would require being in contact with my parents and I have fuck all intent of ever speaking to them again after what they did. They never even came to my aunt's funeral.

I open my fridge and sigh at the contents—useless sauces and a hunk of cheese, furred green. I scrape off the mould and eat the cheese for lunch. My tea tastes awful without milk and sugar, but at least it's warm. I pair it with a cheap glass of wine since there's no such thing as drinking too early on Christmas, then slump in front of my laptop.

I've stopped checking my sales figures. Too depressing. I have no job and too few fans. Nobody cares. The money I've saved won't cover bills for the next two months. If my books don't pick up, I won't make it past spring.

I gulp wine and search the internet for credit cards, applying for one that has a ridiculous interest rate, but that I'm more likely to get compared to the others.

Approved. Shocking.

I toast the screen, red liquid sloshing in my glass. Now I can pay for ads, my only hope for more sales. The risk is not making a profit and running up a credit card debt into the thousands, but what the hell. Maybe I can declare bankruptcy, curl up in bed and never move. Mrs Dounray will come knocking, weeks later, to complain about the smell.

I hope she enjoys the sight of my rotting carcass before she bulldozes my cottage for her fucking extension.

A little buzzed from the wine on a mostly empty stomach, I open Kade's Twitter page. A few tweets disparage my new release, *Demon Fire*. It got twelve two-star reviews the day it went live. A third were removed after I complained. The fifteen five-star reviews it received would have made me ecstatic BK—Before Kade.

Sometimes I wish he'd just killed me in Cabaret Voltaire.

Torturing myself, I scroll through photo after photo of beautiful Kade with a parade of beautiful women, smiling and laughing. Images of his Porsche. Designer clothes. Expensive food.

No one questions the blurriness of the pictures, the sparks of light shading his eyes and mouth. People seem to throw money at him for sneezing, for god's sake. No wonder he doesn't need to work a day in his life. Maybe being a monster helps.

The photos continue—Kade in his big, warm house. A freaking penthouse, of course. Nothing but the best for this incubus demon. A bed the size of a swimming pool. Balconies, wood and glass, a hot tub on a private roof terrace filled with bikini-clad nymphs. A view over The Meadows towards Marchmont.

I slurp my wine and pour another, spilling crimson drops on the desk. The neck of the bottle clinks on the edge of the glass. I gulp the bitter liquid.

"Well, I know where *you* live, you little fanny." I laugh, drink, and spill wine in my crotch. "You really should be careful what you share online, Kade Mc-bloody-*Kade*."

I should go over there and confront him. We're long overdue. I should have punched his smug face in The Spark House. Made him not so pretty anymore.

I knock back my glass and shove to my feet. The room sways and twirls around me. I slap a hand on the damp desk. The wine bottle appears to be empty. How did that happen? Should probably soak up some alcohol with food.

I stumble into the kitchen. My Christmas dinner consists of two handfuls of Cheerios scooped straight from the box, the honey and wheat cereal clumping to paste in my mouth.

Cock-sucking Kade. Bet he has a roaring fire and a whole turkey. All the trimmings. Roast potatoes and gravy, stuffing and Brussels sprouts.

My stomach rumbles for everything but the Brussels sprouts. Awful, tiny balls of cabbage.

I should interrupt his fun. Show up unannounced and berate him. Return the favour. Ruin his Christmas. The insufferable bawbag deserves a piece of my mind.

I'm half-way round Duddingston Low Road before I realise I've forgotten my jacket. Fuck it. I keep pedalling, my bike wobbling on the empty road. My harsh breaths puff in clouds of white. The streetlights ping on and sparkle on the frost.

Only the brightest stars shine in the clear sky. Cold nips my fingers and turns my hands to red claws on the handlebars.

My front wheel hits a pothole. The impact judders through the rusted frame of my bike and wrenches my arms. I sail into a ditch by the side of the road, slamming onto the solid ground and knocking my breath out. Ice crackles, and freezing water soaks into the shoulder of my grey hoodie. My mouth gapes frantically until my chest relaxes, and I whoop in air that sears my lungs with frost.

I clamber onto my bike, my hip and shoulder smarting, and pedal faster, teeth gritted. Tears trail down my cheeks from the wind. The lights of Edinburgh start a headache pounding between my temples. I cycle past Pollock Halls and the Royal Commonwealth Pool, then zig-zag to The Meadows, zooming between the trees of North Meadow Walk, the only soul crazy enough to be outside instead of tucking into Christmas dinner and falling asleep in front of the telly. By the time I reach Simpson Loan, the cold and the throb from my fall have evaporated the alcohol in my system, leaving me sore and queasy.

What a stupid idea this was. I should go home. Curl around a hot water bottle and lick my wounds.

But what if Kade never leaves me alone? Maybe I can appeal to his better nature.

I manage not to snort, mostly because my teeth are chattering. More likely, he'll see the pathetic specimen he's reduced me to and retire the victor.

I wheel my bike around the three apartment blocks and abandon it in a bush near the vestibule where the buzzer reads 'McKade'. A warm yellow light shines invitingly through the glass of the front door. I push the top button and tuck my stinging hands in my armpits. Shudders wrack my body. There's a ragged hole in the knee of my black leggings, my skin scored and oozing blood. Mud streaks my hoodie and probably my face, the material at my shoulder dark with water. I have red wine seeped into my pants for Christ's sake.

I need to get the hell out of here. What was I thinking?

The speaker crackles. "Hello?"

My tongue freezes to the roof of my mouth. I clamp my teeth and stay silent. Violent twitches jerk me on the spot.

"Hello-o? Anyone there?"

A wave of exhaustion weakens my knees. I rest my forehead on the chilled stone of the vestibule.

"You've proven—your point," I whisper into the speaker, my lips numb. "You can—leave me—alone now."

"Reiley?" Kade says.

Living in my cottage should have got me used to the cold, but my bones are iced over and I can barely stay on my feet. My skin feels raw.

"Just leave—me alone, Kade. Please."

The door buzzes.

"Come up."

"Fuck yourself," I hiss.

I may be an idiot for cycling out here in the freezing dark with no coat, but I am not idiot enough to voluntarily trap myself in his house so he can slice me open for Christmas dinner.

"Then I'm coming down," he says, and hangs up.

Oh, *shite*. Run away!

I lunge for my bike, fumbling with deadened hands. The frame catches on the bush and refuses to budge. I tug, cursing, branches rattling together. Evergreen leaves flutter to the stone walkway. The door behind me shushes open. My heart would race if it weren't trapped in ice.

"Come inside, Reiley," Kade says, his voice gentle. "We can talk."

"Piss off," I say to him and the bush that's munched my escape vehicle.

"You're hardly in a condition to cycle home."

"Is that a threat?"

He chuckles, and I whip around to give him a good glare, but my brain must still be a little pickled on alcohol or woozy from my tumble. I list sideways, and Kade catches my elbow.

"Fuck, Reiley, you're freezing!"

I yank my arm from his grip, overbalance, and topple into the bush to join my pinioned bike. Kade coughs into his fist, then tries to help me. I slap at his hands, my skin stinging, sensitised by the cold. My struggles weaken, and he pulls me to my feet. For a second, I'm cradled against his firm chest, his arms around me.

God, he's so warm.

I shove him away. "Don't touch me."

He holds his hands up in surrender. "Come inside and thaw out at least. You leave in this state and you'll have an accident or catch pneumonia."

I snarl at him. He retreats and opens the door. Hot air unfurls around me. I shiver harder, my vision blurred.

"Fine," I say. "But no funny business."

He smirks. "None whatsoever."

"Arsehole," I mumble, and trail him inside.

9

The interior of the apartment block feels so warm, it hurts. My skin is tight and aching, my knees literally knocking together. Kade leads me into the lift in the centre of the hallway, a flight of stairs extending to the left. Everything is shiny and grey. The doors slide shut, and panic twists my stomach. The walls are narrow, barely wider than my shoulders. The space would be claustrophobic with one person. With an incubus demon, it's damn tiny. Intimate. His body heat bakes through my clothes. He smells like summer and hot grass.

Funny, I always expect the stink of sulphur.

He reaches for me. I leap backwards, slamming my spine into the wall. He plucks a twig from my hair and drops it at his feet. He holds out a tissue.

"What's that for?" I growl.

"Your nose is running."

And I thought getting fired in front of him was humiliating.

I snatch the tissue and face the mirrored wall. A line of snot glistens from one nostril.

Fantastic.

I swipe at my bright-red nose. My eyes and cheeks are red, too. My hair frizzes in all directions, more wild than usual. I look pale and pitiful beside Kade with his perfect bone

51

structure and slim-fitting jeans. His t-shirt hugs his shoulders and flat belly. It's the same grey as my hoodie, though mine is streaked with mud.

"Bit late to be nice to me." I turn to face him and notch my chin higher, tucking the snotty tissue into my hoodie pocket.

Kade smirks. "Who says I'm being nice?"

The ice around my heart crackles and my pulse finally speeds. I stay pressed to the wall. His eyes and mouth make me dizzy.

So stop staring at them, idiot.

"What are you hiding?" I snap. "Elliptical pupils and fangs?"

He smiles slow, and my stomach rolls.

"Maybe you'll find out," he says.

The lift glides to a stop and opens into another hallway with a single entrance straight ahead. Kade sweeps his arm towards it.

"You first," I say.

He steps out. I'm tempted to mash the 'Doors Close' button and run for it but no doubt he'd find me, bleeding in the road after spilling from my bike, my legs numb. Feeding on me would be like sucking on an ice lolly.

I stumble into Kade's house and swallow a moan at the wash of heat. The entrance shuts. My skin prickles, Kade standing close. Chattering voices echo from a room down the hall.

Lots of voices.

"Nope," I say, and lunge for the doorknob, shouldering Kade out of the way.

"Don't be scared, Reiley. I won't let them hurt you."

The bastard is smirking at me again.

"I'm not fucking scared. I am, however, sick of your harpies slagging me off every chance they get."

The door cracks open but lodges on Kade's foot.

"You care what they think?"

"Couldn't care less," I say through my teeth.

He moves his foot. My tug swings the door back, and I slam into my second wall of the evening.

"What doesn't kill you, Reiley…"

He tosses me a grin over his shoulder and walks towards the sounds of laughter and clinking crockery. The heavenly scents of roast turkey and potatoes beckon me to follow.

"I can warm up fine here," I call.

"But we're having dinner." His smile issues a challenge. "Join us."

He disappears through the doorway.

"Vain, irritating cockwomble," I mutter.

This is just a continuation of his plan to kick me while I'm down. I doubt he'll murder me in front of his women or that they'd sit placidly while he did so. He won't want to expose what he is. Still, nothing good can come from spending the evening with him and his harridans.

But damn if my mouth isn't watering at the thought of a proper Christmas dinner. And who can say no to free food?

I sigh loudly and shut the door, running my fingers through my tangled hair and dabbing at my nose. Certain the night will be a disaster, I hover in the entranceway and survey the room.

The wide living space stretches to a wall of glass, the blackness beyond unbroken. A large dining table runs parallel to the window, five of the seats occupied by women. A holly-trimmed cloth drapes the table, the surface laden with platters of steaming food and glasses filled to the brim. Crumpled Christmas crackers lie on the laminate floor. Kade claims his place at the head of the table.

Of course.

"Have a seat, Reiley," he says, indicating the chair opposite since the women are clustered close to him.

Five unfamiliar faces turn to me. I stop myself from patting at my stained hoodie and ripped leggings. I march to the far end of the table and plonk myself onto the plush cushion.

"Don't you have any male friends?"

"Who needs friends?" Kade says.

"You could at least add variety—have some with more brains than boobs."

"I have a PhD," sneers the woman on my right. Glitter sparkles on her chest, framed by the plunging neckline of her dress.

"Then how can you be happy with"—I wave my hand at the competition—"this?"

"Look at him—he's rich, gorgeous." She licks the tines of her fork. "The sex is amazing."

Kade salutes me with his wine. Garnet liquid clings to the inside of the glass.

I jerk my gaze away. "Do you know anything about him? Have you ever had a proper conversation?"

I don't have conversations with my sexual partners, but that's necessity rather than choice, thanks to the demon smiling faintly at me from the head of the table. My life would have been so different if I were just like everybody else.

"There are better things to do with your mouth than talk," Dr Glitter-tits says.

"Great sex isn't worth fighting for his affection."

"Said by someone who's never had great sex."

I open my mouth to argue about my fantastic sex life, then

wonder what I'm doing. The good doctor returns her focus to Kade and continues to fellatio her fork for his amusement.

"She stinks of wine," slurs the lady on my left, her hazel eyes unfocused.

I smile sweetly. "Maybe it's you."

Kade chuckles and tells the woman next to him to fill me a plate. She pouts but does what he says, adding an extra shimmy to her step as she sidles around the table. She slaps the plate in front of me and skips back to Kade's side to simper at him. His harem ignores me, vying for his attention with fluttering lashes and lots of cleavage.

What exactly is his game plan? Five ladies are quite a lot to handle, even for an incubus demon. How does he satisfy them all? Or maybe he just stretches out, naked, and they do stuff to him.

Did it get warmer in here?

I jam a forkful of food in my mouth. A moan slips out at the explosion of flavours, my tastebuds weeping in gratitude after weeks of boiled noodles and toast. My eyes roll back. When I finally open them, everyone is staring at me. Kade's hungry expression tingles from my gut to my toes, or maybe that's me getting feeling back.

"And I thought starving artist was a stereotype," says the woman who delivered my plate.

I tear my gaze from Kade and shovel food into my mouth. My skin warms. My belly fills. I'd forgotten what being full felt like. I add a second helping. Slurring lady stops wiggling her chest at Kade long enough to gape. From the cleanliness of her plate, she only ate a Brussels sprout. No wonder she's sloshed. I wipe up the last of my gravy with a hunk of bread and pop it in my mouth, slumping in my chair.

"Better?" Kade says.

I manage a frown, though the rest of me wants a nap. "This doesn't mean you're forgiven."

He gives me a wicked grin. "Then I guess I'll have to try harder."

"You really are a dick."

"I know."

His women bicker about who gets to win his favour by clearing up and brewing coffee. They disappear through another doorway that must lead to the kitchen. A set of stairs heads up to a second floor. His bedroom? I yank my gaze down. Kade watches me.

Why is he always watching me? Has he never met another person who can see he's not human?

"What's a Diviner?" I say.

He tilts his head. "You are."

I grind my teeth. "So there are others? Are they organised?"

"Why? You thinking of joining?"

More teeth grinding. "Where are they based? How can I find them?"

"Why would I know that, Reiley?" Kade smiles. "I tend to stay far away from them."

I glance at the kitchen door. Female chirping and the clatter of dishes filter through.

"You've got yourself pretty set up here, haven't you?" I say in my best mocking tone. "Fancy house. Fancy car. Women waiting on you hand and foot. Where do you even find them?"

"They find me."

"Do you kill them all?" I say quietly.

"Do *you* think I kill them?"

I meet his pale-blue gaze, his face gorgeous and unreadable.

I look at the table, and he laughs.

"I think you drop them when you get bored, leaving them broken," I say. "Weak."

"Is that what I've done to you?"

My head snaps up.

"You will never make me weak," I growl.

Another of his slow smiles squiggles into my stomach.

"You're an intriguing woman, Reiley MacEwen."

"But not one of yours," I say, and give him a smirk in place of a one-fingered gesture.

His victims return with mugs of coffee, flapping around him to ensure he has milk and sugar and as much ego boosting as one man could possibly want. I hug my coffee in two hands and inhale the steam, savouring the sweet, creamy scent as it filters to my chest.

"Will you stay for dessert?" Kade says, refilling his cup.

"Um, if it's some kind of cake—yes. Anything else—no."

He grins. "Spoilsport."

And there's my cue to flee.

I stand slowly. "I should get going. It's late."

I wait for him to refuse, to drag me to some kind of torture room, but he walks me to the door, though I tell him not to. His women pout at his lack of attention. My skin jumps, very aware of him behind me.

"So, thanks," I say, "for not being an arsehole one day this year."

He chuckles and his warm breath brushes me as he leans across to open the door.

"You're welcome."

I pause on the threshold. "Are you going to leave me alone now?"

"Where's the fun in that?" he says. "Merry Christmas, Reiley."

I slam the door in his face.

10

My New Year's resolution is to be a successful author and rub Kade's face in the failure of his plan to destroy me. He had me in his clutches last year, pushed me to the brink, but I'm tougher now. Committed. No little demon is going to keep me from doing what I love.

I channel my anger into my work, waking at 5am to switch on my laptop and check my ads, researching and adding new ones to promote my books. I contact bloggers and influencers, start doing interviews and podcasts. When people question me about the Twitter personality who took a dislike to my stories, I laugh and say I'm flattered he read my books, though if he hated them, he should maybe have stopped after the first. That always gets a chuckle from the presenter. I tell the listeners I've been working hard to change his mind, but they should give my novels a chance and see what they think.

Why let one man dictate what's good?

They ask me about the takedown notice and I brush it off as someone acting out of spite. Or they thought my books were so amazing, they couldn't bear the competition. Another chuckle. I say that the claim was false as the accuser failed to respond to my counter notice, so it's doubtful they had any actual evidence of infringement. Other authors contact me after facing the same nightmare.

My Twitter followers double. Triple. My mailing list swells from a paltry twenty six to over thirty thousand. Not curious browsers or freebie chasers, either, but ravenous fans who buy everything I publish and rave about it on their platforms. Together, they are louder than one man will ever be.

If he were a man.

I release *Demon Lover* in January and experience the best launch I've ever had, with three hundred copies sold on the first day and one hundred five-star reviews. I changed the ending. Originally, the demon renounced his kind and chose the Seer—what I called the Diviners before I knew they were real. They skipped off into the sunset, hand in hand, to have lots of hot sex. In the new ending, my protagonist kills her demon lover after she discovers his plot to betray her to his brethren. Moral of the story—never trust a demon.

I write until midnight most days. Afternoons are for engaging with fans, and marketing. My books appear on the bestseller lists and stay in the top one hundred. Publishing *Demon Born*, my seventh novel, in February becomes my best launch of all time. I start writing my eighth.

Write, publish, repeat.

I collapse into bed every night, my eyes burning from staring at the laptop screen, and fall asleep instantly. I wake groggy after only five hours, but the thought of increasing my screw-Kade safety net spurs me into the cold and gets my bum in my writing chair.

March is my leanest month in terms of available cash. My savings have dwindled to nothing despite my careful thriftiness, the payment demand letters building up. October to December were the bad months and my publishing platform only pays two months in arrears, so my first royalty payment from my excellent sales in January is due at the end of March.

The weather slowly warms, but not enough to wear anything less than two wool jumpers and a cardigan in my cottage. Mrs Dounray appears at least once a week to complain about my missing tiles or the crack beneath the chimney or my overgrown garden. I spend a couple of hours weeding and trimming old growth to save her eyeballs from the horror of a dead plant during her morning ablutions.

I'm back to eating noodles and toast. What seemed like failure last year is a walk of triumph this year, knowing the payments are coming. February's sales were even higher. March's sales have kicked off strong.

I count down the days to the twenty ninth of March—pay day. Snowdrops sprout in my garden. Fresh, green shoots herald the spring, my favourite season. New life. Sunshine and flowers. I take walks around Arthur's Seat for exercise, hoping I bump into Kade.

I have a lot of gloating to shove right up his arse.

My royalties ping into my bank account on schedule. I stare at all the zeros and sob for about thirty minutes of pure relief. Then I turn the heating on.

Kade falls silent. At the beginning of April, his Twitter account disappears. Maybe he's buggered off somewhere else. I'm sure he's left a troop of broken-hearted women pining for him.

But this woman isn't one of them.

I stock my cupboards, my fridge and my freezer with food that's not in Asda's value range. I splash out on Marks & Spencer and Waitrose because I deserve to celebrate with top-quality, expensive fare.

My hard work got me here, got me past everything Kade threw at me, though it didn't seem like it at the time.

I think about returning to the clubs. Defeating Kade has got me all horny. Or I could order in from PegLeg, my hook-up app of choice, though I had a bad experience about a month before I met Kade.

Might still be too soon, as much as I feel the urge.

I get the roof and the crack in the wall fixed. Goodbye damp. A new boiler purrs in the corner of my kitchen. For the first time in five months, I can finally relax.

It's over. The campaign of terror is over.

Kade has lost.

11

Rain splatters on the window of the breakfast nook, the street-lights on Old Church Lane shining through the thrashing branches of trees beyond the blurred glass. Wind howls down the chimney flue in my living room, the grate locked tight against the storm. I sip my peppermint tea and watch leaves swirl past, cosy in just a black, oversized t-shirt that says 'Screw bookworm, I'm a book dragon.' My laptop glows softly on the desk, two thousand fresh words typed on the page. I yawn and glance at the time in the bottom right corner.

Midnight.

A knock thunders on my door. I jump but manage not to spill my tea, for once.

It's a bit late for Mrs Dounray. Plus, there's nothing left for her to whine about. Every time she spots me in the street now, she has a face like a slapped arse and quickly hustles in the opposite direction with a tense, "Come along now, Chesington," to her puff of a dog.

She really wanted my land for herself.

Another knock, though not as loud. A palm slapping on wood.

"Who's there?" I say calmly, squeezing the fireplace poker for reassurance.

No answer. I throw open the door and brandish my weapon. Wind flaps the t-shirt against my thighs, rain peppering my bare feet and legs. The light from the hall paints a bedraggled figure and casts his shadow on my flagstones.

Kade sways in the pouring rain, half-naked and shivering, his jeans soaked. His feet are also bare, but dirty and bleeding. His hair is plastered to his cheekbones, so wet it looks brown. My mouth gapes wide enough to drive a tram through. I think I squeak his name. The poker droops at my side.

While it is surprising for him to darken my door on a stormy night in April, it's the rest of him that leaves me stunned.

His eyes are solid black—no trace of white or husky blue. No more wavering, either.

Is he too weak to shield?

Bloody furrows mark his chest and ribs. A bruise colours one perfect cheekbone and the corner of his mouth, his lip swollen.

"I had nowhere else to go," he says, and his legs collapse.

The poker clangs on the hallway tiles. I lunge into the deluge without thinking. My arms wrap around Kade's chest and hug his back, my chin over his shoulder. The shock of the contact zips down my spine. It's the first time I've touched his bare skin. He's solid, but icy. Demons usually run hot.

What the hell am I doing? I should have let him crumple on my flagstones, and slammed the door.

I stagger under his weight, reversing into my house, his feet dragging behind him. The door sways wide, wind licking hungrily into the cottage and splattering water on the tiles. The dim glow of streetlights through the windows leads me to the bedroom. I twist and try to lower Kade gently, but topple at the end, overbalanced by his leaded limpness. We bounce on the mattress, my face pressed to the covers, the rest of me pressed to Kade. My t-shirt inches dangerously high. His eyes stay closed, his thick, black lashes brushing his cheeks. I sprint to the front door, slam it, and sprint back.

Kade hasn't moved. He lies half on my bed, his long legs trailing to the floor. I hoist the rest of him onto the same level, then just stand and stare.

The gouges slice from his left shoulder towards his sternum where bone flashes through a ragged hole. More claw marks trace the curve of his ribs. My scars pulse in sympathy.

Demons did mine. Whoever did his, it looks like they were aiming for his heart.

The wounds ooze and merge with the rain on his skin, forming slick puddles on the planes of his chest and stomach. The blood shimmers ruby red with swirls of ebony. I touch a finger to it, and my skin tingles.

Would he make it appear human red if he were conscious and uninjured?

I scan his face but he lies still, and breathes. My tingling finger eases his top lip higher to reveal a dainty fang.

Is this where vampire stories came from? Maybe they were all incubus demons. Beautiful, arrogant, and deadly.

I swipe my fingers on my t-shirt and grab a towel to stop Kade from leaking all over my bed. His eyelids flutter to reveal black half-moons.

"What the hell happened to you?" I say, and press roughly on his scratches.

"Demons," he hisses.

He watches me. Or I think he does. Those black, shining orbs are a little unsettling. A shark's eyes. I drop my gaze to my hands splayed over his chest, and nerves ping in my gut.

I have so many questions. But I ask the most important one of all.

"How do you know where I live?"

His mouth twitches in the semblance of a smirk. A bead of dark blood wells from his swollen lip.

"Followed you—on Christmas." His eyes slip shut, but he keeps talking. "Wanted to check—you got home."

He's known my address since December. What has he been waiting for? He could have killed me that night.

"Why did the demons attack you?" I say.

Kade's ripped chest rises and falls beneath my hands. I shove his ribs like I'm doing CPR, and he bares his teeth. The sight of his fangs shivers from my eyeballs to my toes.

"*Why*, Kade?" I manage to say.

His head flops on my pillow. "They were at Cabaret Voltaire. They saw you, too."

Goosebumps flare on my arms.

"Did you tell them where I live?"

My head snaps up, my neck craning to scan the room for hulking monsters with horns and scaly lumps. There's nothing but the usual furniture—bedside cabinet, fabric chair in the corner, built-in cupboard and door to my en-suite. My aunt's decorative knife in its mounted display case.

"Thought—it would be enough," Kade sighs.

My gaze latches on his pale face.

"What would be enough?"

No response. I shake him, but he appears to be unconscious. The arsehole.

I yank on a pair of leggings, then check my doors and windows, peering into the street for suspicious figures lurking in the darkness. Kade stays unresponsive. Blood seeps through the towel. I grab my first aid kit from the kitchen. Bandaging his wounds means getting up close and personal to unroll the material around his ribs and diagonally across his chest from shoulder to hip. He smells like salt and hot concrete. His carved abs and slim waist draw my eye. His sopping jeans sit low, two perfect lines disappearing into the waistband.

Maybe I should take them off.

I jerk upright and slam the lid of the first aid kit.

Goddamn incubus demon. Messing with me even when he's passed out.

I curl in my chair and hug my knees to my chest. Kade's eyes roll beneath his lids. He breathes through his mouth, flashing fang.

"Kade?" I shout, and he flinches. "Did the other demons follow you?"

His head lolls left, then right. "Lost them on Arthur's Seat."

What was he doing running about on the old volcano in the dark, fighting his own? His brethren. In his bare feet.

"Why are you here?"

"It's safe," he says. "And I'm hurt."

"One of your floozies could have played nursemaid. I'm not Florence-bloody-Nightingale."

His black gaze meets mine. My heart flutters.

"They've never seen me like this."

"How lucky for them," I say drily.

"And the demons were looking for you," he finishes as if I haven't spoken.

My breath lodges behind a lump in my throat.

"So why did they hurt you?" I wheeze. "Why aren't they here to finish what you started?"

"I broke a rule."
"You have rules?"
"Just one."
"What?"
He wrestles his drooping eyelids, struggling to focus on me. I hug my legs tighter, my chin on my knees.
"Kill your kind on sight," he says, and faints.

12

Kade drifts in and out of consciousness. Ebony-red seeps through his bandages, the damp and stained towel discarded on the floor. My eyes burn, my head nodding on my knees.

Something tells me I won't be getting up at 5am tomorrow. Today. Should I sleep on the couch since there's a demon in my bed?

I toss a pillow at him, and he gasps awake.

"How long until you heal and leave me alone?" I say.

"I can't."

"Sure you can. You've been blissfully quiet the last few months."

"Can't heal without help," he croaks.

"Help?" I splutter. "Why the hell should I help you? You nearly ruined my life."

He coughs, then I realise he's laughing but his eyes are screwed shut, his hands clenched in my covers.

The arsehole thinks this is funny.

I stand, brandishing another pillow from my chair. Maybe I can suffocate him. I've never tried it before, but something's got to kill them, right?

Kade stops his painful chuckling and looks at me, tears shining in his freaky black eyes.

"I *saved* your life, Reiley," he says.

"Don't talk shite," I snap. "You enjoyed making me miserable. What was your plan—drive me to suicide? Would that follow your stupid rule?"

"I didn't want you to kill yourself." He gives me a slow smile and licks the blood from his lip. "I love your books."

"You called them trash," I growl, easing closer with the pillow mashed between my fists.

"Thaddeus and Myron were watching me."

"Thaddeus and Myron—really?"

"We can't all have cool names," Kade says.

"So I'm supposed to believe, what—you attacked my livelihood to placate your friends—"

"Not friends," Kade grunts.

"—and protected me like some kind of saint? Pull the other one, mate. Your plan failed. I beat you. You got into a fight with your *friends* and you turning up here is just some other way to screw with me."

"They would have killed you in the club."

"So why didn't you let them? Why haven't you killed me?"

"I don't kill people."

I snort and throw the pillow back on the chair. "Some of your women looked pretty damn starved."

"But not dead."

He closes his eyes, his breathing shallow. His pulse flutters in the hollow of his throat. The circles under his eyes are as bruised as his cheekbone.

"If you help me, I can help you," he says.

"I think I'll take my chances with the other demons."

"They're not like me."

"Good. The last thing I need is another pain in my arse."

Kade slides me a glare. "They'll eat you alive."

"Figuratively?" I say hopefully.

His chin jerks side to side, and I huff.

"Fine. But then will you leave me alone?"

"We'll see," he says.

I throw the other pillow at him. "God, I hate you."

The cushion flops across his stomach and waist, his long legs stretching towards the metal bed frame. His feet are delicate for a man, though scratched and bloody.

"I know." He grins, and I wish for another pillow. Or a brick. "But you wrote your best stuff after you met me."

"Don't you dare take credit for my success," I hiss. "The only thing you did was make my life harder."

He shrugs his uninjured shoulder. "Whatever you say."

My teeth grind together. "New plan—I help you heal and you bugger off. Immediately."

"You can't fight Thaddeus and Myron by yourself."

"Neither can you." I sweep a look over his prone and bleeding form. "But I don't need to fight them, I just need to hide."

"They'll find you. Is your name on the house, the bills, the Electoral Register?"

Shit. Would it really be that easy? Will I spend every night alone, lying in the dark, eyes wide, listening for the scrape of claws outside, the flap of a wing, the tinkle of glass?

Fear solidifies in my stomach.

At least Kade is harder to kill than I am. He can be my shield. And he's not scary, like all the other demons I've met. A benefit of his 'make love, not war' mentality, perhaps?

"Fuck's sake, *fine,*" I say. "How do I help you heal?"

He manages a full smirk. "Blood and sex."

"Goddamn incubus demon," I sigh. "Does it have to be my blood? I could find you a chicken. Or a stray."

His mouth twitches. "Has to be human."

Damn. No feeding him Mrs Dounray's pissy little dog either, then. And it's not like I can just drag someone in off the street.

I cross my arms and hug myself tight. Kade's eyes are huge and black in his pale face. His breathing seems more rapid. Still shallow. Sweat glistens on his skin.

He really is sick. Can demons kill each other?

I fidget under his waiting stare, exposed in only my sleep shirt and leggings. I wish I had more clothes on.

"You stop when I tell you," I say tersely.

He nods, barely moving his chin.

I can't believe I'm doing this.

I thrust my arm out and frown at the wall above the headboard. Icy fingers cradle my wrist. Every muscle screams at me to run. Soft, cold lips kiss the delicate skin over my pulse. It yanks my gaze to his face. His eyes are pools of drowning black. Not a shark's eyes, but a doorway—a portal to a starry sky. I sway.

"No!" I gasp. "No bedazzling shit. Just bite me already."

Kade's lips curve against my wrist. "This is exactly how I imagined it."

"You *imagined*—"

Fangs slice skin. Sucking and the lap of his tongue replace the sharp pain. My pulse jumps beneath his mouth and echoes deep in my belly. I drop to my knees, my hand tangled in the sheets. Kade watches me with his skin-prickling, black stare. His throat works, each swallow tugging low in my body. An ache grows between my legs. A yearning for his mouth in other places. My eyes flutter shut. His tongue strokes the same spot over and over in time to the sucking. Drawing my blood to the surface until I'm throbbing with it.

Oh god, I'm going to—

"Stop," I moan. "Please, stop."

He licks my wrist in a long, slow line. I squirm. He releases my arm, and I scrabble backwards into my chair like a startled hermit crab. Kade's eyes close but his tongue catches a spill of blood from the corner of his mouth.

"You taste good," he says, and I shiver.

His breathing deepens. A tension I didn't know was there eases his arrogant face to softly stunning. I sit and throb in the chair. Two tiny marks show on my wrist surrounded by a circle of red. It's not even bleeding, only a faint sting to indicate his teeth ever penetrated. I stare at Kade's mouth. Half-parted lips, the glimpse of fang on each inhalation. The clean lines of his jaw. Powerful muscles for sucking.

What would he do if I sat on his face?

"Fucking incubus demon," I say, and shove to my feet.

The bastard used his powers on me. Awakened sexual arousal. If I hadn't made him stop, I would've orgasmed from his bite.

But he doesn't get to have that control over me.

A cold shower fails to cool my flushed and swollen skin. I touch myself and the climax explodes with such force, I slide down the wall, my fist stuffed in my mouth.

Okay, so maybe Kade has some control.

13

Kade's groans wake me. Darkness still presses beyond the curtains, my eyes gritted from lack of sleep. Kade writhes on the bed. A flush pinks his cheeks, but his skin is cold and clammy. Redness creeps from under the bandages. I shake him awake. Black, dazed eyes blink at me and sparkle as if filled with stars, making me dizzy. His spine bows, breaking my gaze. The cords in his neck sing with strain.

"Why isn't the blood helping?" I say.

He struggles to focus on me. His ribs heave. Fresh garnet stains the bandages.

"Need more." Another seizure wracks him. "*Fuck*, it hurts."

I wince, but hold out the same wrist. A faint bruise marks the press of his mouth. He shakes his head and squeezes his eyes shut. His heels shove at the mattress.

"Not enough energy," he pants.

"Energy?"

His teeth click. "Sexual energy. Need to bite where it's more powerful."

"And where is that?" I say, the suspicion clear in my voice.

His eyes are slits of black. "Inner thigh."

My muscles quiver, and I press my legs together.

"Nope. No way."

He spasms on the bed, a whine in his throat.

"Then sex," he croaks. "But don't judge me. I'm not at my best."

"I am not having sex with you, Kade."

His limbs thrash, hands flailing. I grab one without thinking. Comforting him.

"Um, you're not going to die though, right?" I say.

A shudder runs through him. His grip tightens and crushes my hand. I manage to tug free before he breaks my fingers. He thuds onto the floor and crawls towards the door.

"Where the hell are you going?" I say, backing up.

"Outside. So I don't burn your house down."

"I thought bursting into flames was a myth."

That would explain what the police found close to my aunt's body. They thought a dog had attacked her. But they couldn't understand why there was ash scattered in the grass.

I always knew it was demons. No dog would have mauled her body that way. I've carried the guilt for her death since I was twenty. I'm the one who can see demons—I should've been able to protect her. Maybe they killed her while looking for me. But who killed them? Did one of the mysterious Diviners come to her aid, but they were too late to save her?

Thinking about my aunt's last moments gives me night-mares. Especially since, one day, they're likely to be mine.

The current demon in my life continues to crawl for the door. Dried blood stripes his back beneath the criss-cross of bandages.

"For Christ's sake, Kade, get back in bed before you make yourself worse."

I jam my fingers in his armpits and hoist him to his feet, with some assistance. We stumble a couple of steps to the bed.

His legs collapse and we flop onto the mattress, me on top. He pushes at me.

"Get off," he mutters. "You'll burn."

His heart hammers against my chest. His body goes limp.

"Reiley," he whispers into my hair, "I don't want to die."

I huff into his neck. "God, I hate you."

"I know," he says.

His chuckle turns into a cough, and I shove up on my elbows. His hair is mussed and flopping all over the place, quite unlike its usual perfect, boy-band style.

"How much pain are you in?"

His mouth twitches. "You might have to do all the work."

I climb off him. "Wait here."

I grab a few things from the cupboard and lock myself in the en-suite, spreading the items on the counter beside the sink. Incredulous eyes meet mine in the mirror.

"Well, what am I supposed to do?" I grump at my reflection. "Let him die?"

Probably. Okay, so he looks a state, but the whole dying thing could be a lie, like all the bullshit about harassing me to protect me. What are my options, though? Watch and wait with a fire extinguisher, just in case?

I've prayed for his inglorious end numerous times over the past few months, most of it by my hand. Now that it's here, I find myself baulking. I've never killed a demon. Guess I'm not starting now, either.

"This is insane," I say to my reflection.

She agrees.

I pull my t-shirt and leggings off and drape them on the side of the bath. My arms cuddle my nakedness, my palm splayed to hide the scars on my ribs. I turn and look over my shoulder at the slashes and punctures on my back, shiny and white now.

Kade doesn't get to see them. He doesn't get to see me.

Am I really going to have life-or-death sex with a demon? At least he's pretty. Otherworldly with his fangs and bottomless eyes.

I put on my favourite violet corset with black lace and stays. The material hugs my ribs and lifts my breasts, padding on the chest for extra enhancement. Nerves squiggle in my stomach.

I bet I'm the shortest and most flat-chested woman Kade's ever been with. All of my wobbly bits are real, not silicone. Though he's about to get some silicone.

Guaranteed no woman has ever done this to him before.

My next dilemma is what toy to use—double-ended for my pleasure, but no underwear so my arse is bare to the world, or underwear with a toy on top for clitoral stimulation only? Choices, choices.

Screw it. If this has to happen, I'm damn well going to enjoy it.

He should, too. Just thinking about popping his cherry speeds my heart and pools heat between my legs. No guy has ever left my bed without a smile on his face after a session.

Except for the last one.

Maybe this is a bad idea.

I step into the straps and pull them up my legs. Silky silicone slides inside me, and my head falls back. I fasten the harness around my waist, adjust the elastic, and glance in the mirror. I wiggle my hips.

I look fantastic.

Taking a deep breath, I walk into the bedroom. Kade's eyes widen where he's sprawled in the centre of my bed.

"What the hell is that?" he says.

14

I smirk at the wide-eyed demon in my bed. "If we have to have sex, I'll be the one fucking you, not the other way around."

Kade's throat bobs. His uncertainty sends a fizz of excitement to my gut. I kneel on the foot of the bed. Kade scoots until his shoulders press against the headboard, his gaze on my crotch. I wrap my fingers around the curved shaft of the purple strap-on. The silicone flares at the head for a semi-realistic shape, the material flexible and smooth for easier penetration, though I'm sure Kade doesn't care about that.

He will in a minute.

He clears his throat. "Can't we just have normal sex?"

His gaze flicks between my face and the bobbing dildo. I thrust my hips to make it dance and the other end shifts inside, teasing me.

"My bed, my rules," I say a bit breathlessly. "Or would you rather die?"

His eyes narrow. "You're enjoying this."

"Now I am." A wicked smile stretches my mouth. "Time to take your punishment, little demon."

"Isn't getting clawed for you punishment enough?"

"You say that but, somehow, I'm finding it hard to trust you."

He curses and grinds his teeth, another wave of pain

shuddering through him. I ignore a small pulse of guilt.

Is not giving him a choice too close to rape? He can't exactly say no. Though he's not giving me much of a choice, either.

Let's see how far he'll go. If he's fibbing about dying, I'll find out soon.

"Lie on your back," I say.

He hesitates, then uncurls himself. I crawl up his legs and unbutton his jeans. His pulse jumps in the hollow of his throat. I slowly lower his zip. He watches me, all cheekbones and black eyes. His fingers tap a rhythm on the covers.

"Hands on the headboard, and keep them there," I say.

He wraps his fingers around the bars. It arches his back and stretches his stomach, silky skin sliding with each rapid breath. My own fingers ache to stroke that taut, flat expanse, run up his ribs, follow the curve of his shoulders. His wounds ooze garnet blood into the bandages. I curl my hands in his waistband and peel off his jeans.

Must keep touching to a minimum.

He's long, hard and smooth. No hair to distract from the carved lines and firm muscles. Of course he has a fantastic body, he's a bloody incubus demon. Slim, but powerful. I almost ache to feel him inside me, but that would be a mistake.

And I'm full up at the moment.

My hands brush his ankles, and he jumps.

"Nervous, Kade?"

"What about oral?" he gulps. "I'm great at oral."

"If I won't let you bite my thigh, your mouth is definitely not going there, either."

I gently bend his legs. His hands tighten on the bars.

"This isn't what I had in mind," he says, his voice a decibel higher.

"You thought you could just waltz into my house, spin some heroic tale, and have your wicked way?"

He shakes his head, his hair flicking across his eyes. "I had nowhere else to go."

"Looks like you need friends after all."

He lifts his head off the pillow. "And is this what friends do?"

"This is what happens when actions have consequences." I grin. "I hope you can handle it, little demon."

I squirt lube into my palms and work it over the dildo until it's slippery. Kade's breathing quickens. Hell, *my* breathing quickens. The tingles in my belly are something else.

It's been too long since I did this.

I massage down his thighs to his exposed arse. My thumb brushes his puckered hole. He leaps about a foot off the bed, then winces.

"Lie still," I say. No mercy.

"Reiley..." he pants.

His arms tremble, his hands mottled around the bars. I stroke him again, and he clenches under the light touch. I rub until his body relaxes, then slip a finger inside him.

"Oh, fuck," he says.

I circle my finger and he wriggles, a whine trapped in his throat. He's tight and warm. Definitely not as hot as he should be. He really is quite ill.

Well, he's about to get a shitload of sexual energy.

I push his knees higher and tease him with the lubed tip of the dildo, one hand wrapped around the base of the shaft near the harness. Kade tosses his head and struggles to look at me.

God, I want to drive myself hard and deep. But it's too soon for that, especially for his first time.

First and only time, I remind myself.

I nestle between his bent legs, his thighs and calves gripping my ribs. I plant a hand on either side of him. His chest heaves.

He licks his lips, his expression desperate. "Reiley—"

I tilt my hips and ease the strap-on inside him. Whatever he planned on saying dissolves in a long moan, his body arching beneath me. It drives the dildo deeper, both inside him and inside me. I bite my lip on my own moan, my heart already thundering. I glide in and out, the toy rubbing my g-spot whenever I move inside Kade. The effort quivers through my stomach muscles, tightening others, the tension building. Each thrust grinds my clit against the textured material at the front of the strap-on.

And this is why it's my favourite.

That warm, heavy weight swells too soon. This may be a record. Kade's noises don't help.

I love pegging because I'm in control and there's nothing sexier than a man confident enough to be dominated. Every sound he makes is because of me, because of what I'm doing to his body.

And Kade's sounds are *hot.* Wild, frantic. Untethered. Noises I never thought I'd hear from the self-assured incubus demon.

His head is thrown back, the cords in his neck taut. I'm fascinated by the throb of his pulse. His skin glows brighter than the white of his bandages, not that there's much white left. Muscles bunch in his arms, his shoulders, his stomach. He rocks his hips to match me, and my eyes roll.

"Please let me touch you," he groans, clenching and un-clenching his fingers. "I want to touch you."

My rhythm falters.

"Keep your hands on the bars," I growl.

He whines, but I increase my pace, nailing his prostate, and it becomes a strangled, "Oh-fuck-god-Reiley."

I slam into him. All my blood throbs where the dildo is buried between my legs. Kade sobs my name. My muscles tremble.

God, I'm so swollen. So close. So tight.

The orgasm bursts in a tingling rush, and a guttural cry spills from my mouth. My spine bows, driving everything deep. Wave after wave washes through me and explodes to my fingertips. I'm vaguely aware of Kade crying out. Pulsing flesh. Something hot splashes my arm, but my eyes are shut as the last of the pleasure rides me. My head flops forward, my hair tumbling across my face. My arms shake with the effort of keeping myself propped up when all I want to do is collapse on top of Kade and pass out in the afterglow.

Though collapsing on Kade is a bad idea, and not just because of his wounds. The poor guy is a mess. Spunk glistens on his flat stomach, his chest, his bandages. There's even a glob on his jaw and in his hair. His hands drop from the headboard, leaving two melted imprints of his fingers on the bars.

Fucking hell. What if he'd been touching me?

I pull out of him as gently as I can. He manages a whimper, but his eyes stay shut, sweat slicking his brow and pooled between his collarbones. His legs flop akimbo. I leave him to recover in private.

Removing the strap-on in the bathroom is enough to give me breath-stealing aftershocks. I wash the dildos, letting the toy air dry by the sink. I step into black underwear and keep the corset on after checking Kade didn't hit me with anything.

Toilet paper catches the spot near my elbow. He got most of it on himself. When I return to the bedroom, he hasn't moved, though his eyes are open. He blinks at the ceiling.

"Kade?"

No response. I climb on the bed and kneel beside him. He rolls his head to look at me.

"Are you all right?"

He blinks and breathes in answer.

Oh dear. I've broken him.

"Come on," I say softly, "let's get you cleaned up."

I coax him to the edge of the bed. He mumbles something. I tilt his chin and swipe the glob from his jaw, rolling it between my fingertips. I smile at his dazed expression.

"You just got pegged, little demon," I say.

I guide him into the tub and leave him standing under the spray from the shower, the dragon-patterned curtain pulled across.

He feels warmer. Not as hot as he should be, but getting there.

"Don't take the dressings off," I say to his shadow through the curtain. "I'll change them when you're done."

I swap the bedsheets, stained with his blood and more recent fluids, then return to check on him. Water patters on ceramic.

"How're you getting on?" My voice echoes on the tiles.

Still nothing. I peek around the curtain. He stands where I left him, wet hair sticking to his cheekbones and framing those disconcerting eyes. His arms hang at his sides. Creamy stuff clings to his chest and it's not shower gel. I step into the bath, misted by the spray pummelling his back.

Is he in shock? Can you get orgasm shock? I mean, the intensity was surprising, even for a pegging veteran like me.

Or is he traumatised? He wasn't exactly enthused by the idea. Will his passivity switch to embarrassed rage when his senses return?

Despite a rigorous vetting process, I had to call the police on the last guy I hooked up with from PegLeg. Some men aren't confident enough in their masculinity. They crave the act, but feel emasculated after. Ashamed for enjoying it, as if it makes them gay, which is beyond ridiculous.

Like getting pegged by women only? Hello—not gay.

As soon as it was over and before I could bask in the languid afterglow, the guy started screaming at me. Breaking things. Advancing on me with fists clenched. He hated me for 'making' him enjoy it. I locked myself in the bathroom until the police came. It was a little humiliating to explain, but the officers were nothing less than courteous. I stressed that I had the guy's consent, helped by our message exchange planning the meet up. Saying how excited he was.

But did Kade really give me consent or did I just force him?

Tits. What have I done?

"Kade," I say, gripping his shoulders and looking up into his eyes, "I need to know you're okay. Talk to me. Please."

He wraps his arms around me and buries his face in my hair. He's shaking. I rub his back in soothing circles, his skin slick beneath my palm.

"I'm sorry," I say. "I should've warned you—the first time can be overwhelming."

I hug him until he stops shivering, then ease him back beneath the hot spray, the front of my corset sticky. Fluid glistens on my upper chest. I squirt shampoo into my hands and wash Kade's hair. He closes his eyes against the bubbles. My palms glide over his smooth chest, the roughness of bandages, his ribbed abs. Now he smells like lime and mint instead of bleach and summer grass. I cup his hand and dribble in a generous blob of gel.

"I think you can take it from here," I say.

He massages his fingers where I left off at his bellybutton. Moves lower. A lather builds. His eyes stay on me. The heat of the shower pounds in my temples, making me dizzy. Or it's him. Bubbles glide down his thighs. Water trickles under my corset, my pants sticking to me. He strokes himself and starts to get hard.

"Looks like you've got this all in hand," I squeak, and back away until my heel hits the rear of the tub.

I stumble out of the bath instead of succumbing to the ache to press him to the wet tile and slide myself on all that long, firm length.

I fuck him, not the other way around. It can't be the other way. I don't trust him. Or myself.

I change into leggings and another black t-shirt. The water shuts off in the bathroom.

Did Kade get himself off or was the show just for my benefit?

He hesitates in the bathroom doorway, a towel around his hips. His hair sticks to his cheekbones in spikes. A fang grazes his bottom lip.

God, he's beautiful.

The cocksucker.

"You able to talk yet?" I say, striving for nonchalance.

He clears his throat. "Maybe."

His voice is a little croaky, but then he was quite vocal.

A little frisson of lust curls in my stomach. He was the best partner I've had, though I'll never tell him that. Responsive. Sexy in his undoing. Followed commands.

"Sit on the bed," I say.

I remove his sodden dressings, my knee pressed to his towelled thigh. The claw wounds have dried and scabbed as if they're a few days old. Best to let them breathe. Kade's head nods, his eyes half-lidded. I tuck him into the fresh sheets, limp and unresisting, and he immediately falls asleep.

Poor little demon, all tuckered out. I did that.

The sun has risen while we were occupied, the sky a perfect blue to balance out last night's storm. It's still early. I could do with another hour or two's kip myself.

I curl in my chair and drift off to the soft sigh of Kade's breathing.

15

Kade is still sleeping when I wake a couple of hours later. He's in a ball under the covers, hugging his knees to his chest. He looks delicate beneath the sheets. I stretch and my spine pops, my muscles cramped from napping in the chair.

Stupid demon in my bed.

I pad into my kitchen, open the fridge, and swig orange juice straight from the carton. I transfer the used bedsheets and Kade's jeans from the washing machine to the tumble drier. The appliance clicks on with a satisfying rumble.

Like in Cabaret Voltaire, I feel the prickling heat of Kade's gaze before I meet it.

He lingers in the doorway, the towel around his hips. The scratches, though healing, are stark against his chest. Despite his energy booster, his eyes are still solid black and bottomless.

I've seen him at his most vulnerable. This is where the insecure guys have a rant. Or call me a whore.

"Do you eat food?" I say to his unsettling silence. "Or are you a liquid-only diet?"

He quirks a brow. "I eat food."

"Then take a seat."

I sweep my arm towards my high table in the centre of the room. It used to stick out from the breakfast nook before I jammed my writing desk in there. Kade slides gingerly onto a stool, and I turn away to hide a smile.

Poor little demon must be sore. Crap, that's sexy.

It's not something I get to see—the morning after. Though, technically this is the same morning. Once without any time for awkwardness is enough for me until the urge returns in a month or so. Then it's on to someone new. No chance of a relationship.

I pop bread under the grill and whip up a pan of scrambled eggs. My stomach rumbles at the scent of coffee and hot food. I slather butter on the toast, pile it with eggs, and plonk a plate in front of Kade beside a steaming mug of cardamom coffee. I put my own plate opposite him and hop on the stool.

No soreness for me this morning, just a pleasant ache.

Kade scoffs his portion and I watch, fascinated. It's the first time I've seen him eat. I scrape the last third of mine onto his plate, my belly full.

"Hungry?"

He pauses with a forkful half-way to his mouth. "You know, I think I'm starting to hate *you*, Reiley."

I grin at him, and he laughs, then rubs his shoulder. The wounds seem angrier close up, though the bruise has vanished from his cheek, his lip its normal, pouting softness rather than swollen. I come around the breakfast bar and put the back of my hand on his forehead. Kade goes very still, his fingers wrapped around his mug.

"You're not as warm as you should be. Why haven't you healed?"

He rolls the cup between his palms. "Some of the energy escaped."

"Is that why you melted my bed frame?"

He ducks his head. He can't be—

Oh, wow.

"I never knew demons could blush," I say, delight tightening my throat.

Kade scowls at his coffee. "It just took me by surprise."

"I bet it did," I purr.

He blushes harder. How cute.

For fuck's sake, he's not cute. He's the goddamn incubus demon who made my life hell, good intentions or not. Plus, I'm pretty sure he's screwed half the female population of the northern hemisphere.

Let's not forget how easily he gets bored.

I have to be careful. No emotional involvement. Pegging is great for that—they're exposed, I'm not. A lot of the guys wear masks so it's anonymous. Hot sex with mysterious strangers. They don't stay the night. But letting someone inside me takes trust. Intimacy. It's hard not to get emotions tangled in it.

Stupid female hormones. Men are better at the whole pump 'em and dump 'em thing.

"What would've happened if you'd been touching me when you did your metal-melting trick?" I say, and reclaim my seat.

He sips his coffee. "It would've felt amazing."

"Away and shite. My skin would've sloughed off."

"Healing energy doesn't hurt."

"Tell that to my headboard."

He slides me a look. "I'll need more blood."

"No guesses where from. I believe my answer was 'nope' and 'no way.'"

"Fine, if you're happy feeding me from your wrist over the next few weeks. Gives Thaddeus and Myron plenty of time to find us."

I suppress a shudder. "So take more in one go."

"I can't."

"Why not?"

The silence stretches. I force myself not to squirm under his scrutiny.

"Because you'll get sick," he says softly.

"Oh."

Does he actually care? I play our interactions in my head. He didn't follow me home from the club. But he did bad-mouth the books I spilled my heart and soul and truth into. He tried to have them taken down for copyright infringement. He nearly ruined me. Am I to believe he was just making it look good to fool his brethren that he was torturing me, driving me to suicide?

I shake myself and blow out a breath. "You're a manipulative twat."

He smirks, flashing fang. My stomach squiggles.

"Is that a yes, Reiley?"

"One feed and you'll heal, *completely?* Then we deal with these demons and you leave me alone?"

"If that's what you want."

"Kade, that's what I've always wanted."

Something flits across his face, too fast to read. He jumps off the stool and pats the seat, his expression back to smug and arrogant. I sigh to hide my wobbling knees on the journey around the table.

"I really hate you," I say, and strip my leggings off, revealing my silky black underwear.

Why did I choose sexy? Wishful thinking? I *wish* I'd chosen granny panties.

Kade drags his gaze upward. Quite a different gaze from

when he was staring at the strap-on. No uncertainty.

"I know," he says, and gives me a slow, wicked smile. "But I really like *you*."

I perch on the stool. Kade kneels at my feet, not touching, but heat flares everywhere his eyes graze. I press my legs together.

"No funny business," I bark. "Keep your hands to yourself and no incubus voodoo crap."

"It'll hurt unless I—"

"Let it hurt."

Better to hurt than leave me craving more. More Kade. More sex until I become one of his women, fighting over the scraps of his attention.

He shrugs, but doesn't move. He watches me, and I give a tense nod. Tentative fingers touch my knees. I swallow hard and spread my legs, glaring at the ceiling instead of him, my cheeks hot.

God, I'm turned on. The motherfucker.

He kisses the inside of my thigh, and I jump. Another feather-soft kiss tugs deep in my belly. I open my mouth to growl at him, but the words die at the hunger on his face. From my perch, I can see the perfect dip of his back to where the towel sits low on his hips.

I want to peg that sweet arse again already.

Fuck.

Kade sucks gently on my thigh, yanking my gaze to his. His lips curve against my tingling skin. Then he bites. My teeth snap on a yelp. I grip the wooden edge of the table behind me. Sharp pain flares when he sucks but, unlike the feeding from my wrist, it doesn't fade. He keeps sucking and the pain swells, pressure expanding from his mouth to my gut. He stares at me with his depthless eyes. His face is so close to my crotch, his breath brushes the material of my pants. Hot against the damp.

Uh-oh…

The next pull of Kade's mouth draws pain, but it changes. The sucking becomes a throbbing line connecting his mouth to the apex of my thighs. He watches me and drinks, his hands gripping the legs of the chair. The pressure builds, heating and swelling with each suck, dancing between pleasure and pain.

"I said no tricks," I gasp.

"I'm not doing anything." He licks a spill of blood from my thigh. "I swear."

He bends his head, and feeds. I struggle not to squirm.

Maybe he's lying. Or I'm a masochist.

Oh, god, I can't orgasm from this, surely? His fangs in my thigh. Sucking. Licking… but it feels amazing.

My hips twitch, desperate for him to move an inch higher. I want to grind myself on his face. Have that scorching mouth fasten on me, fangs pressing intimate flesh, tongue exploring, teasing—

I tremble on the edge. My breath catches in my throat.

Kade eases away. "That's probably enough."

I swallow a groan.

The goddamn wee shite.

I slide bonelessly from the stool. Kade catches me, his fingers splayed on my ribs, my t-shirt rucked up to my waist.

"Are you all right, Reiley?"

I have to blink a few times to focus on his face. He smirks at me. Blood paints his bottom lip.

"You taste good," he says.

I don't know what happens next. Temporary madness. My shields are down. I'm horny and vulnerable. Woozy from blood loss.

My hands cup his face. His eyes widen.

"Prove it," I say.

I kiss him. I taste copper, then it's all Kade—heat and smoke. He presses me tighter against him. I realise I'm sitting in his lap. And his towel is unravelling.

Kissing him was a bad idea.

But I'm finding it hard to stop.

He nibbles my mouth. His tongue teases mine. He's careful with his teeth, though the press of them against my lips reminds me of his mouth on my thigh, and my body pulses. His slim fingers slip under my t-shirt and scorch a path up my ribs. I arch my spine, grinding myself into his lap, which is not helping me climb back into my head to call a halt to this insanity.

For Christ's sake, I'm snogging his face off.

He lifts me without effort, and I wrap my legs around his waist like it's the natural thing to do. His towel stays on the floor. My fingers knead the firm muscles of his back while his thumbs stroke me through my bra. Push-up, but not stuffed, thank god. He carries me to the bedroom, kissing me the whole way.

I hate to admit it, but I'm breathless.

He lays me on the bed and covers my body with his. Completely naked. I feel him through my underwear, a wisp of nothing separating us, and it's tempting, so tempting, to let him slide inside. I wouldn't even have to take my pants off. He could just tug the material out of the way and fill the ache inside me.

I fist my hands in his hair, his mouth merciless on mine. His palm slides down to my hip, then across my thigh. He lifts himself higher.

"No sex," I blurt into his mouth.

He groans and drops his head on my collarbone. "You started with the kissing, why am I being punished?"

"Because I don't trust you."

He pouts at me and, dammit, I'm kissing him again.

Kissing is okay. I love kissing. I don't get to do it enough. This is fine. I can control myself.

We snog on my bed like a couple of teenagers. I suck his tongue into my mouth, and he moans.

Fuck. I can't resist a man who makes a bit of noise.

We try to climb inside each other, mouths first. I can't breathe. My lips are swollen. My pulse throbs everywhere; he must be able to feel it. His heart thrums against my chest. His hands pet me—sides, hips, thighs. He grazes my breasts, but goes no further. It's maddening. My stomach is hollow. Now I'm the one making little begging noises in my throat.

Oh, bollocks. I'm grinding on him again.

I rub that sweet, throbbing spot against his erection. I grab his tight arse and buck harder. He starts to thrust his hips, stroking himself over and over my soaked knickers. He never breaks the kiss. The pressure builds, that warm, heavy, glorious weight. I'm going to scream his name.

Kade. Kade McKade.

Frantic, I roll until I'm on top. Then, before I let his wicked mouth distract me again, I fling myself right off the bed and thud onto the floor.

Not the most graceful escape—but effective.

I blink at the leather-bound book under my bed, now in my

line of sight.

So that's where I put it after I got drunk on Buckfast. I have a few more entries to add in the incubus demon section.

My heart slams against my ribs, hard enough to wobble my whole body. The chill of the floor cools the heat from Kade's skin. The throbbing lasts longer. I listen to Kade panting on the bed. Neither of us speaks for a long time.

What the hell was I thinking? How could I have let it get so far?

Goddamn incubus demon can kiss.

The bed frame squeaks as he shifts his weight. I roll my gaze up to the edge of the mattress, bracing myself for his face peeking over. Smirking. Triumph in his eyes from getting under my skin.

"So… you *do* have a knife."

His voice sounds casual, but there's effort beneath the words. It soothes my battered dignity.

Though I have no idea what he's talking about.

"Huh?" I sit up carefully.

He's propped on his elbows in the middle of my bed, a sheet across his hips to protect his modesty. If he has any. The position tenses his abs. No wounds mar the perfection of his chest or the curve of his ribs. His lips are swollen. Ripe. His hair flops into his eyes, mussed as if someone has been running their fingers through it.

That would be me.

My shoulder and hip throb from slamming into the floor. Prickling heat climbs up my neck.

I literally had to throw myself off of him to stop. Otherwise, there's no doubt I would have kissed him until we were both naked and he was buried inside me.

What the hell is he made of—crack?

He nods at the wall opposite the bed. I drag my gaze from him to the knife in its glass display case.

"It was my aunt's," I say.

"She was a Diviner?"

"She couldn't see demons. But she was the only one who believed I could."

"She lied to you, then."

I whip my head around to glare at him. "She didn't lie."

"Why would she have a knife if she couldn't see them?"

"What's your fascination with the knife?" I say, annoyed at Kade's accusation. "It's decorative. A collector's item."

My aunt wouldn't lie to me.

"Pick it up," he says.

I frown at him. His expression reveals nothing. We stare at each other for over a minute.

"It won't hurt you, Reiley," he sighs. "You said you don't trust me. Maybe this'll help."

I climb to my feet and tug my t-shirt down. Unfortunately, it's not as long as my sleep shirt, so there's a lot of leg on display and about half a chunk of bum cheek.

Would it be cowardly to back towards the case?

Probably.

I narrow my eyes at Kade's sprawled form. "Tell me what will happen."

"Christ's sake," he snaps, sounding like me, "I'll touch it first."

He whips the covers free. I yelp and throw up a hand, shielding my eyeballs from the sight of his crotch. A naked Kade is too much for my fragile mental state. I grab a pillow from the chair and toss it at him.

"Really, Reiley?" he chuckles.

My cheeks heat, and I risk a peek. Kade holds the pillow in one hand at his waist, everything covered. He steps towards me, and I skip a retreat to stand beside the display case rather than let him lead.

I do not need to see his bare arse right now.

"Do you have the key?"

I shake my head.

"Nail file?"

Wordlessly, I hand him my metal one. He slots the tip into the keyhole, jiggles it a bit, then gives a rough twist. He raises the top panel and scoops the knife from its stand. I suck in a breath. Nothing happens. I hold out my hand.

He pulls the weapon closer to his chest. "We can't touch it at the same time."

"Why not?"

He places it on the stand. "Reiley, I swear it won't hurt you, but it's better if you see for yourself."

I narrow my eyes, then turn my gaze to the knife, examining it from every angle. Glints of silver glitter in the handle to the smooth, gold bolster between the handle and the silver blade. The blade itself is etched with whorls, and looks sharp. Steeling myself, I grab the handle, my shoulders tense. My palm tingles, and I almost drop the knife, but nothing hurts. Blackness consumes the silver of the blade. I gasp, and it slips from my fingers to clatter on the floor. Kade leaps clear, nearly losing his grip on his modesty pillow. The blade stays black, though it swirls along the silver, as if the metal is filled with smoke.

"What is that?" I whisper.

Kade eyes the knife, toes curled. He lifts his solemn gaze to mine.

"Now you can kill a demon," he says.

I glance between his serious face and the swirly black knife. "But why this one? Why not all the other ones I've tried?"

"You've tried…?"

I bend and close my fingers around the handle. "Do you know how irritating it is to stab a demon in the chest and have them laugh at you?"

I straighten, and Kade takes a step back, his fingertips rubbing his sternum. He seems to realise what he's doing and drops his hand to his side.

"It's the silver content," he says.

"What happens if you touch it?"

Wary black eyes flick between me and the knife. "It burns."

"Will it stay like this?"

"As long as you're holding it."

"What if I drop it?"

"It'll go back to normal after a few minutes."

I give the blade an experimental poke. "And you can hold it when it's just silver?"

He nods.

"But if I slip it between your ribs like this, then what?"

He licks his lips and raises his gaze from the blade.

"Then I'll die," he says quietly.

My fingers tighten on the handle.

16

I stare out the taxi window at the passing scenery. A shimmer of gold covers the gorse bushes on Arthur's Seat, everything green and growing and alive. Including the incubus demon sitting beside me.

Alive, that is.

He stares out his own window, only his nose and the plane of one cheek visible. My maroon hoodie hugs his shoulders, loose on me but perfect on him, like everything else. He's back in his jeans, but I had no shoes that would fit so he's wearing a pair of my thick socks. My fingers itch to stroke the knob of his spine peeking above his hood, then slide upwards to the vulnerable nape of his neck. I could grab his hair and twist his face around, claim that damn—

I sit on my hand and frown out the window.

We've been silent since leaving the cottage, lost in quiet contemplation. I don't know what he's thinking about, but my mind is whirling with thoughts of the knife and my aunt.

And let's not forget about the book.

Did she really find it in an indie bookstore on West Nicholson Street? Maybe she had it all along and used the other demon books as cover.

Why would my aunt lie to me? If she was a Diviner, she

could have taught me how to fight. We could have taken her knife and hunted them together instead of turning into a pair of reclusive bats flapping around her cottage for the two years after my release from hospital. I could have protected her on the bleak expanse of Duddingston Loch that awful winter. I wouldn't have been left an orphan.

Okay, technically not an orphan. But I've not spoken to my parents in almost eight years.

The taxi turns off Duddingston Low Road onto Holyrood Park Road, the driver picking up our signals and not bothering to talk, though her eyes keep flicking to Kade in the rearview mirror. She had a good goggle at him when she pulled into my driveway. I don't think she even noticed his socks in lieu of shoes.

I slide a glance at him under my lashes. His hands are in his lap, his slim fingers playing absently with the seam of his jeans, running up and down the ridged material. Up and down…

Oh, for god's sake. How? How is that enough to send a bolt of desire deep in my gut? Fine, the guy is lust on legs. But I need to ignore it.

The flat, green expanse of The Meadows opens up on our left, the pathways lined by beech and cherry trees, the flowers a froth of pink. Groups of people meander in the spring sunshine, several playing Frisbee or football. The park disappears behind buildings as we head further up Buccleuch Street, away from the route I took on Christmas day.

That was the last time I saw Kade until he knocked on my door four months later.

I risk another peek and look straight into his husky-blue eyes. I manage not to gasp this time, just a tiny flinch, but my heart skips. He rewards me with a smirk—damn him—and returns his attention to Potterrow slipping past.

"What?" he'd said to my reaction when he stepped into my living room, dressed to leave.

"Sorry, I just—I didn't expect… I mean, of course I expected…" I shut my stupid, stammering mouth and tried again. "You look weird."

Much better.

He grinned at me. No fangs. The wavering was barely noticeable, but the vertigo seemed to be worse, especially when I raised my gaze to his eyes.

"You think human is weird?" he said.

"I guess I got used to your normal face."

His grin softened to a pleased expression that did funny things to my stomach.

"This is my normal face, Reiley," he said. "For everyone but you."

At which point, I scuttled away, inexplicably flustered.

The taxi zooms down Lauriston Place, then left onto Nightingale Way, almost to Kade's house. Excuse me, fancy-pants penthouse. I touch the knife at my hip for reassurance, the blade sheathed in its custom holster and tucked into my jeans. The zip of my dusky-gold hoodie is lowered enough for me to reach in and draw the weapon.

I've practised.

I've also been arguing with myself ever since Kade told me to pick it up. I never would have discovered its properties without him. He could have said nothing and I wouldn't have been any wiser. Unarmed, vulnerable, and reliant on him to protect me. Why would he give me a weapon that could kill him? Is it just about gaining my trust? Maybe he has an ulterior motive. Maybe I'll relax my guard and he'll spring his trap.

What's the moral of my own book, *Demon Lover?* Never trust a demon.

"Here we are," the taxi driver says, stopping in front of Kade's apartment block and turning to flash him a winsome smile.

I pull a tenner from my wallet and wave it in her face to get her attention. She graces me with a bland lip twitch and accepts the fare.

"Anytime you need a ride, just call me." She presses a business card into Kade's palm. *"Anytime."*

She purrs the last word. I roll my eyes and shove out of the car, though I'm thankful for the reminder.

Kade is an incubus demon. Women drool at the mere sight of him. The quicker I get shot of him, the better.

He joins me on the concrete path and rummages in his pocket.

"I could've paid," he says.

I open my mouth to make some comment about me being rich and successful when I notice a 'Sold' sign sticking out of the ornamental bush that trapped my bike on that cold Christmas day. The number on it is Kade's apartment. Keys jingle in his hand.

"You're moving?" I say.

Is that disappointment in my voice? Surely not.

"It's fake. Thaddeus and Myron were looking for me. I was hoping it would throw them off." He glances at me on his way into the vestibule. "Worried you'd miss me?"

"Did you really run all the way from here to mine in bare feet?" I say, glaring resolutely at the bush.

"Well, I was being chased." A lock clicks and the door

whooshes open. "There was a brief jog on Arthur's Seat. And some hiding."

Kade stands and holds the door for me. I hesitate in the vestibule.

Is this a stupid idea? To be honest, I needed a distraction. I have a weapon and Kade is healed. Why not see if the demons are still at his place and get rid of them all in one day?

I'm really not trained for this.

"We don't have to go in, Reiley," Kade says, giving me that soft look again. "We probably have a couple of days to plan."

I stride past him and mash the button for the lift.

A couple of days alone with Kade is too long. He's only been back in my life for less than twenty-four hours and I've already pegged him, let him feed off me—twice—and snogged him until I was breathless.

Another day and I'll want to bloody marry the guy.

17

Splotches of brown dribble from Kade's hallway into the living room. Dried, his blood passes for human. Would it look different under a microscope? Rectangular cells instead of a biconcave disk, perhaps? I always enjoyed biology in high school. Maybe I should poke Kade with a needle and discover his other secrets.

I draw my knife, comforted by the swirling black. Kade nearly presses himself to the wall.

"After you," he says.

I smirk and enter the living room, the sun starting to set and blazing through the wall-to-wall window. The dining table has a royal-blue cloth this time. A shattered wine glass sparkles on the floor in the sitting area next to a coffee table, a spill of maroon staining the floorboards. One of the trio of couches framing the coffee table is canted. Dried blood crinkles the leather and clots in a sizeable pool on the laminate.

"Drinking alone, were we?" I say drily, though a curl of nausea roils in my stomach.

"A guy's got to rest." Kade's smile is fleeting. "But lucky I was. I know what they would've done if anyone else were here."

I shudder and turn for the stairs to the next level, eager to get away from the signs of a struggle.

"Let's search the other storeys," I say.

I shake my head to dispel the image of Kade skewered on the claws of a massive demon, his bare feet kicking at air, his hands wrapped desperately around a corded forearm, the second demon closing in, intent on punching through his ribcage.

He must have been scared.

The stairs bend in a dog-leg, then open into a corridor ending in more glass. The first door swings inward on a study with a desk and bookshelf and the obligatory windowed wall. The door opposite leads to his much larger bedroom, the curtains partly drawn. Two loungers and some potted plants take up most of the space on the balcony. There's furniture in his bedroom, a door to an en-suite, but I can't stop staring at his bed.

The thing is *huge*. I could roll across it five times and still not reach the edge of grey silk sheets. What's bigger than super-king? Super-duper-sexy-king? It's freaking orgy sized.

Perfect for him.

"Are you petting my bed, Reiley?" Kade says, and I jump.

Shit. My fingers are stroking the silky sheets. The material is cold, but I bet it warms up quickly.

I take a rapid step back. "This room's empty. Let's check the next."

"Don't you want to search the en-suite?"

And picture him in his no-doubt-giant shower or bathtub, all slippery and wet? No thanks. Plus, I've already seen the show.

It's spectacular.

"You do it," I say. "I'll stand guard."

Stupid, smirking, smarmy-faced *arse*.

The third level has a cinema room and a gym, then it's on to the roof with a three-hundred-and-sixty-degree view of Edinburgh. The hot tub is accessed through a private garden and sits next to the glass of the balcony, looking down on The Meadows.

I'd spend all my time up here, soaking in the water in a tiny bikini, a tumbler of wine perched on the tile. Watching the sun rise and set. Leaning back against the firm heat of Kade. His hands gliding on wet skin to slip the straps from my shoulder and—

Nope.

Let's not forget he had all this luxury while I shivered in my cottage, belly rumbling, my income dwindled to zero.

I sheath my knife and stomp downstairs.

"I'm going to pack some clothes," Kade says on the second level, disappearing into his bedroom.

No way am I going back in there. And, hello—presumptuous much?

"Maybe you should stay in a hotel," I mutter.

"What?"

"Nothing," I say.

Instead of fidgeting like an idiot, I head into his study for a nose about. The desk is high quality, the Apple Macbook on it worth about ten of my laptops. A beanbag sits beside a low table next to the window. I plonk my bum in Kade's padded leather chair and scan his bookshelf. Lots of fantasy, some sci-fi. I recognise most of the names. Then—

"You little shite," I whisper.

There, on a shelf to themselves, are all seven of my published books from the *Demon* series. Creases mar every spine.

He really did read them.

A jumble of emotions churns in my stomach. My throat closes with the ridiculous urge to cry. The books blur, and I spin on the chair to face his desk. The desk where he sat on his Macbook and trolled me online. I yank open the lid. The screen brightens to a familiar image—a graphic I made to showcase my work, the seven books spread out equally on a fiery background and there, in the eighth space, a little smiling picture of me.

I stuff my fist in my mouth. My breath hitches. The chair rattles into the bookcase. I power-walk around the desk and through the doorway. Kade steps from his bedroom, a bag over his shoulder.

"Are you all right—"

I barge past him. "I need to get out of here."

"Reiley, wait—"

I barrel down the stairs, swinging myself around the dog-leg.

And right into a scorching wall of flesh.

18

Black spines arch from the demon's back, two ram horns curling from its forehead. Leathery wings brush the walls. Its eyes are yellow, though not solid like Kade's, the cornea jaundiced.

"Hello, Diviner," the demon says, baring teeth the same colour as its eyes.

All my breath rushes out. I lunge for my knife.

Black claws flash, short but wickedly curved, like a cat's. The demon slashes at my stomach, hooks my jumper, and tosses me over its massive shoulder. I sail into the back of the couch and skid to a stop, blinking at the ceiling.

"Reiley!" Kade yells.

I turn my head, which seems heavier than before. Slower. My knife lies half-way between me and the stairs. The demon blocks Kade with flexing wings of mottled grey.

"I should have known, *incubus*," the monster spits, as if it's a dirty word. "You cannot resist fucking them."

"Jealous, Myron?" Kade says.

A lick of pride burns my gut. The demon growls and bunches his huge fists.

"Your kind should be gutted at birth. Barely demon. Pretty plaything for the humans." Myron snaps his teeth. "I'm going to ruin your face."

Kade swings on the banister and slams his heels into Myron's chest, catapulting him backwards into the living room. Talons screech on laminate. Kade lands easily at the bottom of the stairs, light on his feet, now clad in black trainers with a white tick. Myron struggles upright, a sweeping wing spinning my knife closer. Red puddles shimmer between Kade and the demon.

Did the fall injure Myron that much? Why am I still lying down? I need to help Kade.

I try to sit up, but there's something wrong with my abdominal muscles. My hand flails for the back of the couch.

Is Kade shouting my name again?

I hoist myself an inch off the ground, but struggle to get higher. My head flops forward, my chin bouncing on my chest. There's blood on my shoes. I frown at it. My hoodie has rucked up to my diaphragm, the golden hem ragged and stained. The material seems to have unravelled onto my stomach and changed to red. Crimson liquid dribbles down my sides when I breathe, like waves lapping over the edge of a rock pool. There's purple, too. Pinky-grey bulges.

A dull ache starts deep in my gut. Nausea flares, pulsing with each heartbeat. My eyes finally grasp the meaning of the pink and grey and purple.

I'm looking at my own intestines bulging through slashes in my skin.

My numb fingers slip from the back of the couch. I thud on the floor, and a sharp, stabbing pain steals my breath.

"Hold on, Reiley," Kade says, his voice strained.

My head jerks towards him. He ducks a swinging right hook and rolls to avoid a slashing wing. His cheek swells, his lip bleeding again.

"Your weak human will not survive." Myron chuckles, the sound like stones grinding in a blender. "I will feed on her death. The taste is so much sweeter than sex."

His foot pistons out. Kade flies over the dining table and thumps into the window, disappearing behind a forest of chair legs. Myron stomps over to him and scoops him up, claws hooked in his hoodie.

That's another one ruined.

I laugh, but it comes out a groan. A fire sizzles on my exposed organs.

Myron swings his arm. Kade streaks through the air towards me and the couches. Glass crackles. I turn my head to the other side and meet his dazed black eyes through the space under the sofa, the coffee table shattered in a twinkling carpet that crunches underneath him.

"Ow," he says.

My little demon is getting tossed around some.

Myron's footsteps thunder into my ear. Kade disappears. The air swirls above me. Kade skids on all fours through my blood. He grits his teeth. Myron grabs him by the throat and lifts him upwards. Kade's left arm punches Myron in the neck, and Myron shrieks. He drops Kade and stumbles back, garnet liquid spreading on his shirt.

"We will find you wherever you hide, *incubus*," he hisses.

In two bounds, Myron launches himself through the window and leaps over the balcony. My eyes struggle to follow what happens, my vision feathered white and red. He appears to become a wavering cloud and drifts off into the sky. My knife clatters to the floor. Smoke curls from Kade's palm.

Once more, I blink at the ceiling. It *is* a nice ceiling—

comforting lights. They start to dim.

That's good. I'm quite tired all of a sudden. I drift like Myron the wavering cloud.

What is that curious slapping noise?

I crack open one eye. Kade kneels beside me, masturbating furiously.

"That's not calling an ambulance," I croak.

"Help me," he says, his eyes desperate.

His cock hangs limp in his fist. His face furrows in concentration.

I doubt he can conjure enough sexual energy to heal this.

The stabbing pain increases. Sweat trickles down my temples to dampen my hair. I gulp hard to keep from throwing up, afraid my guts will unravel out of my mouth. Tiny wings of regret buzz in my chest.

"It's a shame," I gasp, each breath another stab, "that I never got—to peg that sweet arse—one more time."

"Fuck, Reiley," Kade groans.

Hot liquid splashes across my stomach.

Brilliant. He's spunked on my intestines.

I stare into eyes as solid as the night. Pinpricks of light sparkle in their depths.

"You have stars in your eyes." My voice sounds tinny and far away.

"Follow them, Reiley," Kade says softly.

What a lovely idea.

His eyes fill the ceiling and become the sky. Somehow, I'm falling. Or floating. Cocooned. The stars surround me, warm instead of cold. They smell like summer. The lights wink out, one after the other, until I'm swallowed by blackness.

"I'm sorry," the night whispers. "I'm sorry."

19

Something very warm is wrapped around me, breathing softly.

Is this heaven? The lazy scent of summer. A heartbeat against my shoulder.

I open my eyes and marvel that I *can* open my eyes. I'm lying on my back, blinking at my bedroom ceiling. The warm thing snuggles closer. I try to move my head, but can't bend my neck. My gaze rolls down to see what limpet creature is clinging to me.

Blond hair flops over a scraped cheek, dark lashes fanned outward. The rest of Kade's face is buried in my throat. Goosebumps flare at the tickle of his breath on my skin. He's cuddled into my side, my arm pinned by the firm line of his body, his arm flung across my chest. Scabs crust the palm of his left hand, the skin in between shiny and red. His leg traps my thighs. I wriggle, but he hugs me tighter. An ache flares in my stomach. The ghostly slash of claws.

How healed am I?

"Kade," I whisper.

He grunts. I say his name louder.

"Ssh," he mumbles. "Sleeping."

I raise my head, but his arm blocks my view. I flick my fingers to get his attention and accidentally catch him in the crotch. He startles awake and stares at me out of one, solid-black eye.

It reminds me of being swallowed by the night. The beautiful sparkle of stars. A swoop of vertigo.

"Dammit, Reiley," he says. "Do you know how many times I had to wank over you? I'm *tired.*"

My mouth flaps for a full minute.

"I hope you cleaned me up after," I say lamely.

His eye narrows. "Do you feel sticky?"

His lips brush my neck, and I forget the question. Tingles zip to my belly and my muscles protest, though it's not as bad as the ache that preceded the stabbing pains. My breath catches anyway, but that could be the thought of Kade opening his mouth. The lick of his tongue. The delicious bite of teeth. The sucking…

Nope. Just the pain.

Kade shoves up on one arm, and I shiver at the sudden loss of heat.

"Are you still sore?" he says.

A violet bruise blooms on his other cheek, a scab on his lip. More bruises circle his throat from Myron's fingers.

"A twinge," I say, his worried expression not helping the tingles in my abused stomach. "It's fine. Did you not have enough energy to heal yourself?"

He glances down at the scores on his arms from his collision with the coffee table.

"I barely had enough to heal *you,*" he says.

The urge to look is too much. I plant my elbows and try to heave myself upright. Kade scolds me, but flutters to assist, bracing my shoulder and piling cushions behind my back.

I'm wearing a t-shirt and pants. A clean t-shirt. Meaning

he partially undressed me. He had me spread before him in only my underwear.

Okay, so my disembowelment was probably a turn off.

My eyes flick between my outfit and his—a t-shirt and boxers, tight in all the right places to emphasise the curve of his shoulders, the slimness of his hips.

"You were a bit sticky." Kade clears his throat. "And bloody."

I lift my top to below my ribs, and avoid his gaze.

He's seen my pants already. And my bra. And at least one scar. Why am I embarrassed? He's watched me parade around in a strap-on, for god's sake.

Rough, purple lumps of healing tissue mark the path of Myron's claws slashing across my stomach. All my insides are back where they belong. My muscles quiver, as if the sight of the scars is enough to make them hurt.

"I'm sorry it's not great," Kade says in a rush. "I could have healed you completely but…"

"But what?"

He glances at me, then away. My stomach churns.

What is going on down there?

"I didn't have your consent," Kade says, and quirks his mouth. "I told you I like my women awake."

Yes, when he preys on them. So I could've had no scar if he'd… shagged me while I was unconscious. But where's the fun in that?

The room gets hotter.

"Thank you," I say without looking at him.

Those wicked eyes are a bit much for me right now.

"Are you hungry?" he says.

My belly rumbles in answer.

"Wait here, I'll make you something."

He slides off the bed, and I laugh.

"You, cook?"

He pouts at me. "I can make toast. And coffee. I'm great at coffee."

He likes to brag he's great at other things, too.

Best not go there.

"I'd like to get up, anyway," I say, and swing my legs to the edge of the mattress. "I'll make the toast, you make the coffee."

"Reiley, you should really—"

"I'm fine, Kade. You did good."

I stand up and he hovers around me, as if afraid I'll keel over. My legs wobble, but there's no pain. The muscles of my stomach feel a little tight from healing. Kade skips a step ahead as I shuffle towards the kitchen.

It's cute how worried he is.

Did Myron die? And where is my knife? I forgot to look for it in the bedroom.

"How long has it been?" I unwrap the bread and stick four slices under the grill.

Kade clicks the kettle on. "Just over a day. You slept that night and all yesterday."

"Any sign of our demon friends?"

I lean my bum on the counter next to the cooker. Kade prepares two mugs, seemingly comfortable padding around my kitchen barefoot.

"Not yet," he says.

"Maybe they think I'm dead. Maybe they're not even looking for me anymore."

Good news for me, but not so much for Kade. Myron sounded pretty fanatic about flushing him out no matter where he hid.

"They know I can heal," Kade says, and perches on the stool where he fed from my thigh.

What if he did it again? Would he heal me completely? Not that I care about the scar. It just makes sense. We're in the middle of a war. I need to be at my best.

And the heat of his mouth on my thigh… The sucking…

Kade sniffs. "Is something burning?"

Bugger.

I scrape the worst of the char into the bin and slather butter on the rest. Our happy munching fills the room. We each have two more slices, then sit in silence, drinking coffee. Soft rain patters on the window of the breakfast nook. The space is cosy, rich with the scent of coffee and cardamom. A refuge against the monsters.

Though, technically, there's a monster at my kitchen table.

He doesn't look monstrous, even with his fangs and black eyes. A little battered. Sleepy. He inhales the steam from his cup and sips with his eyes closed.

I want to heal the bruises on his perfect face.

"Did you mean it?" he says quietly.

I jump.

Shit. Did I talk out loud?

He ducks his chin, his gaze on his fingers around the mug.

I lick my lips. "Mean what?"

"Your one regret."

He raises his head. Dark, deep garnet swirls through the black of his eyes. His fang catches on his bottom lip. I struggle to breathe under the heat of his gaze. He is every inch the incubus demon—seductive, dangerous. Hot as fuck.

God, he's so *hungry*.

But we can't. Shouldn't. Too risky, and not just because of

the two demons that could find us at any moment.

I open my mouth to pass off my outburst in his penthouse as some kind of dying babble.

"Tell me what you want, Kade," I manage, my voice trembling out.

"I want what you want."

My pulse speeds at the thought of having him again. He was so wonderfully responsive. And we could both do with some healing.

"Take off your clothes and lie face down on the bed," I say.

He stands without a word and pulls his t-shirt off. Bruises trail across his chest. Smirking, he tosses his top at me and strides for the bedroom. I catch it, waiting until he disappears through the door before I bury my nose in the warm material. Smells like him—summer wind and hot grass. I drop the t-shirt on the floor. My feet carry me towards the bedroom.

This is a bad idea. A *terrible* idea. But, as with most things involving Kade, I find it impossible to stop.

20

Kade is temptation and lust, lying on the bed, the sheet low, baring his smooth back. I pause just to stare at him. My fingers long to trace the spread of his shoulders, the dip of his spine, the swell of his arse modestly hidden by the sheet. He looks gorgeous and vulnerable. He turns his head.

"Don't move," I say.

He follows my progress out of one eye. I walk around to the headboard and pull silk ropes from my bedside cabinet.

"You're not going to let me touch you again, are you?" he says.

"My bed, my rules."

And touching is dangerous. Letting him touch me… It excites me too much to risk it.

Kade huffs. "Can we at least cuddle after?"

"You're quite clingy, for a demon," I smirk.

Binding his wrists to the bed speeds my heart rate. He tugs on the ropes, the muscles in his shoulders and back gliding under his skin. His pulse pounds against the side of his neck.

"No one else gets to tie me up," he growls.

"No one else gets to peg you, either."

He shivers, and pleasure curls in my belly, hot between my legs. I change into my corset and strap-on. This one has a

119

ribbed surface against my clit instead of a double dildo.

I'm too turned on already. I'll last about three minutes with the extra penetration.

I stop at the foot of the bed and slowly tease the sheet off of Kade, exposing his bum and thighs and slim calves. I crawl between his legs. His hands clench, his face pressed to the mattress.

"Reiley, wait," he blurts.

I cock my head. "Wait?"

"You're not too sore for this, are you?"

I open my mouth. Close it. An inexplicable tightness gathers in my throat.

"Reiley?" Kade says, though he's still a good boy and doesn't move.

I lick my lips. "If I said yes, would you really ask me to stop?"

My fingers brush the backs of his knees and tickle up his thighs to the curve of his firm little arse. He groans into the pillow.

I place a kiss on the small of his back and nuzzle all that silky smoothness. "Do you really want me to stop, Kade?"

"No, but—"

I bite the mound of his buttock and he spasms on the bed, arms yanking at the ropes. I nibble his other cheek.

"Just as well I'm not too sore, then," I chuckle.

He mumbles, "Thank fuck," into the pillow.

I tap his butt, pink from my teeth. "On your knees."

He sticks his arse in the air, breathing hard.

Christ, he looks spectacular.

My fingers ache to curve around his hips and stroke his muscled length. Grip his cock while I plunge deep, pumping my hand while I pump my hips. The orgasm from that would have him drooling after me, not the other way around.

I shove the urge away and massage my thumb into his taint, his balls tight to his body. He's trembling already. I slide a lubed finger into his arse, and he rewards me with a moan. I play with him, slowly, circling my finger and brushing his prostate until he writhes.

"Please, Reiley," he pants.

"You want more?"

He nods. His breath catches in his throat and the noise sends a pulse between my legs.

God, I'm not going to last long. He's too perfect.

I rub a palmful of lube into the dildo, black this time. I tease Kade with the head of the silicone cock. He strains backwards, spine bowed, shaking against the pull of the ropes, and guides me inside him, whimpering at the penetration. I grip his hips, my fingers scorched by his skin, and glide in and out of him with long, slow strokes. Kade grunts at the apex of each thrust.

Jesus, he makes me so horny, I'm throbbing. It drowns a twinge from my rapidly healed stomach muscles. Their quivering weakness only adds to the sensation.

My clit grinds the textured material at the front of the strap-on. Heat and tension build between my legs, that wonderful ache swelling outward. I increase my pace.

"Reiley," Kade gasps. *"Fuck."*

I groan, my head thrown back, my teeth clamped.

No way am I screaming his name.

I drive myself inside him, and he cries out. My cry joins his, the tension bursting in a tingling, nerve-sizzling rush. Kade's hips buck. He comes so hard, I hear the liquid spurt of him on my sheets.

The second orgasm blasts me out of nowhere. Somehow,

it starts in my hands clamped on his hips. Heat scorches up my arms and drops to my belly, pleasure clenching every muscle. I convulse against Kade, slamming deep, and that sets us off on another cycle of squirming and moaning. I scream, wordlessly, soaked to my knees. Sparkles dance in my eyes. My heart lodges in my raw throat and kicks like a mare in heat.

Finally, the sensations fade. I collapse, boneless, onto Kade's slick back. His ribs heave. I nestle my cheek between his shoulder blades and listen to the thunder of his heart. He shudders on his knees.

I could stay here forever. Soothed by his heat. Buried inside him. Safe and no longer alone.

I force myself away when I find my fingers petting his arms, up and down from the ropes at his wrists to his shoulders. Untying the silk leaves red bands on his skin. I clean up quickly in the bathroom, and pull on underwear. Kade is sitting up on the bed when I return.

"Well look at you, recovered already," I say. "I obviously didn't peg you hard enough."

He grins at me—a grin of pure, uninhibited delight that exposes his fangs and hits me between the eyes. Light-headedness weakens my knees, and I grip the bed frame to keep from staggering.

What the hell?

"I, um, made a mess," Kade says, his face flushed.

A bead of blood glimmers on his lip where he's bitten it. White glistens on his chest and belly but most of it streaks my bed.

How can he still be unbearably sexy while covered in his own spunk?

"Christ," I say, "I'm going to have to get you a tarp before I run out of sheets."

He laughs, then winces, shuffling gingerly to the edge of the bed.

I smirk. "Is my little demon a bit sore?"

My fingertips brush his cheekbone, no longer marred by a bruise, the marks gone from his neck. He freezes. I freeze.

Bollocks. What did I say?

"*Your* little demon?" Kade breathes.

My hand appears to be glued to his face. My traitorous thumb traces the curve of his bottom lip. I'm standing between his legs. His very naked legs and other bits.

"You're healed," I squeak.

He shows me his left hand, the scabs replaced by normal skin. Keeping my gaze, he places his palm on my belly over the stiff stays of my corset.

"You should be, too."

I inch closer. His thighs hug my legs.

"That's what that was?" My voice quavers. "The second one?"

"It can be that way every time, Reiley."

His thumb slips lower to stroke the thin band of skin between the corset and my underwear. My stomach goes all squiggly. A feeling close to panic bubbles upward.

The evidence of our sex hasn't even dried on his chest and I want to climb into his lap. Get all sticky. Kiss him senseless. Be kissed senseless.

Stop this *right now*.

I snatch my hand back and jerk out of reach. "Go clean up. I'll strip the bed."

He hesitates, then steps around me and pads into the

bathroom, comfortably nude. The stupid lump is back in my throat.

I was supposed to be careful. To enjoy him, but not let him get close. To never forget what he is.

But I haven't been careful enough.

21

Kade must leak some kind of incubus juju crap, even if he doesn't mean it. It's the only explanation for my intense reactions to him. He has addictive pheromones. It's probably why he smells like a blissful summer day, his scent and heat enough to make you want to strip.

Speaking of, I should put more clothes on.

I change the sheets. *Again.* The new sheets are the ones Kade covered in other bodily fluids and not just his happy juice. I wasn't kidding when I said I needed a tarp.

Wait. How long has the shower been off? Is there time to get dressed?

The bathroom door opens. Steam curls around the frame. Kade takes a tentative step into the room, wearing a pair of jeans and nothing else. I stare resolutely at his face and not his lovely collarbones. His gaze bounces from me, to his feet, to the bed, and back to his feet.

I sigh, and hold out my arms. "For god's sake, come on then."

He flashes a grin. Before I can recover, he bounds across the room and scoops me into a hug, his fingers in my hair, his other hand just beneath my shoulder blades on the stiff material of my corset. My face is suddenly pressed into his chest over the comforting lub-dub, lub-dub of his heart. My fingers glide around his ribs to grip the firm muscles of his back, his skin damp from the shower. I inhale a little harder than necessary.

He's a mojito sipped on a beach at sunset, the heat of the day still baked into the sand.

I rise on tip-toe and bury my nose in his soft, warm neck. His arms tighten, and he rests his cheek on the top of my head. My body relaxes into him, as close as I can get.

The damned guy can cuddle.

Like kissing, I don't get enough of it. Sex in a nightclub bathroom or with a stranger after I've ordered in doesn't really end in cuddles and a heart to heart. Plus, I don't want to give them the wrong idea.

How many people have I slept with in comparison to Kade? Wouldn't it be funny if we were close? And I thought I had the moral high ground.

"I'm sorry, Reiley," he says.

"What for?"

My lips brush his throat, and he shivers. I tell my pulse to behave itself.

"For hurting you," he says.

"When did you hurt—oh, right."

His thumb strokes my skin just above the line of my corset. "I thought they'd get bored before I had to go too far."

The touch awakens the squiggles. I suck a slow breath in and out until I'm certain of my voice.

"I saw my books in your study."

"Is that why you wanted to leave?"

"You've—" I clear my throat. Damn lumps. "You've read them. Multiple times."

"I love them," he says.

His thumb continues its slow, tickling caress.

"You really know the way to an author's heart," I joke.

His thumb stills. "Do I?"

Said heart flutters into my stomach and I'm pretty sure Kade can feel it. How long have we been cuddling? This is too intimate. *Way* too intimate.

Oh, bugger. I'm nuzzling his neck. Why does he have to smell so good?

His hand slips from my hair and kneads the small of my back, his fingertips grazing the narrow band of skin between the bottom of my corset and my underwear. Desire sizzles from his touch.

It would take so little. A slight lean back. A tilt of my head. His lips finding mine. My caution—and my panties—thrown to the wind.

"Have you looked?" he says.

I mumble, "Huh?" into his throat.

"At your stomach," he says patiently. "To see how well it healed."

"Oh. No. It's... I'd have to take the corset off."

He sighs into my hair. Goosebumps prickle from my scalp to the nape of my neck.

"I thought you were going to die. On the drive here, you were so still."

"But you spunked me back to life."

He chuckles. "It's a talent."

The weight of the moment, heavy in my stomach, passes with a tug of disappointment. I ease out of his arms and he lets me escape to the bathroom.

I add cuddling to the list of things I can't do with Kade. Time to add everything on there. The pegging was an emergency.

A voice whispers—*both times, really?*—and I shove it away. It was an *emergency* and it won't happen again. The sooner we deal with our demon problem, the better. Kade can return to his gaggle of women and I can return to… What? My lonely hermit existence with no real intimacy?

I tell myself to shut up.

What's the alternative—ask Kade if he wants to be my boyfriend? Don't be ridiculous. He may not be the little demon wankstain he pretended to be, but he's still an incubus. I'd rather keep my pants on and my dignity intact than have a few nights of fantastic sex before spending the rest of my life craving him when he inevitably flits on to the next woman, and the next, like a sexy butterfly.

Kade is someone you fuck, not someone you spend the rest of your life with.

But I *am* tired of meaningless sex. Maybe I needed Kade to show me that. I want a relationship. Love. Someone I can be myself with, feel safe with. Talk about demons with. Who better than someone exactly like me? A Diviner. Kade and I haven't done well with Thaddeus and Myron, both of us barely escaping alive. We need help. We need the Diviners. And if one of those Diviners happens to be a hot guy I fall in love with and we live happily ever after hunting demons together, so much the better. That's what I need.

Not Kade-bloody-McKade.

22

"Who wrote this bit?" Kade says, sprawled on my sofa, my aunt's book spread open on his lap.

I follow his finger to the incubus demon section. After a neat paragraph of precision-printed letters about feeding on sexual energy and enslaving the loins of women, there's a scrawl that reads 'annoyingly gorgeous'.

I vaguely remember drinking all the Buckfast after Kade and the coffee shop. Swinging between anger and melancholy. Then I misplaced it under the bed and couldn't find it when Kade confirmed the mysterious Diviners were an organised group. There must be something in the book about where to find them. I searched the rest of my aunt's belongings in the attic, but there was nothing.

"Probably one of the original authors," I say, ignoring the heat in my cheeks.

I can't believe I desecrated the book when I was drunk. Stupid Kade.

Shame it's true, though.

Kade peers at the vellum. "But the style is different. And it looks more recent."

"What are you—some kind of graphologist?"

I snatch the book and flop on the couch, hard enough to

jostle him. His shoulder bumps mine, and I slide away.

No more touching, especially not snuggling or pegging or kisses. We have a job to do and it doesn't involve getting naked.

I flick to the front of the book and check the spine and bindings for slips of paper or hidden messages. The endsheet of the inside cover is glued tight. I turn each page slowly, scanning the drawings and text for anything that looks like code. Kade inches closer. I ignore him.

He's pulled on a grey, zip-necked cashmere jumper over a crisp, white shirt. The collar frames the hollow of his throat, the cuffs of the shirt turned back over the sleeves. Like all of his clothes, they hug his slim figure and complement the jeans.

I jerk my gaze back to my aunt's book. Every passage is familiar. I pored over the text numerous times with her. I fan the empty pages and reach the end, the sheet stuck tight to the cover like the front. I sigh and slump into the couch.

"How are we going to find the Diviners in time for them to help us?"

"Are you sure we need their help? They're not exactly going to like me, Reiley."

"You got clawed half to death and I got gutted. We need help."

We figure we have a day, maybe two, before Thaddeus and Myron trace my address. I'm not on the Electoral Register, but there are other, non-legal means for acquiring information. Kade has booked us into a hotel from tonight since it's no longer safe to stay here.

And I hate that. My cottage has always been my sanctuary.

A polite knock raps on the front door. Kade's eyes switch

from solid black to human blue in a blink. He jumps up to answer and I stay on the couch, absently rubbing my fingers across the endsheet of the book. A voice drifts from the hall.

"That's the cameras installed outside, too, mate. Just need to show you and the missus how to work it."

I snort. *Missus.* As if Kade would ever have a wife.

One woman could never be enough for him.

My fingertips play on smooth vellum. I trace it absently.

Maybe there's a message written on the *inside.*

I jerk forward. Kade and the security man appear in the living room doorway before I can whip out my knife and slice at the endsheet. The man towers over Kade, his shoulders twice as broad as the demon. Muscular legs bulge beneath a pair of khaki combat trousers. He looks like some kind of special-ops soldier.

We should ask him to help us.

"Right-o," he says, not meeting my eyes, "this here tablet is the main hub of your new system. The Microsoft Surface Pro X is one of the best devices for monitoring your CCTV."

Reluctantly, I leave the book on the sofa and join Kade and the man in a huddle near the fireplace. My fingers itch to tear at the endsheet.

What if it's there—a name and address, a number, an email? Maybe it's tiny, tiny writing with exact directions to Diviner Headquarters. Or maybe it's invisible ink that needs lemon juice wiped on it to reveal a secret message. Very cloak and dagger. I feel like a spy.

God, I can't wait to be able to talk to someone about demons without them looking at me like I've gone doolally.

Kade not included, of course.

The security man angles his hefty frame away from me and

addresses all the instructions to Kade, his giant paw palming the tablet. Usually, I'd be annoyed, but I'm not even listening. And Kade is paying for it.

He called a guy, mentioned a huge sum, and the security team were here in less than an hour to install cameras inside and out. Of course, they spent the first twenty minutes cooing over Kade's Porsche parked at the side of the cottage, out of sight of the main road.

Finally, Kade ushers the man from the house. I leap onto the couch and scoop the book into my lap, my heart beating hard. I draw the knife from my homemade wrist sheath, covered by the sleeve of my thin hoodie, lilac this time. Murmuring a plea of forgiveness, I slice the border of both endsheets and peel them back.

Nothing. Shit. Perhaps I need that lemon juice. I'll douse the whole damn book in it.

I twirl the knife between my fingers and thumb, the blade pointed down. My nail catches on a seam at the butt of the handle.

"This thing is cool," Kade says, walking back into the living room and jabbing at the tablet. "I should get one for—"

His eyes widen at the swirling black blade. I peer at the seam. There's a gap, and some kind of catch. My pulse kicks. My nail slides the catch along the seam. The butt of the handle pops open. I tilt the knife, and a scroll of paper slides into my waiting fingers.

Kade hugs the fancy Microsoft tablet to his chest. "What is it?"

"A note." I flip the unscrolled parchment and show him the text. My aunt's looping scrawl pricks at my chest. "It says 'Reiley, I hope you never find this because that means you were searching for it, and you need it. I never wanted you to be a part of this world. I'm sorry.' Then there's a number."

I grab my phone and start dialling instead of thinking about my aunt lying to me. How could she know of the existence of demon hunters and not tell me?

"Are you sure, Reiley?" Kade says, still not coming closer. "Now we have the cameras, we can watch your house from anywhere. We could ambush Thaddeus and Myron when—"

"It's ringing," I say in a hushed voice.

Kade perches on the chair near the fire. My knife lies on the seat he vacated to answer the door, swirling softly.

Another ring. Another. I bounce on the sofa. The ringing stops. I hold my breath.

"Where did you get this number?" a woman says in a neutral tone.

Is she asking for some kind of password? If I say the wrong thing, will she hang up, the number ringing out, and I'll never find them again? Never know what my life could be like as a Diviner.

Surely I'm supposed to be one of them? I just got lost.

"In a knife," I whisper. "It had a hidden letter. From my aunt."

Crap, I'm babbling.

The silence burrows into my stomach. I jiggle my leg. Kade frowns.

"Who is your aunt?" the woman says, her voice warmed by curiosity.

Is she Scottish? She sounds Scottish. Maybe she can be my best friend.

"Isabella MacArthur," I say.

The woman sucks in a breath. I press the phone so hard

into my ear, it aches.

Please, *please,* let her like me. Let her help me. I mean *us.*

I glance at Kade, back to showing his demon eyes and fangs. He chews on his lip and makes himself bleed. The woman clears her throat, and I jump. My hand sweats around the phone.

"We've been looking for you, Reiley," she says.

23

The glow from the dashboard pools shadows in Kade's cheekbones and glints in his eyes, reminding me of being swallowed by stars in the whispering night.

Can he do that whenever he wants—capture me in his gaze and coax me unconscious? Bedazzle me into submission?

The darkness of the interior folds around me, cradling me in its hush despite the rumble of the Porsche's engine. The heated leather seat hugs the curve of my spine. Every breath smells like Kade—sunshine and magic. His panic-inducing proximity is worse than in the lift of his apartment building.

He steers the Porsche easily through the traffic lights past Edinburgh Royal Infirmary, heading south towards the City Bypass. Slim fingers flick the little gear paddles on the wheel.

The woman on the phone gave me a time and a place—10pm at some kind of farm west of South Queensferry. Kade argued about going. I told him he didn't have to come. I'd cycle there if I had to. He huffed and agreed to drive. I spent the rest of the day fidgeting and watching the clock while Kade watched me. We packed our bags for the hotel just in case.

Maybe the Diviners will let us stay with them.

Kade zooms down the sliproad onto the City Bypass. The speed pushes me back in the seat and grips my chest, the roar of the engine vibrating in my belly. The car is like its owner—sleek, hot, and predatory.

The teenage girl in me wants to squee at being in a sports car with a sexy boy. My teenage years weren't exactly normal—moving frequently for my dad's job so I never made friends, hiding in the house to avoid seeing the wavery people who tried to kill me.

"You always went out with two women at a time," I say to distract myself.

Kade glances at me, not bothering to hide his demon eyes in the car. "So?"

"Where did the other one sit?"

Our bags barely fit in the boot, and the car is a two-seater.

"In the other's lap," he says.

I roll my eyes. "Of course they did."

More silence, heavy in the cosy intimacy of the Porsche.

I'm pretty sure he's grumpy about asking the Diviners for help, him being a demon and all. I'm not sure why I'm grumpy. Maybe it's the thought of all the pert little bottoms that have graced this seat before me.

"How many women have you slept with, *Kade?*"

"I don't count, *Reiley.* How many men have you slept with?"

I think I'm in the forties somewhere, which sounds like a lot.

I cross my arms and say, "None of your business."

His fingers tap on the wheel. Streetlights strobe across his face, and I get angry at myself for noticing how gorgeous he is.

"I don't sleep with all of them," he says almost to himself.

My muscles unclench. "What do you mean?"

He guides the car onto the M8 motorway with another burst

of heart-jolting speed.

"Some of them only think I have." He slides me a tentative grin. "I'm mostly human. I get tired."

"But how do they…?"

"You haven't seen me in my full power. I can make them believe whatever they want. And biting helps."

My cheeks heat, and I'm glad for the dimness of the car.

I'm well aware of his orgasmic bite. Him sucking on my wrist and my thigh nearly drove me over the edge, and I doubt he was even trying.

I hide a squirm by crossing one leg over the other. Kade keeps his eyes on the road, though the prickling heat tells me he's peeking at me through his peripherals.

"I saw the bruises," I say. "But you didn't… I mean, my bruises. You always healed them."

I never noticed when he did it. It wasn't after his first pegging since most of that energy melted my bed frame. Bet none of the floozies ever got that reaction from him. He could have done it during our kiss. There was definitely a lot of sizzling energy.

The Porsche flies up the long, curving sliproad onto the M9. Kade sneaks a glance at me.

"They didn't know what I was, so I had to pass the bites off as hickeys. And I got a kick out of marking them as mine. But I… I don't want any marks on you."

Of course he doesn't. I'm not one of his.

By *choice,* I tell the stupid bloom of hurt bubbling between my ribs.

Being around Kade has really screwed with my confidence. Maybe the Diviners can save me from more than just Thaddeus and Myron.

The Porsche purrs contentedly under my arse, the tyres hissing on concrete. We glide through the bend onto the M90, close to our final turn off.

Kade clears his throat. "What junction is it again?"

"Queensferry. A904."

I stare out the window at the passing night, the sky clear and twinkling with stars now we're out of the city. A slice of moon bathes the surrounding fields in silver.

"If these people really are the Diviners, then your aunt must have been one of them," Kade says.

"She told me she found the book. And I didn't know she had the knife."

Kade cocks his eyebrow.

I hug myself. "But why would she lie? We could have hunted demons together. I could've been with other people like me."

Kade glances at me, his hands steady on the wheel. "Maybe she just wanted you safe."

"But I wasn't safe! After she died, I blamed myself. I went hunting. Alone. Unarmed." I glower at the window.

"Is that when you got the scars on your ribs?"

My reflection gives a grim smile. "That was the year of many wounds, but those scars are from when I was thirteen. They're not my only ones."

"How many demons have you met, Reiley?"

I smirk at him. "It's nowhere near the number of men I've slept with."

His face is serious in the dashboard lights. "Any one of them could have killed you. *Should* have killed you."

"Right—your only rule. Seems they all lacked commitment, though they tried."

"How did you get away?"

"Same as you—I ran and hid."

We exit the wide swathe of motorway for a smaller road lined by trees. The Porsche's headlamps chase shadows through the leaves. Kade turns down a pitted track running parallel to our destination, wincing at each scrape along the underside of his beloved car. The hardened dirt peters into the forest about half a mile in. The engine rumbles to a silence as thick as the trees.

I stroke the knife beneath my sleeve. "At least now when I meet a demon, I can do something about it."

"You're sitting right next to one," Kade says.

I shrug into my fleece, wriggling in the restrictive confines of the car. "You don't count."

"Why don't I count?"

"You're… Kade. I guess we're… friends?"

"Friends don't see each other naked."

"You haven't seen me naked."

"Semantics," he snaps, and unfolds himself from the Porsche. He's in a weird mood tonight.

I follow him into the woods, watching where I place my feet to avoid clumps of nettles or snapping twigs, my vision slowly adjusting. Kade ploughs ahead, a grey smudge in the dark with a bright white collar and cuffs. The chill leaches into my jeans and creeps under my fleece. Soft cursing reaches me before I trip over Kade, his trousers snagged by a hummock of brambles.

"Don't demons have nifty night vision?" I snigger.

He tosses me a glare. "I guess I'm not demon enough."

I move to help him, but he yanks his leg free, the rip loud in the quiet of the forest, no wind to stir the branches. He stomps ahead, manages fine for twenty metres, then falls on his face in a slick of mud.

My body shakes as I try not to laugh. "Wow, you really are a city boy, aren't you?"

"Fuck's sake," Kade growls at the leaves.

He clambers to his feet. Dark splodges stain his knees and his lovely cashmere jumper that probably cost a couple of hundred pounds.

"Would you like me to lead?" I say, deadpan.

He brushes at his clothes. "Reiley?"

"Yes, Kade?"

"Who's the pain in the arse now?"

"Still you," I say, and flounce past him.

He rewards me with a chuckle. I ignore the sudden warmth in my chest and get us safely to the edge of the trees. We crouch in a bush that smells of cat pee. A dry ditch and a strip of tangled grass line a pot-holed concrete road. On the other side, overgrown fields surround an area of piled bricks. All that remains of the farm is a large, metal barn, patches of darkness showing where the walls have rusted. No lights shine from within.

"What time is it?"

Kade tilts his wrist to the glowing hands of his fancy— probably expensive—watch. "We've got half an hour."

"Let's do a quick scout."

We slip across the road like a pair of foxes and circle the outside of the barn. Our shoes crunch on glass. Kade accidentally kicks a stone. It clatters across the concrete.

"And I thought your Porsche would be the loudest thing here. Don't you know how to sneak?"

He pouts at me. "I can sneak."

He precedes to tip-toe in an exaggerated fashion, all arms

and legs.

My breath snorts white. "You look ridiculous."

The inside of the barn smells of straw and cold metal. Leaves choke the central concrete runnel and form piles in the corners. We hustle back to our bush to wait, me shivering, Kade perfectly warm in his thin jumper. I force myself not to scoot closer. After ten minutes, headlights flare as they turn off the main road, the vehicle hidden by the trees.

"Stay here," I say.

Kade's hand whips out and snatches my sleeve. "You're not going in alone."

"Well, you can't come with me. They won't listen to anything I say if I rock up with a demon."

"What if they're not who we think they are?"

"They're the Diviners—I know it." I wriggle my arm in his grip. "It'll be fine. Just stay here."

"No."

"But you're usually good at following orders."

"That's in the bedroom, Reiley," he says, and stuns me with a smirk, "not out here."

Damn incubus.

"*Fine*. Hide where you can hear through the wall, but for god's sake be quiet and don't peek. We'll introduce you later when I've warmed them to the idea."

He squeezes my arm, his fingers blooming heat through the material of my sleeve.

"Be careful," he whispers.

He disappears in a rustle of grass and leaves, vanishing around the side of the barn a second before the headlights bathe the metal in white. Gravel crunches under tyres. I hunker lower as a dark-coloured car purrs past and eases to a stop. Gears crunch. The vehicle reverses into the building, headlamps pointed out of the doorway. The engine cuts out. Three doors slam. I hold my breath, certain they can hear my heart pounding on my breastbone.

This is it. This is really happening.

I'm finally going to meet people like me.

24

"Hello?" I call, as if I've just strolled up the road and not scrambled out of a bush.

A figure appears, and I squint against the headlights of the car in the barn.

"Reiley MacArthur?" says the woman from the phone.

"Actually, it's MacEwen now. I changed it."

"That explains our trouble in tracking you down," she says, amused. "We checked your parents, of course, though they don't have the Sight. Goodness, they didn't even know where you were or where your aunt lived, though neither did we."

Sadness tinges her voice at the end.

"Hold out your hands and turn in a slow circle, please, Reiley," a man's voice says—a second, shorter figure haloed against the light. "A precaution, you understand."

I do as he says, then fidget on the spot. "I have a knife. In my sleeve."

Their laughter floats from the barn.

"We'd be disappointed if you didn't," the man says. "If you wouldn't mind showing it to us?"

I pull the knife out and blackness swirls along the silver blade, eerie in the stark lights of the car.

It only does the swirly trick if I'm holding it. It doesn't

seem to activate when it's just strapped to my skin, which is probably a good thing. No accidental burning of Kade.

Not that he's ever getting that close again.

"It belonged to—"

"—your aunt," the woman finishes.

"Was she really a Diviner?"

"One of the best. We were heartbroken when we learned of her murder."

"Filthy demons, the lot of them," the man spits.

"Come inside, Reiley," the woman says. "We have a lot to talk about."

I tuck my knife away and step into the barn, blinking my eyes to clear the spots from the glare of the headlights. Three people gather at the rear of the car—the man and woman and a second, smaller woman. I force myself not to look for Kade since I won't be able to see him. He can't risk peeking without the prickling heat giving him away.

"I'm Annabel," says the woman from the phone, her smile warm. "This is Bryce and—"

"Elsie," chirps the other woman.

Elsie is smaller than me, but curvy to make up for it. Her brown hair is streaked purple and sits in choppy layers around her face, framing piercing, cobalt-blue eyes.

My gaze bounces around my three new friends. "And you can see it, right? The wavering when demons hide their true form?"

Annabel laughs. "The blurriness of their glamour. Yes, we see it."

My throat gets a little scratchy. I clear it and pretend my eyes don't have some blurriness of their own.

Glamour. Kade will like that.

I stop my eyeballs from scanning the pocked sides of the barn.

"Isabella didn't tell you about us?" the man—Bryce—says gently.

He's a little taller than me, a wool hat pulled low on his forehead. Spikes of black hair frame warm brown eyes. A scruff of stubble roughens his jawline unlike the smooth and perfect Kade.

I shake my head. "I didn't even know the word Diviner until a few months ago."

My stomach clenches. Crap. I shouldn't have said that. I can hardly say a demon told me.

"I live in my aunt's house," I babble. "I was going through her things. That's when I found the knife and a book about demons."

"You mean you had no weapon before that?" Annabel raises a hand to her mouth, her manicured nails slicked red. "My goodness, how did you survive?"

She towers over the three of us, her white-blonde hair in a long ponytail, a silver spike flashing in the arch of her left ear. She seems almost Slavic with her high cheekbones and pale-blue eyes, though the accent is Scottish.

She's exactly Kade's type.

"I'm good at running," I say.

They all laugh, and it heats me to my toes.

"Isabella never told us she had a niece," Bryce says in the same gentle tone. "It was only after her death we learned about you. How you were in Leverndale. The psychiatric hospital. Before you moved in with Isabella. We tried to find you after her murder."

I stare at his ripped jeans and skater shoes until my eyes

stop prickling.

"Don't be embarrassed," he says. "From all the drugs I was on, I can't even remember my childhood."

"We're just glad we've found you now," Elsie gushes, bouncing on her high-tops. "Isabella was legendary. Well, until…"

A look passes between the three Diviners.

"Until what?"

"Until, um, she left us. We missed her. But here you are! You look like her. Same eyes. Same 'screw you' tilt to the chin." Elsie giggles.

I take a few years off her age. I'm tired just standing next to her.

"Elsie, goodness, let her breathe," Annabel says. "Sorry, Reiley, this must all be a touch overwhelming."

"It's fine." I cough. "I was actually looking for you when I found the letter. I need your help."

Elsie claps her hands. "Yes, a hunt! Please be a hunt. I've not been on one *for ages.*"

"Demons in Edinburgh?" Bryce's fingers rasp through the stubble on his jaw. "It's been a while. In fact, not since—"

"—my aunt."

"—Isabella," he says.

"There are two searching for me. They saw me at Cabaret Voltaire."

"The Cab!" Elsie says with more bouncing. "I *love* The Cab! Did you have a unicorn juice?"

Annabel pinches the bridge of her nose. "Elsie, we can get the details later. It's time to head back. Will you join us, Reiley? You'll be perfectly safe and we can come up with a plan for your demon problem."

"Join you where?" I say instead of yanking her into a hug

and crumpling her silk shirt.

"We have a compound on Loch Fitty about twenty minutes north of here."

"It is *the* compound where we learn to kick demon arse all the way from central Scotland to the Borders," Elsie says, followed quickly by a maternal sigh from Annabel.

"We can swing by your place to pick up your things," Annabel says. "I would love to see where Isabella lived. Did you drive here?"

"I, ah, got the bus."

Damn. Most of my stuff is in the boot of Kade's Porsche. What the hell is he going to do while I'm gallivanting around a compound in Fife?

Again, I stop myself from looking for him through a rent in the wall.

Elsie tugs on my arm. "You can sit in the back with me."

Annabel gives me an apologetic smile and climbs into the passenger seat, Bryce slipping behind the wheel of the Volvo SUV. He plugs my address into the sat-nav. I settle into the rear of the spacious car with Elsie chattering away, seemingly content without a response from me. The car pulls out of the barn and rocks easily over the potholes in the old road. I strain my neck and glimpse a streak of black behind us.

I imagine Kade crashing through the woods to his Porsche. Falling in more mud. Cursing. Tearing his expensive clothes on the same brambles. Arriving at his car, panting and dishevelled while I recline in the comfort of the Volvo, basking in the glow from my new friends. I laugh, and Elsie laughs with me.

I think we're going to get along fine.

25

The birch forest ends in a flat expanse of open space and a huge, white house on the edge of Loch Fitty, the shine of water just visible through more birch trees scattered on grass. The house itself glows like the moon in the dark. The Volvo purrs down the road towards it. I grip the driver's seat to peer through the window, craning my neck to the blackness of the woods behind us, unbroken by headlights.

Where is Kade? His Porsche growled past us on the way to my house and I saw it parked further up Old Church Lane. It was still there after I'd packed another bag of clothes, minus any toiletries since Kade has those. I had to stop myself from turning around on the drive to the Diviners' compound in case Elsie interrupted her stream of chatter to ask what I was looking for.

"Do you not have a fence or a gate?" I say when she pauses for breath. "Guards or cameras to watch for demons?"

Annabel twists in the passenger seat, her ponytail whispering over the material. "Don't worry, Reiley. It's perfectly safe. We have the whole area warded."

"Wards are a thing?"

That must be the symbols in the notebooks in the attic. I was surrounded by Diviner paraphernalia and never even knew it.

My three new friends laugh. Bryce's normal, human-brown eyes crinkle at me in the rearview mirror.

"If a demon tries to approach the house, we'll know," he says.

"And he'll soon regret it," Elsie chirps, mock-stabbing the back of Annabel's seat.

My gut clenches. I hope Kade has the sense to stay away. But what if he parks, and sneaks through the woods?

I stifle a snort. They'd hear him before he tripped the damn wards.

Still, I'm going to have to creep out and warn him since I don't have his mobile number. An incubus demon waking a house of Diviners at midnight is probably not the best way to introduce him. That was poor planning on our part, though this is the first time I've been free of him since he knocked on my door.

The distance is a good thing. It'll clear my head. It's bloody exhausting being around someone so intensely sexual.

"How many people live here?" I say, unbuckling my seatbelt and climbing into the cold night, my breath puffing out.

A mournful call drifts over the water. Some kind of loon? I'm not well-versed in bird song, but it doesn't sound like an owl—too haunting and beautiful.

"There are twenty of us," Annabel says, joining me at the front of the car. "We'll let you settle into a room tonight and give you a proper tour in the morning. Marianne will want to make the introductions."

"Who's Marianne?"

"I suppose you'd call her our leader—"

"Commander in Chief of the Central Scotland Diviners."

Elsie bounces between us and tosses a stiff salute.

Annabel shakes her head, and smiles. "But please don't call her that."

I sling my bag over my shoulder and follow the three Diviners up the porch steps and into the house. The white door opens on a wide, wood-panelled hallway lined by framed pictures of the loch across the seasons—frozen in winter, brilliant green reeds feathering the edge in spring, the trees on the far bank a blaze of gold and bronze in autumn.

"Used to be a fishing lodge, this place," Bryce says, aiming for a set of red-carpeted stairs. "Though we've extended it a bit."

Muted lamps give a buttery-yellow light. The air smells like coffee and pine and animated talks into the night with people who could be family.

Okay, that last one doesn't have a scent, but the longing for it aches in my bones.

The red carpet and wood panelling continue down a corridor on the first floor. We stop in front of a door near the end, a window looking east along the edge of the loch.

"Sorry, all the loch-facing rooms are taken, but this one should be comfortable enough."

Annabel swings the door open on a compact room with a single bed and an en-suite. The window has a padded seat and looks out over the sloping porch roof to the birch wood we entered through.

"Sleep well, Reiley," Annabel says, then turns to Bryce. "I'll let Marianne know we're back, though no doubt she does already."

I trail them into the corridor. Annabel strides towards the stairs, her ponytail shimmering.

Elsie bounces two doors down. "And we're practically neighbours! See you in the morning, Reiley."

"If you need anything, I'm on the second floor." Bryce walks backwards. "Or just shout and someone will help."

He waves and slouches away in his ripped jeans and skater shoes, the grunge style and friendly demeanour quite different to the expensive tastes and arrogance of a certain somebody.

Stop comparing everyone to Kade.

I shut the door and lean against it, yawning hard. Is it really still the same day where I woke up after being gutted, and pegged Kade for the second time?

Not that I'm counting.

I shove away from the door and change into a black hoodie. The house creaks and settles. Murmuring voices fade from further down the corridor. I flush the toilet and run the water in the sink in case anyone is listening. In the dark, I release the window catch and ease the frame upward, jiggling it when it sticks. Cold air caresses my thighs where I kneel on the padded seat. I slither onto slick tile and scoot on my arse to the lowest corner. Most of the windows on my level are dark, Elsie's bedroom glowing yellow through the drawn curtains two windows down. My heels catch in the ancient metal gutter running along the porch roof. I hug my knees and peer over the edge.

The swoop of vertigo is like staring into Kade's eyes, be they demon or pretend human.

Wishing I'd just waltzed out the front door, I roll onto my belly, the sloped roof digging in to where my intestines so recently bulged out. I take a second to marvel at Kade's healing skills. My legs kick air. I start to slide, and panic jolts my heart into my mouth. My fingertips scrabble on the slate tiles. My shin barks against something solid. I bite my lip on a curse, wrapping my legs around the pillar and shimmying down. I breathe a little easier when my feet are on the ground.

No way am I getting back to my room via the same route. I don't have the strength to pull myself up, though that should change after some training with the Diviners. I imagine it will be rigorous and in-depth. Hunting demons must take skill and stamina.

I sprint across the grass, my shoes quickly soaked by dew. On the edge of the trees, I glance back at the house.

I can see myself living here. A relaxing coffee with Annabel on the back porch, watching the sun rise, the hour too early for Elsie and her exuberance. Training in the afternoons until I'm panting and covered in sweat, Elsie still bouncing around and making me feel old. A communal dinner. Laughter and conversation. The occasional demon hunt. Reclusive lump of knitted cardigan to warrior and Diviner.

I hope my aunt would be proud.

Swallowing a confusing tangle of emotions, I slip into the trees. The grassy undergrowth muffles my steps, the drooping branches brushing my hair. I angle for the road, which stretches empty in both directions.

"Kade?" I whisper.

No answer.

Maybe I'm still too close to the house. Will I feel the wards? Have I passed through them already? Shit, will that warn someone I'm wandering around?

I jog to a T-junction, the right fork leading to a main road into the village of Kingseat.

"*Kade*," I hiss.

"Reiley?"

I jump at his voice. A slice of darkness peels itself from a larger shadow on the road to the left. I walk into the prickling heat of his gaze and spot him beside his Porsche. A new streak of mud paints one cheekbone and the cuff of his no-longer-quite-so-white shirt.

"Fall much?" I say.

"Having fun with your new friends?"

I smirk. "Jealous?"

"I'm the one who has to wait in the cold."

"You're a demon, you don't get cold."

"That's not the point."

I roll my eyes. "All right, Mister Huffy. I came out here to warn you the place is warded. And to get my things."

"I assumed it was warded," he sniffs. "I'm not an idiot."

He opens the compact boot of his Porsche, then leans his arse on the edge and raises a brow in challenge.

What is with him tonight?

He refuses to move. I bump his shoulder, rummaging through my clothes for my toiletry bag and stuffing it in my hoodie pocket, leaving the rest. My skin goosebumps from his gaze, the heat of him so close. I step away, and the night seems colder.

Why do I never remember my jacket?

I clear my throat.

Great. Back to twitchy and uncomfortable in his presence.

"Have you tripped a ward before?" I say casually. "Does it hurt?"

"No, but it tends to bring a bunch of annoying people with pointy things."

I snort. "Well, they seem very nice."

"I'm sure they do. To you."

He slams the boot, and it echoes. I wince, but it turns into a full-body shudder.

Kade's face softens. "Do you want to sit in the car? I can turn the heating on."

Sit in the intimate confines of his Porsche, breathing his scent, bathed in his warmth? Sounds like a bad idea.

I shake my head. "I should go back soon. But give me your mobile number so I can keep in touch."

He holds out his hand. I hesitate, then pass him my phone. A little electric sizzle vibrates down my spine at the brush of his fingers. He frowns at me, and I blow on my hands for good effect.

Just cold. Nothing else.

He turns his disconcerting eyes to my phone, the light from the screen reflecting in their black depths and tingeing his face blue-white. His hair flops over his forehead.

"You don't have to stay here all night, you know," I say to his silence. "You could go to the hotel."

He slides me a look, and taps his finger on my phone.

"They're giving me a tour of the place tomorrow. I've not seen them in action yet, but I bet they can get rid of Thaddeus and Myron, no problem. In fact, you could stay in the hotel until it's done."

What a great idea. I wouldn't have to tell the Diviners about him and risk them turning against me. Kade can go back to his penthouse and life of debauchery.

He cuts me a glare. "So now you have human *friends,* you don't need me?"

"That's not…" I drop my gaze to my feet, unable to meet his eyes. "You'd be safe in the hotel. They probably won't let me help, either. Like you said—I'm untrained."

I risk a peek. He seems to be considering whether he's going to stay pissy. His expression thaws.

"Do you worry about me, Reiley?" he purrs.

Dammit. The squiggles are back.

I hold out my hand and ignore the slight tremble. Kade places my phone in my palm, and steps closer. I dance backwards.

He sighs. "Let me hug you. You're shivering."

"I'm fine," I say. Are my teeth chattering? "This is fine."

He bristles. "You're the only woman I have to beg to touch. Why is that?"

The arrogant little arsehole. It must kill him that I'm not drooling at his feet.

I jam my phone in my pocket without looking at the screen. "So because they throw themselves on your dick, I should let you do what you want?"

"No," he huffs, "that's not—"

"Trying to shag me is like breathing for you," I snap. "Something you have to do. It's not exactly flattering, *Kade*."

An expression I never thought I'd see flits across his usually self-assured face.

I think I just hurt his feelings.

My heart immediately drops into my stomach. I open my mouth to apologise, but Kade spins on his heel and yanks on the driver's-side door of his Porsche.

"Nice to know what you really think of me, Reiley," he says, ice crackling in his voice.

"Kade, wait—"

He slams the door. The engine snarls and the headlights bleach the darkness. Tyres squeal. I stumble back, shading my eyes against the glare. The Porsche leaps forward like an enraged jaguar and streaks down the road in a blur of muscle. The angry red of the rear lights disappears long before the rumble of the engine.

<h1 style="text-align:center">26</h1>

I wake up scratchy, irritable and guilty after six hours of tossing and turning. My eyes burn from lack of sleep. Doors open and close elsewhere in the house, voices heading to the ground level. The smell of coffee and bacon creeps into my room to tantalise my nostrils. I reach for my phone and search for Kade's number.

Nothing under 'K' or 'McKade'. Did he delete it?

I scroll through my contact list and find him at the bottom. The entry reads 'Your Little Demon'. A ridiculous urge to cry grips my throat, and the words blur.

Crap. I guess I am fond of the stupid incubus.

I open a text message and type *I'm sorry. I didn't mean it. Forgive me?*

It's kind of a lie. I did mean it, but I didn't *want* to mean it.

I'd like to be special.

Cursing myself, I roll out of bed and dress in my lilac hoodie and jeans, the cuffs no longer damp from last night's—or this morning's—dew. I hesitate at the top of the stairs and press myself against the wall as a large, chattering group passes through the hall. The front door opens and slams shut. I creep down the steps and sniff my way to the kitchen.

"Morning, Reiley," Annabel says, standing at a huge range

cooker. "I was about to make a fresh pot, would you care for some?"

Her ponytail swishes against her summer-blue silk shirt tucked into grey linen trousers.

I imagine it wrapped around Kade's fist, his mouth on the taut line of her throat. She'd moan his name and let him do anything he wanted.

Stop it, Reiley.

Did he go to the hotel and feed on a random woman? Thrust her to one orgasm after the next until she passed out and he collapsed in a panting, dishevelled, sexy heap?

I said *stop it.*

I nod to Annabel—who's still smiling warmly at me, so I can't have waited that long to reply—and take a seat at a rustic dining table set with covered platters. Smaller tables line the walls beneath mullioned windows. A sliding glass door leads onto a porch overlooking the loch, the water calm and still and glimmering. I peek at my phone under the table.

No messages. Maybe he's still asleep after all the sex I don't care about.

Annabel places a steaming mug in front of me and gestures to the platters. "Help yourself to breakfast. There's cream and sugar for your coffee, too. I trust you slept well?"

I stir a heap of sugar and a swirl of cream into my coffee, and sip. My eyes close on a sigh.

"Not really," I finally say. "It always takes me a while in new places."

And worrying about a certain sulky demon didn't help.

"Goodness, your brain must have been whirring. I'm sure this is all surreal. I can't imagine what it was like living for so long, believing you were the only one who saw the truth."

I investigate the covered platters, and pile food on a clean plate.

"It got lonely," I say.

Annabel laughs, and sips her coffee. "I'll bet. Well, I'll be giving you the official tour today, so I hope you'll be feeling a lot less lonely by the end of it. Our members are very excited to meet the niece of Isabella MacArthur."

I fork bacon into my mouth. "No Marianne?"

"She sends her apologies. She wanted to be here to greet you, but something urgent called her away at dawn."

"Nothing bad I hope?"

"I don't think so, though she and the senior members seemed quite animated. I'm sure she'll keep us informed. There aren't many secrets in this compound."

Apart from the whopper I have. How the hell am I supposed to raise that today? It seemed perfectly valid last night not to mention it at all, but then Kade got all pouty.

Annabel talks about compound life and the other Diviners while I finish my breakfast. She tidies my plate and mug into the dishwasher despite my protest.

"If you choose to be a permanent resident, then you can clean up after yourself but, for now, you're our guest," she says, shooing me away.

"Does everyone choose to stay here?"

"Some people prefer their own space, usually the more senior members, like your aunt, though Marianne has the largest room in the attic. For the others, it can feel a little like student digs."

"Are there other compounds?"

Annabel opens the sliding door and we step onto the rear porch. I suck a breath of crisp air rich with soil and green, growing things. The sun reflects off the loch in shards of light that paint the birches between us and the water.

"There's another in the Highlands and three in England. I remember when there was only one."

She walks towards the loch, and I hurry to match her stride.

"What about in other countries? I travelled a bit after my aunt died. I found a few demons in Europe."

"And without a weapon?" Annabel shakes her head. "Goodness, Reiley, that was so dangerous."

I avoid her gentle, chiding smile. "I didn't know about the weapon thing. I thought I was just really bad at fighting."

Annabel chuckles and steers us on a footpath through the scattered trees. A small beach curves on the edge of the loch with the remains of a bonfire and the legs of a barbecue driven into the sand.

"I shouldn't be surprised that the niece of Isabella MacArthur survived numerous attacks, alone and unarmed, but you were rather lucky. Once a demon knows we have the Sight, they try to kill us."

"Like a rule," I mutter.

"Yes, I suppose you could call it a rule."

The footpath angles away from the loch and into a thicker area of birch and willow. Birds flit between the branches, their feathers bright in the sunbeams dappling the grassy floor. I slide my phone out of my pocket.

Still no response from Kade. I quickly type *Friends don't leave other friends hanging,* then delete it. He got snippy about being referred to as a friend. But what the hell am I supposed to call him—pet demon, comrade in arms, occasional pegee?

Friend is safer.

I put my phone away. I said what I needed to in my first

text. Anything more might seem desperate.

Though he probably wants that. It's as close to begging as I'll ever get.

Crap, Annabel is still talking. Stupid Kade distracting me when he's not even here.

"We have compounds in other countries," she says, moving easily along the rough path. "We even have an international conference once a year, but it never seems to be enough. Demon numbers are growing and they'll only keep growing until we find where they breed."

I trip on a root. "They breed?"

Christ, is that what Kade's doing? Seeding his women with little demon babies?

Annabel glances over her shoulder. "Have you wondered why we never see the females?"

"A time or two," I say nonchalantly.

She ducks under a low-hanging branch. I don't have to. The path ends in a woven enclosure, the sides too high to see over, even for Annabel. Thwacking sounds and shouts of excitement drift from beyond.

"Demons breed in secret clans, but we've never managed to find one, not in this country." Annabel strides for a gate woven from the same material as the fence. "Unfortunately, it's very difficult to get any information out of them. Most demons don't react to sedatives, except for the uncommon races and they're harder to find than their breeding clans. Demon culture appears to abhor anything that's not typical breeding stock. You could call them racist, I suppose."

Myron the generic demon certainly disliked Kade the special little snowflake. Was Kade born in a breeding clan? Would he tell me where it is?

I touch my phone. Probably not something I should communicate via text, especially if he's still in a huff.

"God, there's so much I've got to learn," I say.

Annabel holds the gate open for me. "Oh, believe me, you'll feel like your head might explode some days and on the others, every muscle in your body will ache until you can barely move. Of course, it's absolutely worth it. I wouldn't trade my life here for all the money in the world. We're a family."

It's been so long since I had a family.

I walk through into a small arena of soft wood chip and a row of colourful straw targets along one side of the woven fence, opposite a wooden cabin. I glimpse a cluster of people on the porch and three women standing in a line, frowning at the targets.

"Reiley!"

Elsie bounces from the centre of the line, her purple hair bouncing along with her and blazing violet in the sunlight.

Annabel holds out a cautionary hand. "Knife, Elsie."

"Whoops!" Elsie giggles, and expertly flicks the knife point-first into the ground. Then she wraps her arms around me in a quick hug. "I've been telling everyone about you, Reiley. They're so excited to meet you!"

I squint at the sky and pretend it's the sun making my eyes hazy. She jumps back and scoops up her knife. The weapon flashes bronze in her hand. No black swirls. Annabel catches the question on my face.

"Our Dyrnwyns are too precious for practice," she says.

"Your what now?"

She smiles. "Our Dyrnwyns. They—"

"Ooh, ooh—let me tell it!" Elsie chirps, jiggling on the spot. "We call our demon-killing knives Dyrnwyns from Welsh legend. Dyrnwyn was a sword that blazed fire when drawn by a worthy man. If drawn by an unworthy man, it burned him. *And* the legends say the first demon was killed in Wales. How cool is that?"

I smile at her exuberance. "Very cool, Elsie."

Was I ever this energetic as a teenager? Maybe I just morphed out of a ball of wool.

The two girls who were standing in the line with Elsie when we arrived ease closer. One elbows the other in the ribs.

"I *told* you it was Reiley MacEwen," she says. "You are Reiley MacEwen, aren't you?"

I open my mouth to confirm that I am indeed Reiley MacEwen, niece of the apparently great Isabella MacArthur.

"I *love* your books," the other girl gushes, and receives another jab in the ribs. "I mean, *we* love your books."

I gape at them. "You've read my books?"

Where have I heard that before? Oh, right. I really shouldn't be so surprised that people love my books. *I* love my books.

"We have all of them in our rooms. Would you sign them for us? Please?" They look at me with wide eyes, their hands clasped around their knives.

"Of course I will," I say, and stop myself from gushing right back at them.

Annabel waves at an older woman on the porch of the wooden cabin. "Sorry for interrupting, Iona. We'll let you crack on."

The woman claps her hands, a heavy ring flashing on her finger. "Right, ladies, back in line. No one gets lunch until I've had three bullseyes in a row."

Annabel laughs and shuts the gate behind us. "Iona is a hard taskmaster. I spent many hungry afternoons under her tutelage, but it's amazing what it will do for your focus. You seem to be a woman of many talents, too, Reiley. I didn't know you were an author."

"It's my only talent, really."

She cocks a perfect blonde brow at me. "No need to be modest. I wouldn't have survived as long as you without training and a weapon. None of us would have."

"Okay, so I have a natural ability for running away."

She laughs and hooks her arm in mine. "Well, Reiley, now you no longer have to run."

27

Kade ignores my apology message for the rest of the morning and into the afternoon. I send him a terse *Just let me know you're alive* text, worried he might have crashed his Porsche after tearing off into the night. More likely, he's pouting in his hotel room, sipping Krug and eating chocolate-covered strawberries, enjoying the angst he's putting me through.

I didn't say anything that wasn't true. He's a goddamn incubus demon. He's programmed for sex and manipulation. Okay, so he's also the guy who saved my life and can sometimes be cute and maybe even a little fragile.

But still…

The arsehole has the Pro Plus or whatever the hell the fancy tablet is called. I won't even know if Thaddeus and Myron have turned up at my house unless Kade deigns to tell me.

At least the Diviners are everything I hoped for. After visiting the practise arena, Annabel takes me to the assault course where they have regular fitness and agility tests. They also go off into the woods or up in the hills once a quarter for survival training. They use Loch Fitty for swimming, fishing and kayaking until your arms fall off, according to Annabel. Their social evenings include marshmallows on the bonfire, movie nights and cocktails on the beach.

Basically, it is my heaven.

They hold classes on everything—demon lore, wards, self-defence, and how to lose a pursuer. I think I've aced the last one already, though the hide and seek games they play as part of it sound epic.

Every person we pass, whether outside on the lawn or inside the house, runs over to say hello, marvel about my aunt, and welcome me to the group. They listen, fascinated, to my stories about European demons, asking question after question until Annabel shoos them away. Elsie pops up everywhere, but Bryce and the mysterious Marianne remain elusive.

My favourite stop on the tour is their research and development lab in an annex off the main house where they're trying to create longer-range weapons as effective as the knives—or Dyr-wotsits. One of the metallurgists explains their difficulty with the responsiveness of the silver in smaller proportions, such as in bullets or buckshot. I get to hold a spear crafted entirely of steel and silver. The shaft and the wicked, bladed tip swirl black under my hand. Annabel laughs at my awe and my clumsy attempt to twirl the spear like a badass. The tour ends back in the kitchen of the house with me elated, though exhausted.

The compound is amazing. Everyone here is amazing. I can't think of anything I'd rather be than one of them. Reiley MacEwen—author and Diviner. Except there's that little, worrying niggle.

Where the hell is Kade?

* * *

I spin my phone on the kitchen table, half-listening to Elsie exclaim over passages she's reading aloud from *Demon Born*, my first published book. My number-one fans from the practise arena have her hooked on the series already. Three other Diviners prepare dinner—some kind of stew—while listening to an 80s radio station turned low. The sun slowly sets through the mullioned window in the west wall. The relaxed camaraderie and setting are idyllic.

Why hasn't Kade replied?

I tap my phone screen. No messages since I last checked a minute ago.

Is he trapped in the wreckage of his Porsche, phone crushed, garnet blood dripping as he dangles upside-down? Hoping to his last breath that I'll come find him. That someone will find him. The car finally discovered, on fire or a husk, one small pile of ash inside.

Kade told me he's not as invulnerable to injury as the demons that feed on life energy. Wound him enough, even without a swirly black knife, and he can die.

And if he's not dead or dying and this has all been a vindictive sulk, I'll kick him so hard in the nuts, he won't be able to have sex for months.

I have to phone him. In private. Just in case it goes to voicemail and the sick feeling in my stomach leaks out my eyeballs.

Why is it so disquieting to picture him broken and in pain? A few days ago, such a fantasy was enough to put a skip in my step. But he's not broken. Or in pain. The guy is sturdier than I am. He's probably fine.

Probably.

I stand up. "I'm going to make a quick—"

A streak of brown and white bounds into the kitchen and barrels into my legs, staggering me against the table and knocking over Elsie's glass of water. She yelps and whisks my book clear of the spreading puddle. Huge paws thump on my shoulders, and the brown and white beast pants dog breath into my face.

"Atka! *Down!*"

The commanding voice alone is enough of a clue without the chorus of, "Marianne!" from the Diviners gathered in the kitchen. Atka the Alaskan malamute thuds onto all four paws and stares up at me from belly level with eyes the same colour as Kade's human ones.

"I'm sorry," the voice continues, "she gets very excited around visitors."

I drag my gaze from the massive, tongue-lolling dog to a willowy woman in her fifties who looks too delicate to lead an army. Brown hair falls to her waist, streaked grey and cut into a fringe above shrewd, hazel eyes. Her spring-green dress swirls at her ankles, cinched by a belt at her hips that holds a knife in a sheath. Dark marks speckle her bodice.

"You must be Reiley," Marianne says. "I apologise for not greeting you this morning. I usually like to do the tour myself."

Atka butts my thigh. I place a hand on her thick, but surprisingly soft, head.

"Annabel said you had something urgent come up."

Annabel mops the water spill and gives Marianne a nod. "We missed you, but I think I covered all the bases."

Marianne scans the Diviners in the kitchen before returning her gaze to me. Atka makes a perplexing *wow-ow-woo* noise until I scratch her ear.

"Could I speak with you outside, Reiley?" Marianne says.

"Annabel, you should join us, too."

"Um, sure…" I say, feeling like I'm somehow in trouble.

We troop out of the kitchen into the short corridor that connects it to the wide hallway at the front of the house, Atka trotting at my heels. Marianne shuts the door on the curious faces.

"Forgive me the secrecy," she says. "I wanted to extend my condolences for your aunt. Five years seem like nothing when you're grieving. Isabella and I were close when she was here."

I pat Atka, and she winds around my legs. "Do you know why she left? She never told me she was a Diviner."

Marianne shares a glance with Annabel.

"We can discuss that in detail another time. Annabel tells me you have two creatures searching for you."

"Creat—oh, you mean demons." I play with Atka's curly tail, and she wiggles her arse. "They saw me at a nightclub in Edinburgh. They know my name. It won't be long before they find my address."

Marianne strokes her chin with her left hand, and I try not to stare. She's missing the index finger.

"It seems one of them followed you here," she says.

My hands freeze on Atka's woolly coat.

"Followed me *here?*" I squeak.

"That was the urgent matter needing my attention so early this morning. Come—I'll show you."

"*Show me?*" I squeak even higher.

Marianne spins on her heel and inserts a key into the wood-panelled wall near the door to the hall. The panel swings outward, revealing a set of concrete steps leading down.

"This wasn't included in the tour," I say, my voice returned to a normal decibel.

"Some areas are off-limits except for senior members." Marianne's sandals whisper on the stairs.

Annabel gives me an encouraging smile, but a frown knits her delicate brows. She follows Marianne. I hesitate at the top, unease roiling in my stomach.

"This day has been quite unprecedented." Marianne's voice echoes. "Atka sensed him on our morning walk."

I hustle down the steps to join them in a grey corridor that ends in a single, metal door.

"I thought most demons couldn't be captured," I say, somehow out of breath.

"They can't, so I didn't expect it to be one of the creatures stalking you." Marianne strides down the corridor. "But he keeps saying your name."

My stomach drops to my feet.

No. Oh, no.

Marianne pushes the door open and steps through. Annabel gestures for me to go first. The lump in my throat wants me to scream and sprint out of the suddenly stuffy house. My feet shuffle forward, as heavy as my heartbeat.

Please be Myron. Or Thaddeus. Please, *please* don't be—

"Kade!" I gasp, and every face in the room turns to me.

Every face except one.

28

Dried blood stains the chest of Kade's grey cashmere jumper, and peppers the thighs of his jeans. Mud crusts the cuffs of his previously white shirt. Leather straps at wrist and ankle bind him to a chair.

He never got to the hotel. Marianne said she found him this morning. Did he come back after our fight?

"Kade," I whisper, and rush forward.

A thin but steely arm blocks my path. Atka growls from the doorway.

"Careful, Reiley," Marianne says. "He's drugged and de-fanged, but still dangerous."

My stomach flips. "You pulled out his *teeth?*"

Oh god, they've had him down here all day. Bloody. In pain. While I romped around the compound with Annabel.

"An incubus demon's bite is addictive," Marianne says. "It's one of the many ways they enthral their victims."

Kade raises his head, though it seems to take a lot of effort. His hair flops into his eyes, one eye almost swollen shut from a welt on his cheek. Blood has dried in a rivulet from the corner of his mouth to his chin.

"Reiley?" he croaks.

Annabel gasps. "Goodness, those eyes are just awful, aren't

171

they?"

They're half-lidded. Dazed and disorientated. It's unsettling to be pinned by them.

But not awful.

"Has he talked?" Marianne says, and I finally register the other people in the room.

Bryce leans on a table close to Kade's chair, his wool hat pulled low. The older woman—Iona—stands in the corner, her thick hands cupping her elbows, her chunky ring glinting beneath the fluorescent lights.

Is that what caused the welt on Kade's cheek?

"Since you left, he's been quiet," Bryce says.

Marianne nods. "Hit him again."

Bryce bends to a contraption that looks like an old radio with a large dial and some kind of circular scale. Wires dangle from the side. Bryce twirls the knob. Kade makes a horrible whine and his head snaps back, his spine bowing, slim fingers curled to claws. The wires from the machine disappear under his collar and attach to two metal disks at his temples.

I freeze. My brain struggles to process moving from a kitchen idyll to this scene of torture in the basement.

"Tell us where you came from, demon," Marianne says. "Tell us and your pain will end."

"My car," Kade says between gritted teeth. "I was sleeping— you old witch."

Bryce cranks the dial and Kade convulses in the seat, his body arched as far as the straps allow.

"Stop it!"

My scream bounces off the walls. I dodge past Marianne and fall to my knees beside Kade. He collapses in the chair, panting hard. My fingertips cup his bruised face. His head lolls on the seat back.

"Told you—they wouldn't—like me," he sighs.

I shove to my feet and spin to Marianne. "He's not one of the demons hunting me. He's *helping* me."

A glance passes between the Diviners. Atka cocks her head, her fluffy bum parked on the concrete.

"I know it's probably against Diviner code to fraternise with a demon," I say, trying to keep my voice calm, "but he's not like the others. I was going to tell you about him."

"We don't blame you, Reiley," Marianne says, her smile sympathetic. "These creatures are made to confuse the hormones, but you have to be honest with us—has he seduced you?"

My cheeks heat. "We've not had sex if that's what you're asking."

"Semantics," Kade mutters.

A lump catches in my throat, half-way between a laugh and a sob. I force myself not to look at him.

"He protected me from the other demons. They attacked him, too."

"Has he bitten you, Reiley?" Marianne says softly.

"Well, I... Only because I let him. He was injured."

Telling them I still fantasise about his teeth in my skin, the sucking, the heat of his mouth, is probably too much information.

Rather than disgust, all four Diviners give me similar expressions of understanding.

"We can free you of him," Bryce says, his brown eyes warm, "don't you worry."

I frown at Bryce. "It's not him I'm worried about."

"You're in thrall to the creature," Marianne says in the same gentle tone. "He is magic and pheromones. None of it is real."

Atka chuffs, as if in agreement.

I angle my shoulders to look down at Kade while keeping everyone in sight. He's slumped in the chair, his eyes shut, one cheekbone perfect, the other swollen and weeping. His pulse thuds thick and slow in the side of his neck.

Is he a lie? In less than a day, I let him into my house and into my bed. Only my ragged willpower kept him out of my pants. If he weren't an incubus, would I have slammed the door in his face on that stormy April night?

"I'm not in his thrall," I say slowly.

Marianne graces me with a sad smile. "Isabella said the same."

The world wobbles. My mouth flops open.

"My aunt knew Kade?"

"Another of his ilk. Thankfully, they are rare. She fell under his spell. She was like you—convinced he was on her side. Our side."

"Is that why she left?"

Another look passes between the Diviners.

"Partly," Marianne says. "She refused to see the opportunity such a creature presented."

"Opportunity?"

Atka shuffles and presses herself against Marianne's leg. Marianne pets the dog's head.

"Demons that feed on life energy are stronger. Impossible to capture. But an incubus is closer to human. They can be drugged and questioned." Marianne scratches behind Atka's ear. "We will never be safe from them unless we find their breeding clans. And *he* knows where at least one of them is."

I follow her nod to Kade sprawled in the chair without his

usual grace. No smirk or dark, drowning eyes. Just a bloody mouth and mud on his clothes.

I swallow hard. "If he tells you, will you let him go?"

"He is too powerful, Reiley. Once you are freed from his thrall, you will understand."

"I'm not—" I pinch the bridge of my nose. "What if I can get him to talk?"

"By all means try, but he has resisted since this morning. He is quite stubborn."

That's my little demon.

I rub my suddenly blurry eyes, and crouch next to Kade. Maybe if I get Marianne what she wants, I can bargain for his freedom. Coming here was my idea. There's no way I'm leaving him to be tortured, thrall or no.

I yank the wires, the metal disks popping from Kade's skin, and toss them on the floor. He sucks in a breath, and blinks at me.

Bryce clears his throat. "We're not—"

"The torture portion of the day is over," I say without looking at him.

"Reiley." Kade attempts a smile, flashing gaps where his fangs used to be. "You're still here."

My stomach dips. I cup Kade's uninjured cheek, and he snuggles into my palm.

"I need you to answer a question."

"I didn't go to the hotel," he says. "I was mad. I drove around. But I came back."

"Hush," Marianne says to Atka's growl.

I stroke the hair out of Kade's eyes.

"I didn't want to leave you alone," he whispers.

"Kade—"

His sigh flares goosebumps on my wrist. "But I was alone."

Damn clog in my throat. Nothing seems to clear it.

Kade jerks his arms against the straps. "Why can I never touch you? I want to touch you."

"Where were you born, Kade?" I say a little desperately.

He shakes his head. "I can't—can't remember. Mountains and trees. I ran away."

"How old were you?"

"Nine?" His mouth twitches. "They didn't like me, either."

His gaze floats around the room, not settling, like a dust mote in a sunbeam. It takes him a minute to return to my face, then he gives me the soft little smile that squiggles in my belly.

"Can I get a hug?" he says.

Something hot splashes my cheek. My shaking fingers tug at his straps. Gentle hands coax me away. I fight, but Marianne's wiry strength cushions my feeble protests until I find myself shivering in the corner next to Annabel. Annabel holds out a handkerchief the same colour as her shirt. I ignore it, and swipe at the tears on my face.

"He is very good," Marianne says, turning my back to Kade. "Every word, every action, designed to manipulate. I admit, he almost had me fooled."

Annabel cuddles herself. "I'd forgotten what his kind were like."

"Parasites," Iona growls, and I jump, "feeding on the illusion of love."

She twirls her ring around her finger and glares towards Kade. I try to look at him, but Marianne places her hand on my shoulder.

"You are untrained, Reiley. Of course he has you over-whelmed. This is what makes him so dangerous. Even here, when he's drugged and cannot access his full power, we all feel his call."

Annabel grips herself tighter. Iona twirls her ring—faster and faster. Even Bryce shudders.

Has it been a trick? Magic and pheromones? I thought I was in control, but maybe Kade has been the puppet master all along.

I shake my head, but I'm not sure who I'm disagreeing with.

"We can guide you," Marianne says. "We can teach you how to resist him. Annabel can make a charm to help until you're strong enough."

Annabel nods. "I'll make several. I imagine a few of us will need them while he's here."

"He won't be here long," Marianne says.

I shake my head, harder this time. "You're not killing him. Just let him go."

Marianne shushes me and pets my hair. Atka wriggles into the centre of our tense huddle, staring up at me with Kade's pale-blue, human eyes.

"Then every woman he seduced would be on my conscience."

Marianne stops petting me, and ruffles Atka's fur. Atka's curled tail wags against the floor.

I don't want Kade to seduce anyone else. I want to be the only—

Tits. Is this what it's like to be under his spell? I thought he was real.

"You're not hurting him," I say, my lips numb. "Or killing him."

Marianne slides an arm around my shoulders and steers me towards the door. "Let's talk upstairs. I fear you've been in his presence too long."

"I'm not leaving him down here."

"I promise you he will not be harmed while we're away. Bryce and Iona will watch him, keep him drugged, nothing more."

I blink and find myself in the corridor. Atka and Annabel trot ahead.

"Reiley?" Kade's voice is slurred and confused.

I twist in Marianne's tender yet unbreakable hold. Kade strains against the straps, his hair in his eyes. A flash of skin peeks through the leg of his jeans where he ripped the material on the brambles.

"Reiley, wait," he says.

Bryce slowly—firmly—closes the door.

<h1 style="text-align:center">29</h1>

I cuddle my body around the warmth of the mug, the lemon and ginger steam stroking my face and twining into my nostrils. The tea is restorative, apparently, though I've done no more than breathe it in.

I'd rather have coffee.

And Kade. I feel his presence under the floor. If I listen carefully, maybe I'll hear the smack of Iona's ring on his cheek. His cries of pain.

I shudder and hold the mug tighter, scalding my fingers.

Marianne said they wouldn't harm him.

The living room of the Diviner house looks west and north over Loch Fitty, the windows of the kitchen just visible where the two rooms form a ninety-degree angle. Orange-gold light paints the wall and the door back out into the corridor, shut now, muting the conversation from the kitchen. My bowl of stew sits untouched on the coffee table. Elsie is curled on one side of me, Annabel on the other. More couches and chairs are scattered throughout the room, some roughly pointing towards a large TV. Atka is stretched out on a plush rug, snoring. Marianne blows on her tea in the seat opposite me, her long hair swept over her shoulder.

"Isabella met her demon about eight years ago, though she

kept it secret, and the creature had a year to seduce her from us before we learned of him," she says.

Elsie must have been about twelve. I was, what—sixteen, seventeen?

"Dill or lavender?" Annabel mutters. "Both ward against evil spirits, but maybe we need the additional protection from witchcraft…"

Annabel scoops a bunch of tiny, yellow flowers from the pile of herbs and crystals in her lap and crushes them into a leather pouch on a black cord. A shudder runs through Elsie. She jostles my elbow, and a splotch of hot tea dampens my jeans. I take an experimental sip, and it's like getting kicked in the back of the throat.

"We should kill it now before it sucks poor Reiley in deeper," Elsie says.

Kade has already sucked on me quite a bit, though not where I want him to. No, that place has been neglected by his mouth and his hands and his—

I slurp another mouthful of tea, and wrinkle my nose. The mug clatters next to my bowl on the coffee table.

"What happened to my aunt? Why did she leave?"

Marianne sips her fiery tea without so much as a twitch. "She refused to be parted from her pet. Perhaps your family has a genetic predisposition towards incubi. We tried to help her see the truth of the creature, but she turned us away. Withdrew."

A clock on the wall ticks into the silence. Muffled laughter ripples from the kitchen.

Is Kade hungry? Has he had anything to eat or drink today?

"What happened to him?" I say, though the heaviness in my gut knows the answer.

Marianne examines the contents of her cup. Annabel drops a diamond and an aquamarine stone into the pouch. Elsie fidgets like a puppy.

"We were worried about her," Marianne finally says, meeting my eyes. "She lost weight, became distracted, irritable."

"It could have been something else and not the incubus demon."

"What do you mean?"

"She was in a battle with my parents. They were convinced I needed psychiatric care and wouldn't listen to her. She begged them to give her custody. Instead, they got a doctor to grant me a short-term detention certificate, then extend it under a compulsory treatment order. My aunt helped me apply to a tribunal to have them revoked."

Marianne smooths her dress over her knees, the bodice still speckled with Kade's blood. An image flashes behind my eyes—her knee braced on Kade's chest, pliers clamped in his mouth, her wiry muscles corded. Kade screaming.

Was I enjoying my breakfast while he was losing his teeth?

I swallow hard. "Her incubus demon could've been as peaceful as she described. But you killed him, didn't you?"

Annabel hunches over her lap, scribbling on a roll of paper with a quill.

"Reiley, you must understand—it was for her own good," Marianne says patiently. "Isabella was caught in his thrall. Everything she believed about him was a direct result of his hold on her. If she had let us help her, she would have seen the truth. It is, I fear, the same situation with your creature."

"His name is Kade."

Marianne places her empty cup on the coffee table. "Let us help you where we failed her. I can start your training right now. We can keep… Kade… alive in order to test your resistance. Then you will know what is real and what is sex and lies. I imagine you will not be so adamant about preserving his life."

"Will you at least feed him?"

Annabel and Elsie shiver on either side of me. Marianne curls her lip.

"That creature will get no blood or sex from anyone in this house."

I roll my eyes. "He also eats food."

"In that case, we will do what is necessary to keep him comfortable."

"Thank you," I say, and sit up straighter. "So how do I resist him?"

Marianne climbs to her feet and paces beside the coffee table. Atka cracks open one eye, snorts, and goes back to sleep.

"Elsie, this will benefit you as well," Marianne says. "You and Reiley can practise together."

Elsie claps her hands and bounces on the couch until Annabel scolds her for scattering her dried herbs.

"The charms Annabel is making are only part of your protection against the literal charms of an incubus," Marianne says, her gaze far away. "The rest is visualisation."

I swallow a laugh. Sure, I can just visualise Kade as a potato instead of a tall hunk of sexiness with broad shoulders, slim hips, a wicked mouth and—

Tits. My visualisation is not off to a good start.

Marianne places her fingers on her temples and shuts her eyes. "Imagine a loch—deep and placid, the water dark and cold, like Loch Fitty. Whenever you're in the presence of an incubus, I want you to picture this loch. Picture yourself in the water. You're surrounded by cold and dark, but you're not afraid. You're safe in this icy space. Safe from his heat. Can you feel the water? Feel the chill of its protection?"

I shut my eyes. Water. Dark. Black, like Kade's eyes. *No.* Just dark. Cold, but safe. Who the hell feels safe in the cold?

"I feel it!" Elsie chirps. "I feel the cold!"

I feel stupid. Comfortably warm. Anxious and untethered.

"Describe it for me," Marianne says.

"It's, like, ice water. Everywhere. I'm floating in it. My skin is blue and white and hard as marble! I can see the sun way up through the darkness, but there's no heat. Wait..." Elsie frowns, her eyes squeezed tight. "Damn, I lost it. There's heat creeping in from somewhere."

I notice it, too. A prickling wave of heat swelling closer, throbbing in my heartbeat and rushing my blood through my veins. Annabel's fingers hesitate on tying the thread of the pouch. There's no more laughter from the kitchen.

Marianne's eyes snap open. "The incubus is loose."

30

Atka rolls onto four paws, and growls, her hackles raised. I jump to my feet, mirrored by Annabel and Elsie, though I'm the only one who barks their shin on the coffee table. I grit my teeth on a curse, and watch the door.

Heavy footsteps thud in the corridor.

The heat swells, filling the room with air that's too thick to breathe. Goosebumps flare on every inch of my skin. A pulse throbs deep in my stomach. Elsie pulls her knife, and the blade swirls black. She points it at the door as it swings open. The tip of her knife trembles. Iona stumbles into the room, giggling, supporting Kade on her brawny shoulder. Bryce follows, tucked under Kade's other shoulder, his wool hat knocked askew. He stares up at Kade with a look of pure adoration. I avert my gaze from Kade's face in case he bespells me with his eyes.

"Goodness, I never knew Bryce was bisexual," Annabel mumbles, then shakes herself. She thrusts the amulet pouch at me. "Put this on, Reiley. Quick."

The women from the kitchen spill through the open doorway and surround Kade in a twittering mass. A couple of them fall to their knees and cuddle his legs. I smother a ridiculous burst of jealousy.

Marianne clenches her fists. "This is why you're too powerful to live, demon."

"This is what you made me do to get out of your dungeon, old woman," Kade says, lisping slightly through the gaps in his teeth.

I loop the cord of the amulet over my head and the pouch thumps on my chest. Stones rattle together.

"How do I know if it's working? Should he be hideous?"

"Are you still attracted to him?" Annabel says.

I risk a peek.

"Oh, wow," I gasp.

Kade sags between Iona and Bryce, his cheek bruised, blood on his mouth and dried on his clothes. But he looks magnificent. Stars fill his black eyes, framed by his hair and as mysterious as the night sky. He glows with power and that power pulses into the room, whispering promises of soft kisses, skin gliding on skin and his name moaned in the dark.

"Should have used the lavender," Annabel sighs, and brandishes her knife.

"Release my people from your thrall, incubus," Marianne says, her voice calm. "You are no match for us."

"Wanna bet?" Kade says.

Heat crashes through the room. I brace myself for a wave of heart-thundering, knee-shaking lust, but it parts around me as if I'm a rock in the path of a river.

Maybe the amulet *is* working.

Two knives thump on the carpet. Elsie's face goes slack, her eyes wide and fixed on Kade. Annabel whimpers, her head thrown back. She runs her palms across her breasts and her nipples harden through the silk of her shirt. I jerk my gaze away so fast, I nearly topple. Marianne appears to be in a trance, staring at nothing, her hazel eyes glazed.

Perhaps she's swimming in her imaginary loch.

Atka bares her teeth and bunches her hindquarters. Kade turns his starry eyes on her. She whines and rolls onto her back, paws in the air, belly exposed.

Christ, no female has a chance.

So why am I still standing and not writhing on the floor like the women closest to Kade? I watch them out of my periphery since their hands are going places I don't want to see.

"Sorry, Reiley... I'm trying—stop that," Kade snaps.

Bryce pouts and removes his questing hand from under Kade's cashmere jumper. He wraps his arms around Kade's waist and cuddles tighter into his chest. Iona appears content to draw little circles around and around Kade's nipple. The women clinging to his legs start to nuzzle his thighs.

"Fuck's sake," Kade sighs, and his exhalation whistles through his teeth.

"Are you...?" I draw a blank on the best question to ask. "Okay?"

Should I be visualising my loch right now? Is it dangerous to even look at him? Maybe I should be gripping my amulet and praying to the goddess of granny panties and chastity.

Kade sags harder against Iona and Bryce, his head bowed, hair falling into those bedazzling eyes.

"Are *you* okay? I'm trying not to let it bleed all over you, but the damn drugs mess with my control."

"You mean you're deliberately not hitting me with your incubus juju?"

He manages a weak grin. "I believe you told me no incubus voodoo crap."

"I..." I clear my throat. "Hit me with it."

"What?"

"I want to see what it's like," I say in a rush. "Out of curiosity."

"Reiley, I don't think that's a good—"

"But you can stop, right? Just give me a non-addictive taster?"

He hesitates, but finally nods.

"Then you have my consent," I say, and stand up straighter, holding my hands loose at my sides.

He ducks his head, hiding his expression.

"You trust me to stop?" he says in a carefully neutral tone.

My heart speeds. What the hell am I doing? Asking him to bewitch me is not visualising my cool, happy place. But I want to feel his power. Maybe I'll recognise it and know for sure if he's used it on me before or if he ever does in future.

"I trust you," I say.

Kade raises his face and smiles at me. It takes my breath away.

Is this his power? That sweet, tender smile—

Heat crashes into me. Raw desire. My skin is instantly slick and swollen and aching, *scraping* against my clothes. I need to take them off. Naked. Naked is good. Naked he can touch me. Caress me. Tease me with his lips and brand his name into my skin.

Kade-Kade-Kade.

I need him. I need. I *need*.

The lust recedes. I come to, shaking on the floor and panting into the carpet. My hoodie and t-shirt are rucked up under my breasts, as if I've tried to pull them off over my head. My pulse throbs between my legs. I suspect one touch, even somewhere as innocent as my arm, will make me explode. My knickers are *soaked*.

Kade calls my name in tones of increasing worry.

I claw myself into a seated position using the coffee table and flop against the wood, each breath stirring my hair.

"Holy titcakes, Batman," I wheeze. "You might want to dial it back before you cause an orgy."

Kade chuckles, and I risk the sanctity of my eyeballs to meet his gaze. He sways between Bryce and Iona. Bryce starts to buckle under his weight. Iona is… yup, humping his side.

"Can I at least sit down before I release them and they get their pointy things?" Kade says.

What a selfish idiot I am. The poor guy has been tortured, and I'm making him stand and perform tricks. They yanked out his teeth, for god's sake.

I leap to my feet. My knees collapse, and I land hard on the couch.

"What have you done to my *legs?!*"

"They'll be wobbly for a while." Kade blinks a few times.

I heave myself upright and stagger on quivering, baby-deer legs to Kade. Bryce pouts again as I shoo him away and tuck myself into Kade's side. My arm slides around the heat of his back. I grip his hand where his arm drapes over my shoulder. He tangles his fingers in mine, and my heart skips.

A remnant of the arousal he just gave me. Nothing more.

"Forget sitting down," I say. "We need to get you out of here."

"I might faint soon."

"Can you make it to a car?"

"I don't think I can drive, Reiley. Can you?"

"What if we hide in the woods?"

Kade leans more of his weight on me, and my quivering legs protest. I tilt my head to look up into his face. He manages a half-mouth smile.

"I can't—hold them—much longer."

"They're not going to be happy with you, Kade."

"I know."

Iona and I steer him through a forest of grasping, petting hands to the sofa, and lower him gently. Iona attempts to climb into his lap, and he orders her back to Bryce.

More pouting.

"What's with her?" Kade jerks his chin towards Marianne.

I rip my gaze from his pale face.

"She's visualising a loch. Apparently, the cold, dark water is protection against all your lusty juju."

Kade snorts.

I twiddle my fingers and avoid his eyes. "You could've done that to me anytime you wanted? Just switched it on and *bam*—goodbye inhibitions?"

The silence stretches. Has he fainted? I raise my gaze and meet his beautiful, starry eyes. The world wobbles, though it's probably just my legs.

"Yes, Reiley," he says. "I could've."

"Oh."

I thud next to him on the couch. He snuggles his head on my shoulder. I jump to my feet and nearly somersault over the coffee table.

"We need a barrier," I squeak.

I drag the chairs to form a fort, dodging the writhing and groaning shapes on the carpet.

"Do they all think you're shagging them right now?"

Kade smirks, his eyes half-lidded moons of night sky. "Mostly."

"So you can switch it on and all your women visualise having amazing sex while you're, what—reading a book?"

"How do you think I read yours?"

I perch on the arm of the couch, curse my cowardice, and slide onto the cushion beside Kade. He strokes one finger down the amulet on my chest.

"What's this for?"

"It's supposed to ward off you and your evil spirits."

He sniffs. "Smells nice."

He lifts his feet onto the sofa and curls on his side, settling his head in my lap. I hold my arms up, unsure what to do with my hands.

"Reiley?" he mumbles. "You won't let them kill me, will you?"

I lick my lips. "No, Kade, I won't."

He nods, rubbing his uninjured cheek against my thigh. I brush his hair away from his eyes, careful of his violet bruise, the welt crusted.

"This isn't exactly the best position to protect you from, though," I say, watching his eyelids droop.

"Just one more minute."

His breath sighs out and the tension eases from his body.

Then the shrieking starts.

One of my fans from the practise arena points a quivering blade in our direction and says, "He raped us!"

She stands near the doorway with the women from the kitchen in a clump of bristling, swirly black knives. Buttons gape undone, clothes in disarray, hair mussed from rolling on the carpet.

"I swear he didn't touch you," I say.

"He mind-raped us," Annabel croaks from somewhere behind my chair fort.

"Okay, *that* I'll give you."

Fingers grip the couch back opposite us, and she pulls herself upright. Her gaze drops to Kade. She bites her lip and frowns down at her hands.

"He had no right to make us feel that way."

Kade cracks open one eye. Solid black, no stars.

"You gave me—no choice."

Atka—or what I assume is Atka—whines. Paws shuffle on the floor. What did she see under Kade's power? Kade as a dog? Or maybe he just forced her into heat.

The damn guy does it to me all the time.

Marianne sucks in a loud breath, and shudders. Her shrewd, hazel eyes zip to mine, then narrow at the demon sprawled in my lap.

"Your foul magic did not touch me, incubus," she says, drawing the knife from her belt and slinging a leg over the barricade.

I hold up a hand. "Wait, Marianne. He didn't hurt anyone."

Her gaze sweeps the pale and shaking Diviners. "Define *hurt*."

Bryce's voice whispers, "You bastard… You filthy demon bastard," over and over.

Marianne hops past the chair and lands easily in the space between the coffee table and our couch.

"Move away from the creature, Reiley," she says. "Annabel, get the fire extinguisher."

A brief image of Kade bursting into flames, a knife sticking out of his ribs, flares in my head and rolls nausea through my stomach. I wrap an arm across his chest and cuddle him into me.

"Ow," he says.

His eyes roll beneath bruised lids. He drapes an arm over my legs, his other hand tucked under my thigh.

"Look at him, Marianne," I say, struggling to stay calm with her knife so close. "He's in no state to hurt anyone."

"Exactly. We must strike before he gathers his strength."

"He could've killed you all and waltzed out of the house."

"He is semi-drugged and weak, he could do no such thing. You are being manipulated, Reiley. Manipulated into protecting him."

"I'm *choosing* to protect him. There's a difference."

"Could've killed you, old woman," Kade groans.

"He's right," I say quickly. "You were in a trance, Marianne. He walked right past you."

Her lip curls. "He may have stayed his hand for your benefit, but all demons kill."

Annabel enters the room with a fire extinguisher, hose in one hand, trigger and canister in the other. Kade's original entourage fan out behind her, their blades swirling in the tangerine light of the sunset.

Elsie pops up behind the chair barrier. "Come on, Reiley. You don't want to be next to him when he dies."

"No one's dying," I squeak.

Panic tightens my throat. I fist my hand in the soft cashmere of Kade's jumper. His heart thuds against my wrist.

How am I going to protect him if everyone decides to charge?

"I feed on sex," Kade says, shivering in my arms, "not death."

"I wouldn't have brought him here if I thought he was a threat. He didn't even want to come."

Annabel gasps. "You *brought* him here?"

"He's been staying with me since the demons attacked him. You know—the demons that are actually trying to kill us? He wouldn't tell them where I lived. He saved my life."

"Oh, Reiley," Marianne says sadly, "he really has his claws in you."

"And something else," a voice mutters.

Chairs scrape as the Diviners dismantle my barricade. My heart flops into my mouth.

"You wouldn't listen to my aunt and look what happened. She died because of *you*."

Okay, so that's a stretch, but I'm desperate.

Marianne frowns. "Demons murdered Isabella, not us."

"And if she had her incubus and the rest of you to help her, don't you think she'd still be alive? Grief drove her to

Duddingston Loch that night."

"Her incubus would have abandoned her for his brethren."

"Not if he loved her."

"They can only love you to death. That is abuse disguised as love." Marianne sneers at Kade. "Have you ever loved, demon?"

Kade lies very still in my arms, not even breathing, though his eyes are open.

He glares at Marianne. "Have *you?*"

She returns his glare. "That is none of your business."

"Then ditto."

"Enough of this foolishness. Reiley, release the creature. If you're holding him when we stab him, you'll both burn."

I hug Kade tighter, and he hisses through the gaps in his teeth.

"I am Isabella MacArthur's niece," I say with more confidence than I feel. "You wouldn't dare."

Marianne steps closer, brandishing her knife. Annabel opens her mouth, but seems at a loss for words. Elsie looks like she might cry.

"Goddammit," Kade huffs.

He shoves hard, breaking my hold and rolling off the couch. He thumps onto the floor on his back and blinks dazed eyes at the ceiling.

"Just make it quick, old woman."

I yelp, "No!" and launch myself off the sofa.

I land on top of Kade. His breath gusts out. He's firm and warm and trembling underneath me.

"Christ's sake, Reiley," he groans. "Get off me."

He pushes weakly at my arms. I bury my face in his neck and jam my hands beneath him to grip his shoulder blades. He sighs into my hair. His pulse flutters against my cheek. I bob with the rise and fall of his ribs, the room so quiet, I can hear his heartbeat. I roll my eyes, but all I can see are Marianne's sandals through the tickle of Kade's hair.

God, I've forgotten how good he smells.

"You would let me kill you?" Marianne says.

Tentative hands pat my back.

"Well, not right now, clearly," Kade says.

"But if she were a safe distance?"

Kade takes a deep breath. "Look, old woman, I don't want to die, but if you're going to kill me, I'd rather she wasn't hurt, too."

He sags under me, his head resting on mine, as if the words exhausted him.

"What is she to you?"

"She's my"—another breath in and out—"friend."

He's right. It does suck. No wonder he got pissy.

"Friends don't see other friends naked," I whisper in his ear, and he shivers.

"Climb off him now, Reiley," Marianne says in a firm voice.

"Not unless you promise you won't kill him."

"I promise he will not be killed."

My head snaps up. "Really?"

Kade watches me, all dark eyes and sharp cheekbones. His expression squiggles through my stomach and makes me very aware of being pressed to every firm inch of him. I gulp, and focus on Marianne instead.

She's much less confusing.

She sheaths her knife and indicates for the rest of the Diviners to do the same. They hesitate, but follow her lead. The fire extinguisher clunks at Annabel's feet.

"If he can prove he is benign, then we won't kill him," Marianne says.

"And no more stuff about me being in his thrall?"

She gives me a small smile. "You disobeyed him and don't act as though he's the most wonderful person you've ever seen."

"Well, he can be a real arsehole."

"One time," Kade mutters, though his hands squeeze me a little tighter.

My breath catches. I carefully push into a crouch and reverse-crawl onto the sofa, leaving Kade spread-eagled on the floor. I hug my knees to my chest.

The room seems cooler.

"Perhaps *you* have charmed *him,*" Marianne says, and cocks a brow at me.

I stare at her as if my life depends on it. No need to see what Kade is thinking. Atka saves me from any kind of response by weaving between the seats and lunging for him. He flinches and tries to roll away.

"Don't let the damn dog eat me."

Atka licks his jaw and wiggles her arse in the air.

"You've made another friend," I say, willing my heart rate to slow.

Kade slides me a look and levers himself into a sitting position, leaning heavily on the couch. Atka laps at his cheek, and he waves her away. She trots to Marianne's side, her eyes on Kade. Marianne clucks her tongue.

"It seems you have bewitched my dog."

Kade holds up a finger, then his hand flops in his lap. "*Before* I had to prove I'm benign. So it doesn't count."

"No way—no fucking way." Bryce stalks towards us, his

hands clenched, wool hat so low it almost covers his eyes. "We can't let that thing live. He made me *want* him."

Kade smirks, and shifts his hips a tiny bit. Bryce's furious gaze drops from Kade's face to the hollow of his throat and continues south to where his somewhat stained jumper hugs his chest and flat stomach, the slimness of his waist, the tightness of his jeans over his crotch and—

Jesus Christ. Even rumpled and exhausted, Kade is gorgeous.

Bryce's cheeks blaze red, and he jerks his eyes to Kade's face.

"I can only enhance what's there," Kade says, the smirk dissolving to something more serious. "Consider it payback for the electric shocks."

Bryce bares his teeth and spins on his heel, barging through the gaggle of fidgeting women. Iona is sitting on the floor near the door, twirling her gold ring around her finger and avoiding everybody's gaze. Kade sighs, and his eyes flutter closed.

"I'm taking him upstairs," I say before anyone can agree with Bryce. "Annabel, would you give me a hand?"

"I'm not touching him," she says quickly. "Sorry, Reiley."

Shudders of agreement ripple through the Diviners. Seems I'm the only one who wants to touch him.

Which is the problem.

"Kade, can you stand?"

He peeks at me. "Maybe."

I hold out my hands, and he takes them after a pause. A tingle zips to the base of my spine. With much pulling and straining, I manage to get him on his feet and tuck myself into his side, his arm over my shoulders, fingers gripping mine, my arm around his back.

"Old woman has my keys," he mumbles.

Marianne plucks his car keys from a pouch on her belt and places them in my waiting palm.

"And his phone?"

"In the car," Kade says.

We limp for the door. The Diviners part and watch us go. Iona spits at Kade from her crumpled position on the floor, and he blows her a kiss.

32

There's a demon in my bed. Again. He fills the single mattress with his weak and shivering sexiness.

Fuck's sake. There's something seriously wrong with me, but now I can't blame it on Kade's incubus voodoo.

I toss his trainers on the floor and unbutton his shirt cuffs, pulling the blood-stained cashmere over his head while he clumsily levers himself off the bed.

"I think your fancy jumper is ruined," I say.

"I think all my clothes are ruined," he groans.

Unzipping his jeans sends a little spurt of excitement to my gut.

"Are you in pain?" I say to distract myself from whatever the hell is going on.

"Aches. Though my mouth is throbbing like fuck."

He probes his gum, and winces, his fingertip slicked red. My stomach rolls, and I focus on peeling his jeans off. Bruises and mud darken his knees, his shin scoured by the brambles. Shallow punctures circle his lower leg.

"Damn dog chewed on my ankle."

My throat closes. The poor guy has spent most of his time with me banged up. Thrown around. Clawed. Now tortured.

I have to fix it.

Will his teeth even heal? Growing a body part or two is a lot more than knitting flesh back together. What if he can never feed on blood again unless someone, literally, opens a vein for him? That'll be a little harder to explain than a hickey.

This is all my fault. I forced him to drive me to the farm. Abandoned him for my new friends.

I reach for his boxer shorts. He grabs my wrist.

"What are you doing, Reiley?"

"Well, I didn't pack for play, so it'll have to be mouth or hand stuff."

Okay, so that's definitely on the list of things not to do with Kade, but it's an emergency. I hate seeing him hurt. And I'm still sexing him rather than the other way around, so it's safer.

Makes total sense.

He gives me a slow blink. My pulse bounds under the grip of his fingers.

"I need you healed," I say, my voice higher than normal. "What if the Diviners change their minds tomorrow and we have to run? I wouldn't be surprised when they dream about you tonight."

"Did you dream about me?"

I remember candlelight and slick skin. A wicked smile. Moaning his name.

"I thought you were messing with me, but you just planted the suggestion and—*ta-da!*—instant sex dream."

He smirks, and I twist my wrist free, but he bats my hands away from his crotch.

"No," he says softly. "No more emergency healing. Touch me because you want to, not because you have to."

"Uh, hello? I threw myself on top of you."

"Because you had to." He curls on his side in his boxers and shirt, the cuffs long and flopping over his hands. "But thank you. Though you're heavier than you look."

"Just let me help you, Kade."

He cracks open one, amused eye. "Annoying, isn't it? When you want to touch someone and they won't let you."

"Now you're just being petty."

He grins a pale imitation of his usual smug expression. "Goodnight, Reiley."

I thrust to my feet and cross my arms, glaring down at him. His chest rises and falls, his bare legs bent close. He looks small and vulnerable.

"Pain in the arse," I mutter, and tuck him in.

The ghost of a smile curves his lips. I sit on the chair opposite the bed, my chin propped on my knees. Kade's breathing deepens. The tension eases from his face as he escapes into sleep. His hair falls over his forehead, and I want to brush it away.

Goddamn incubus demon making me want to touch him.

The house settles. Voices argue on the ground floor, hushed but heated. Doors open and close, leaving a silence that weighs on my eyelids. My head nods. I jerk and nearly topple out of the chair. I stand and stretch, and my spine pops. Kade slumbers, all cute and innocent.

Innocent. *Right.*

Instead of climbing in beside him and snuggling into his heat, I grab his car keys off the bedside cabinet and creep out of the room.

* * *

Kade's Porsche is parked on the same bit of road, the nose

pointed towards the blackness of Loch Fitty this time. Thick clouds obscure the sky and pepper my face with rain. I pan the torch of my phone around the car. There, on the grassy verge next to the driver's-side door, is a scuff mark and a splash of blood.

He was asleep and they dragged him from the car, Atka growling and fastened to his ankle. He must have been disoriented until he saw their knives, swirling and pointed at him. Did they hit him with a tranquilliser before he had a chance to try anything?

Chilled, I slip into the driver's seat and shut the door. It's cold in the car, but his scent warms me. Summer and grass and lazy days on the beach. The seat is canted as far back as it will go, but is nowhere near horizontal. I lean into it and blink at the roof, my eyes adjusting to the dark. I imagine I can feel the imprint of Kade's body in the expensive leather. The sweep of his shoulders, the curve of his back where it dips to his perfect, tight little arse. His legs are longer than mine, so I can't reach the pedals without scooting forward. My fingers stroke where he's touched—steering wheel, gear paddles, handbrake. Confident in handling this machine of speed and muscle, like he is with everything else. Mischief in his demon eyes and a smirk on his lips.

I rest my forehead on the steering wheel, and start to cry. Hot tears drip onto leather and a multitude of buttons. I sob out the horror of seeing him in the basement, hurt and confused and strapped to a chair. The way he called my name when I left him. How close Marianne came to stabbing her blade in his lovely chest. My cries peter to hitching breaths and sniffles. I scrub my wet cheeks.

"Okay," I huff. "Not sure where that came from."

I grab his phone from the cup holder. Two unread texts from an unknown number. My finger hovers on the delete button of the lock screen. I release it without erasing them.

Where are all the missed calls and messages from his women? Wondering where he is. Begging him to come back. None of them are afraid to get naked and let him do what he wants.

I shiver, and pick up the tablet from the passenger seat. The Pro Plus or whatever. My finger taps the screen. No sign of Thaddeus or Myron in the motion history, only the postman. I glimpse the time in the bottom left corner.

Shit. I've been gone forty minutes. What if Bryce saw me leave and snuck into our room, Kade alone and unguarded on the bed? Or Marianne reneges on her word and I find them dancing around flames on the grass?

Heart thumping, I scrabble out of the Porsche, sprint a few steps, curse, then fumble Kade's bag out of the boot.

I should never have left him. Bad things happen when I leave him. This was such a stupid idea. I just wanted him to have clean clothes when he woke up.

The locking lights of the Porsche flash orange. I hustle down the road in a breathless rush. The house glows white on the edge of the loch, few lights on bar the one in the porch. No burnt patch on the lawn. No shriek of a smoke alarm from inside.

An ache in my chest eases, though I take the stairs two at a time. Kade doesn't twitch when I stumble through the door and trip over his bag dangling too low in my hand. My heart rate slows by the time I pick myself up, splash water on my flushed face, and brush my teeth. I ignore the bed and its seductive occupant, climbing onto the chair and huddling beneath a blanket.

Once again, I drift off to the soft sigh of Kade's breathing.

<h1 style="text-align:center">33</h1>

An empty bed greets me when I open my eyes. My heart spasms. Images of flames and cackling Diviners streak through my head before the hiss of the shower penetrates. And a soft curse.

That's it. The stubborn arse made his point last night, but now I need him healed. *Want* him healed. The bloody guy can't even brush his teeth, for god's sake.

Heart hammering for a different reason, I throw back the blanket and strip off my clothes. Except my black bra and pants.

I'm still not brave enough to be naked with Kade.

I miss my corset and my confidence-boosting strap-on. Compared to his leggy, boobily enhanced women, I'm a flat-chested midget. With scars.

I lose my courage outside the bathroom door. Water splashes on tile. I shoo away the thought of Kade wet and naked before it can take root.

I can't do this. Barge in on him in the shower. We're not exactly in a relationship where that might be acceptable. I don't know what we are, though it's definitely not friends.

Kade makes a small pain sound. I hang my head, and knock on the door.

"Kade? Can I come in?"

There's a pause. If he says no, I may just crawl under the bed and die.

"Okay," he says.

Crap. Now I have to go in.

My hand twists the knob. I taste my pulse on my tongue. The door swings wide onto the grey-tiled bathroom, steam curling towards the ceiling and misting the mirror. The walk-in shower fills the rear wall, the bottom half of the glass panel opaque to spare Kade's modesty. And mine. He swipes the fogged glass and his eyes widen a fraction, then he frowns at me.

"If this is you proving you want to touch me, you're failing at it."

"How? I'm in my damn underwear."

Those black eyes sweep me from head to toe, and my knees wobble. His hair sticks to his cheekbones, dark with water.

His gaze meets mine in challenge. "Yes, but you're all the way over there. And not naked."

Is it hot in here? Feels hot in here.

"And I don't believe I will be getting naked."

"See? You don't really want to touch me."

I laugh, and it's a tad bitter. "Kade, I want to touch you so badly, I don't trust myself to be naked."

God, my heart is beating hard.

"Reiley," he growls, "get your arse in here."

I stagger to the shower, slide the glass door open, and step into the sticky heat before I can decide whether it's a good idea to do what he says. Spray speckles my feet, but I stay out of range, nearly pressing myself to the tile, as far from Kade as possible in the tiny space.

I used to get anxious trapped in a lift with him, now I'm half-naked and in his shower. And he's very, fully naked.

My traitorous eyeballs follow the path of water from his cheekbones, gliding down his neck, dipping in the hollow of his throat to his chest, rippling across his abs and dripping from his long, hard—

"My face is up here, Reiley," he chuckles.

I jerk my gaze north, and my cheeks flame hotter than the steam misting from Kade. A hint of garnet swirls in the depths of his eyes, making me woozy. Or it's the heat.

Nope, it's him. Stupid horny demon. Stupid horny me.

"What are you so afraid of?" he says.

"You, obviously."

"I'm just a guy, Reiley."

I stare at his feet. Safest part of him. Except they're slim and cute and I want to nibble on the arch until he writhes. A giggling Kade would be a sight to see.

"Maybe I'm not the self-assured and worldly wise girl I pretend to be," I mumble to his toes.

He wiggles them. "What do you think I'm going to do to you, exactly?"

"Break my heart."

Well, that sounds pathetic.

I duck my head and turn my back. The splash of the water changes. His heat goosepimples my skin, but he doesn't touch me. I address the tile since it's less disconcerting than looking at him.

"I've seen who you sleep with, Kade, and they're nothing like me."

"Why do you think that is?"

I shrug, and draw a circle on the damp tile. "You got bored.

I'm sure you'll flit back to your usual type once your curiosity is satisfied."

"Flit? What am I—a butterfly?"

I swallow a laugh. "Sure. A polyamorous butterfly that feeds on sex. One woman would never be enough for you."

"Depends on the woman," he says softly.

Warmth hovers over my back, as if he's splayed his hand an inch above the scars on my skin—three puncture marks on either side where a demon tried to rip out my spine.

I snort instead of leaning into the temptation of his touch. "A monogamous incubus? Don't be ridiculous."

"We'd just have to have lots of sex," he purrs.

Desire pulses deep in my stomach, and my breath catches.

Kade groans. "Fuck's sake. Can I touch you yet?"

I shake my head and hug myself. The rest of me is shaking, too. I force my legs to move, and face him. He's so close, I have to tilt my head to meet his eyes. They're dark—*hungry*—and swirling crimson. My heart skips.

"Reiley," he says, gently and without strain, which, given the state of his arousal, is quite impressive, "haven't you wondered why I protected you; why I haven't tricked you into bed; why you are so different to the other women?"

I clear my throat. "A little."

It is unbelievably hard to keep my gaze from slipping south.

"Because you're"—Kade sucks a breath in and out—"*not* my friend."

I cover my mouth to hide a smirk.

"I'm not your friend?" I snigger into my palm.

Whoops.

He steps closer, and my laughter dries in the heat pulsing off him. The raw need on his face. My hand moves without any command from my brain, reaching out to touch his chest over the heavy thud of his heart. He shuts his eyes on a sigh.

"Friends don't see each other naked," he says. "And friends don't do this."

He holds my hand against his chest and cups my jaw, his fingers slipping into my hair. There's a moment of panic, then his lips are on mine and it all vanishes in the heat and smoke of his mouth. I moan and collapse into him, his skin hot and slick from the shower. I immediately start rubbing against him, my pants already damp from the mist, and clinging to me.

God, he's a fantastic kisser. It's not fair. It makes me want to get naked.

I taste blood a second before he curses and pulls away. We pant at each other, the shower a comforting hiss behind us.

It takes three tries for me to speak. "You need to heal."

He nods.

"Now do you believe I want to touch you?"

A smirk is my answer.

"Good," I say, smirking back, "because until you've healed, you're not allowed to touch me."

"God, Reiley," he says. "I want to fuck you so badly."

Anticipation shivers into my gut and wobbles my legs. Kade does his sexy, growly thing again, and I almost rip off my pants and to hell with it.

I poke a quivering finger in his chest. "Not until you're healed. Now brace your hands on the wall."

He grins and follows my command, hands splayed on slick tile, his body slightly arched, muscles sliding under the pounding water. I kneel at his feet and let the sight of him fill my eyes with what I'm about to do. He moans, and I haven't even touched him yet.

"I may not be able to stand for all of it," he says, sounding somewhat breathless.

I curl my fingers around the backs of his knees and trail my nails up his thighs. His legs spasm, but he manages to lock his joints.

"Just don't let the energy go to waste," I say.

His chest heaves, his eyes a little desperate.

"Can't make any promises."

Now his voice is strained.

I squeeze his buttocks, and slide my mouth over the head of his cock. He sighs my name. I watch the pleasure on his face, his eyelids fluttering, water dripping from his hair and onto me. I explore for a bit, licking and sucking and teasing him like he did when feeding on my thigh. The thought of his mouth between my legs has me whimpering around him, his answering whimper clenching my stomach and throbbing where I ache for him. I wrap my hand around the base of his shaft and pulse in time to the bob of my head. His balls are tight to his body and I tug gently, rolling them between my fingers.

"Shit, that feels amazing," he gasps.

He's slumped against the wall, not so much braced as sagging on it, his forehead almost pressed to the tile.

I love his responsiveness. It soothes my slight performance anxiety at the thought of how many women have been where I am and how much better they might be at this.

Though I bet none of them went where I'm planning for the finale. The poor guy may melt the wall.

I release him long enough to take a breath and say, "Brace, Kade. Your legs are shaking."

"No wonder," he says. "You're fucking glorious."

He manages to look at me, his eyes dazed and filled with a tenderness that makes me dizzy. I suck him deep, and his spine bows. Muscles quiver under silky skin. He whines low in his throat and it takes all my willpower not to hump his leg, frantic for my own release. I increase my pace, sucking, squeezing, swirling my tongue around him.

"Reiley... *Christ*... I'm close."

I hum around him and am rewarded with another sexy moan. His balls draw nearer to his body. Kade holds his breath. I taste him on my tongue in that shivering pause before climax, everything tight and aching.

Then I stick my pinky up his arse.

The shout of my name echoes off the tiles. Kade explodes in my mouth, thrusting deep. I wrestle with my gag reflex, but Kade's legs collapse and he slides down the wall, spurting the rest on my neck and chest and ending in a sprawled, panting heap. I kneel between his splayed legs and enjoy the view.

His ribs heave for a long time. His lids twitch, the bruise and welt gone from his cheek. He blinks sleepy, satisfied eyes at me. His soft smile grips my throat with a feeling close to tears. A chuckle rumbles in his chest.

"You're all messy," he says, and pulls me into his lap.

His mouth steals my breath. That and the very solid length of him pressed to my wet panties. He kisses me woozy, never mind senseless, his skin slick and hot and gliding against mine, driving me mad. I bury my hands in his hair and grind in his lap, the scrap of material between us both frustrating and exciting. I ache for him inside me, but I don't want to stop the kissing or the rubbing. I can come from this. I'm so swollen... so close... I thrust my tongue in his mouth, and something sharp pricks me.

"Your teeth," I gasp. "I didn't think it would be enough."

Kade grins, flashing his lovely fangs. His strong fingers knead my back, and my eyes flutter shut.

"First times are special," he says.

Oh holy god. I'm definitely going to faint.

His lips drink the water from my neck and my pulse leaps, as if desperate to burst the skin and spill into his mouth. A door slams. Voices swell in the corridor beyond the tiled wall. I arch closer to Kade. I need more of his hands on me, in me. Everywhere. His tongue licks up the line of my throat.

"Too special to do it here," he murmurs between kisses. "I want you in my bed where you can scream my name."

His fingers tangle in my hair, pulling my head back, stretching my neck further. I can't breathe past my pulse.

"But your house is miles away." I frown at the ceiling, struggling with his logic, not helped by the teasing caress of his mouth. "We might not get there for ages."

"You're going to think about having sex with me every day until it happens, Reiley." His lips curve on the sensitive skin beneath my jaw. "And I'm not going to let you come until then."

"But Kade… you can touch me now. You can touch me *all over.*"

He nibbles my ear, his breath scorching. His hands press me harder against him.

"I know," he whispers. "It's going to be excruciating. You're going to beg me for it. Plead. You're going to be so horny, it's all you can think about. *I'll* be all you can think about."

He's already all I can think about.

I make a sound suspiciously like a sob. "But Kade—"

"Then, when it happens, when I finally get you in my bed, naked"—he tilts his hips, the head of his cock teasing my opening through my sodden panties—"I'm gonna make you come five times. And fuck the living daylights out of you."

Okay, that was a sob. And an animal, guttural noise I've never made before.

I try to squirm closer, take him deeper. Kade scoops me in his arms and plonks me on my feet.

Oh god, yes, *finally.* He's going to shove me against the tile and quench the desire that's been building ever since he smirked at me in Cabaret Voltaire. I don't know what nonsense he's talking. Waiting? I'm ready *now.* So ready, I may orgasm as soon as he slides inside me.

Two swollen heartbeats later, I find myself blinking in the bedroom, achingly unsatisfied and dripping water on the carpet.

What the fuck just happened?

34

I dress in a daze, my libido wailing at me for putting clothes on when I should be wrapped around Kade. I finally plucked up the courage to have sex with him. *Where the hell is my orgasm?*

Though, somehow, I still didn't end up naked.

He walks out of the bathroom, unruffled, wet hair slicked to the side, while I'm still hopping around trying to get a leg in my jeans. My skin is flushed, swollen from the heat. His hooded jumper is demon-blood garnet, like his eyes get when he's horny. It hugs his shoulders and biceps, two toggles on black cords hanging on either side of a diagonal zip that ends mid-chest. Black jeans encase slim hips.

Red and black—fire and darkness. Perfect for him.

Shit. I've been staring too long.

"This is punishment, right?" I yank on stubborn denim. "You're punishing me for what I said."

"Then we're both being punished."

"So, now I'm desperate to touch you, you're like—nah, I'm all right?" I tug harder. "What the *fuck* is wrong with these jeans?"

Kade stills my hands. The denim slips easily up my thighs and over my hips. He pins me with that damn gaze, fastening the zip, his knuckles brushing me through the tough material.

Slim fingers tease the button through the slit. Kade grins, and I fear it may be at my slack-jawed expression.

"Oh, I want you to touch me. I am *definitely* going to touch you." He hooks his fingers in my belt loops and drags me against him. "I'm just not going to let you come."

My knees wobble, but I notch my chin higher. "Then I'm not going to let *you* come."

"I think I'll be good for a bit." He smirks, and traces my bottom lip with his thumb. "You're very talented."

My cheeks flame, but I lean into him. He steps away to scoop his phone off the bedside cabinet.

The goddamn manipulative twatnozzle.

He taps the screen and glances at me, a damp lock of hair falling across one eye. I remember my texts.

"I was worried about you," I say.

His phone bounces on the bed. His mouth collides with mine, his strong hands gripping my waist and lifting me up. My feet dangle about a foot off the floor and he locks his arms under my bum, pressing me to the firm promise of his body.

"No throwing yourself off me this time," he says.

A gentle glide of lips rockets my pulse. The exhilarating scrape of teeth. His tongue teases mine, and all my blood throbs between my legs. I fist a hand in his damp hair, my other arm across his shoulders, and attempt to climb into his mouth. He makes a begging noise in his throat, then I realise it's me. And it's more than one. Need builds in my gut, aching outward. My fingertips tingle.

This is ridiculous. He's not even using his incubus voodoo. It's all him—smoke and heat and sex.

A tentative knock on the door barely penetrates the rushing in my ears.

"Reiley—you coming for breakfast?" A pause. "Are you okay?"

Kade pulls away, breathing hard, his arms still pinning me against him. A flush pinks his perfect cheekbones.

"Don't worry, I haven't eaten her," he says to the person at our door.

"Then why isn't she answering?"

The voice is familiar, but I can't seem to recall any names at the minute or any words for that matter.

Kade smirks. "Say 'I'm okay', Reiley."

"I'm okay, Reiley," I say.

Kade makes a soft sound and crushes me into a hug, his heart thudding against my chest.

"Reiley?" the person persists.

"Huh?"

"*Are* you okay?"

Elsie! That's who it is!

"Yes," I say. "I mean, I am. Okay, that is. Totally okay."

The sentences are fine in my head, but Kade's hot breath on my neck jumbles them before they reach my mouth. Goosebumps prickle my shoulders and the base of my skull.

"So I'll see you downstairs?"

"Yup," I say. "Downstairs. In a minute."

Elsie ghosts away as silently as she arrived, though she could stomp down the corridor and I wouldn't hear her over my heartbeat.

Kade sets me on my feet. His hair sticks up where I tangled my fingers through it. His eyes are black opal, beautiful and rare, specks of red, violet and gold flashing in their depths.

Honestly, him and his mood eyeballs. They make me dizzy.

He holds out a hand. "We should prove you're okay before

they come at me with their pointy things."

"You know, they have a spear that works like the knives. I've seen it." I lick my lips. God, I can taste him. "They also have a fancy name for them. D-something. From a Welsh legend."

Am I babbling? Feels like I'm babbling. Why am I so nervous about taking his hand?

Kade waits patiently. I swallow a sigh and reach for him. His fingers slide between mine, and my heart skips.

Ah. That's why. I always knew touching him was dangerous.

We walk to the kitchen hand in hand, my demon and me. I sneak glances at him from beneath my lashes.

He looks like his usual confident self but is *he* nervous? Uncomfortable? Marianne and Bryce tortured him yesterday. Iona punched him in the face. They all wanted to kill him. Most of them still do.

Chattering voices reach us first. Kade keeps a hold of my hand, but lets me go ahead through the doorway. All conversations stop. A fork rings on crockery. Spring sunshine sparkles on the loch and slices gold through the mullioned windows. Angry muttering precedes a rush for the door, the kitchen emptying to leave Marianne, Annabel and Elsie at the main table and a couple of women washing up at the sink.

"Would you glamour your eyes?" snaps one. "They're feckin' creepy."

A tiny flinch passes from Kade's hand to mine. If I weren't touching him, I wouldn't have felt it.

"He doesn't have to," I say, my voice hot. "You know what he is. And his eyes aren't creepy, they just take a little getting used to."

The woman turns her back and buries her arms elbow-deep in the suds at the sink. Her companion frowns at the plate and dishtowel in her hands, but says nothing.

"I don't want to get used to it," the woman mutters, scrubbing furiously. "The only good demon is a dead demon."

I tug Kade to the table and we sit with our backs against the wall, me beside Elsie, opposite Marianne and Annabel. He releases my hand and places his palm on my thigh.

"You've healed, I see," Marianne says, sipping something that smells like ginseng and flicking a pointed glance my way.

My cheeks heat. Brilliant. Now she knows we've done something sexual. Though I imagine a few people heard Kade shout my name this morning.

"He can heal other people, too," I mumble.

Marianne shifts her shrewd gaze to Kade. "Is that so?"

"You wouldn't like the methods, old woman."

Elsie shifts in the seat next to me. Annabel fiddles with her mug of coffee. The two women at the sink clatter dishes into cupboards.

Marianne appraises Kade as if he's a new tool she's suddenly acquired. "How strong is this healing ability?"

"Goodness, Marianne," Annabel gasps, "you can't be thinking…"

"I'm just considering the practicalities."

My mouth drops open. "He's not a sexy sticking plaster you keep in the first aid kit—"

Kade coughs into his fist. "No, apparently, I'm a butterfly."

"—that you just peel out and rape when someone gets hurt."

Marianne sips her tea. "He's an incubus. He feeds on sex."

"I choose who I have sex with, thank you," Kade sniffs.

"But do they ever really choose *you*, incubus?" Marianne says with another smug sip of tea.

Kade's hand clenches on my leg, though his face stays a

picture of arrogant perfection. I butter toast and scoop eggs onto two plates in the tense silence. The two women finish washing up and stomp out of the kitchen.

Marianne sets her cup on the table and crosses her arms. "You invaded everyone's dreams last night. I don't believe that counts as benign, demon."

"Did you dream of me, old woman?"

Marianne narrows her eyes. "My dreams are my own. Yet it seems you reneged on our agreement. Shall I stab you here, at the table, or would you prefer outside and on your knees?"

Kade's smile is calm. "I can't control what people dream."

"And I am to take your word?"

He shrugs.

"He doesn't control dreams." I swallow a mouthful of eggs that struggles to get past the pulse in my throat. "It's just a byproduct of his power."

Marianne cocks her eyebrow while I take a gulp of coffee to wash down the food. Elsie stares at her hands, unusually quiet.

What did she dream?

"Even so," Marianne says. "You are not wanted here, incubus. We have graciously spared your life. You can extend us the courtesy of staying elsewhere since you make my girls uncomfortable. There are several hotels in Dunfermline."

"No!"

Was that a bit loud?

"No," I say, quieter. "Myron and Thaddeus could find him if he checks into a hotel."

Marianne doesn't blink at my outburst, her eyes on Kade.

"Then perhaps you can stay in the cabin by the practise arena. It's on the property, but out of the way. There's a camping bed and a stove." Marianne's gaze flicks to me. "It would give Reiley some space and, maybe, some perspective."

"I'm fine, Marianne."

She clucks her tongue. "Very well. One demon problem at a time. Annabel tells me you have Isabella's—pardon me, *your*—cottage covered by CCTV."

I nod, and dab my mouth with a napkin. Kade forks his eggs one-handed, his fingers stroking the in-seam of my jeans. It tickles through the thick material and sends tingles higher.

"Reiley?" Marianne says.

Crap.

"Uh, sorry. Yes. You can watch them all on a tablet. I left it in our room."

Christ, it's 'our' room already.

"I'll get it," Kade says.

"Are you sure—"

"I'll yell if anyone attacks me with a pointy thing." He slides me a soft smile and glides out of the kitchen.

It's ridiculous that I worry about him. He's harder to kill than I am.

I eat my eggs and toast, my ear cocked for a muffled shout or the thump of a struggle.

"Are you sure you're okay, Reiley?" Elsie says.

She swings her legs, her head bent, violet hair falling over her face.

"He doesn't hurt me." I raise my gaze to include Marianne and Annabel. "In fact, he does his best to protect me."

"We can protect you now, better than he can," Marianne says.

"That's why we came to you. We weren't doing so well on our own. And I wanted to find… people like me."

Annabel offers a smile. "You're family now."

"Yeah!" Elsie bounces in her chair. "You can be my big sister."

I stop myself from ruffling her hair. She's not that young.

"There does seem to be a lot of 'sisters' here. Where are all the guys? Bryce is the only one I've seen."

Marianne washes her cup at the sink and sets it on the drainer. "It seems women are predisposed to receiving the Sight. We have men in our ranks, though fewer in number. Our Highland compound has five."

Marianne leans her hip on the counter. Annabel and Elsie stiffen at the footsteps out in the corridor, preceding Kade with the tablet. Marianne holds out her hand.

"Do you need me to show you how to use it?" he says.

She raises a brow. "I may be old, demon, but I'm familiar with technology."

She swipes the screen, tapping through the footage, a slight frown wrinkling her forehead. Kade reclaims his seat and slings his arm across the back of my chair.

"No sign of the demons yet," Marianne says. "I'll deploy a team and have someone monitor the tablet so they can move as soon as the creatures show their faces."

"I want to help," I say, and Kade pinches my arm. "I mean, *we* want to help."

Marianne has the grace not to laugh, though her hazel eyes sparkle.

"Perhaps on the next hunt, after you've been trained." Her gaze flicks to Kade. "You are untrained and cannot hold a blade. Can you even kill your own?"

"I could pin one down, or knock them out, for someone to stab."

Marianne gives him a tight smile. "I think we'll manage just fine without your services."

"We could both benefit from learning how to fight," I say before he can snarl at her.

"He will have to find another way to occupy his time, preferably out of our sight." Marianne shoves away from the counter. "Finish your breakfast and head to the practise arena, Reiley. Your training starts today."

Elsie claps her hands. "Yay! Can I train with her, Marianne? Please?"

"Annabel can teach you both. I trust her to work you hard." Marianne smiles and leaves the kitchen, the tablet tucked under her arm.

Kade huffs. "What am I supposed to do?"

Annabel tidies the breakfast platters away. She glances at Kade, sighs, and stares him full in the face.

"There are DVDs and books in the communal area, though you may want to take them to your room. And try not to antagonise Marianne."

Annabel and Elsie hustle away, bidding me to hurry up and join them.

"Are you sure you're going to be okay by yourself? There are a lot of unhappy people with knives walking about here."

"Go. Have fun with your new friends." His mouth quirks in a slow, sexy smile. "Just remember I'll be waiting for you in our teeny, tiny bed."

Then he leans over and kisses me silly.

35

I stumble into our room at 11pm and sag on the closed door with a sigh. All I can see are Kade's bare feet and the hem of his jeans, but I'm too tired to move further.

I haven't spoken to him since breakfast, grabbing food in between training sessions with Annabel and Elsie. The hours disappeared, laughing and joking and sweating with them. When Annabel finally called a halt, the nerves returned at the thought of being alone in the room with Kade. Alone with one teeny, tiny bed.

I doubt he'll let me sleep in the chair tonight.

He swings his legs off the mattress and pads towards me, still in his shoulder- and bicep-hugging garnet jumper.

"Hello, Reiley." He places a light kiss on my lips. "I missed you."

The little ache I had under my ribs all day says I missed him, too. But I'm not going to tell him that.

I dodge around him and kick off my shoes, unstrapping my blade and laying it on the beside cabinet.

"Annabel made us throw knives at targets for *hours*," I say. "I can barely lift my arms."

"I can fix that."

Magical fingers knead my shoulders. My head falls back

on a moan. My knees hit the bed, and I crawl on top. Deft hands unzip my hoodie and pull my t-shirt off before I can blink. I flop on my front. Kade straddles me, brushing my hair to the side, and works his fingers into my weeping muscles. His warmth seeps into my body. He massages me to the consistency of a cooked noodle.

"How does that feel?" he purrs.

I groan, loud and long, into the pillow. Strong hands sweep from my lumbar muscles to my shoulders, and I arch my spine.

Wait. When did he unfasten my bra?

The sneaky little fucker.

He repeats the movement, his thumbs brushing the curve of my arse under the waistband of my jeans. His fingers trail up my ribs and graze the sides of my breasts. My heart bounces from my chest to my stomach. Heat flares at the press of his hands and an ache starts between my legs.

"I'm terrible at knife throwing," I blurt to distract him or me or both.

"It was only your first day. Give it a chance."

His wicked fingers knead my neck to the base of my skull, and my eyes roll. I float on the bed, my tongue as loose as the rest of me.

"It was your fault," I murmur. "You were in my head."

He chuckles and lies on his side next to me. "I was thinking about you, too. Thinking about this."

The light clicks off. He gathers me into his solid chest and I make a small, protesting noise in my throat, my bra slipping off my arms.

"It doesn't count as naked if I can't see," he whispers in the dark.

Scorching hands splay on my stomach, but no higher. I can't

stop a little wriggle, my breasts bare to the world.

He's touching me. Kade McKade is touching me.

His lips nuzzle my neck right over the throb of my pulse. A delicate fang scrapes my skin, and my breath catches.

His mouth curves. "Your heart is hammering, Reiley. Why is that?"

Hot air goosepimples my throat and sends a sizzle to my belly. My heart beats harder, ping-ponging between my ribs and no doubt playing a tattoo on Kade's chest. His teeth close, ever so gently, on my jugular. My body dissolves in his arms and spills my secrets to the soft night.

"I want you to bite me," I say and it's almost a sob. "I can't stop thinking about it."

He stills against my back, his fangs firm in my skin, but not hard enough to break it. My pulse leaps between his teeth and swells between my legs. The danger of his fangs, the glorious, sharp pain, the sucking, my blood spilling into his mouth to warm his belly, the taste of me on his tongue. God, it does it for me. It fucking does it.

Kade buries his face in my shoulder, breathing heavy. His arms tighten, wrapping around my midriff and brushing the underside of my boobs. A tiny shiver transfers between us.

"Are you okay?" I say softly.

His head shifts, but it's impossible to tell if it's a yay or nay. Have I pushed him too far?

"Everyone else—" He clears his throat. "They want the human or they don't want me at all."

I swallow a laugh at the absurdity.

"That can't be true."

I stroke his arms. Fine hairs tickle my fingertips, my senses enhanced by the blackness. He snuggles closer, nearly crushing my ribs.

"I showed myself to a human, once. I thought…" Definitely a head shake this time. "She was horrified. Called me evil. Refused to see me. I tried to explain. She… took her own life."

"Oh, Kade, I'm sorry."

He shrugs. "I was young and naive. Sick of hiding. I just wanted to be myself."

"Not to speak ill of the dead, but she was an idiot."

He chuckles into my neck, and I shudder.

"Are you horrified by what I am, Reiley?"

"Do I feel horrified?"

He kisses my throat, and my slowing pulse bounds into my mouth.

"I felt that," he whispers, something like awe in his voice. "You really mean it."

"Of course I mean it. It's been driving me mad. Both times you bit me, I was so goddamn close, then you stopped."

"And that was without any incubus voodoo."

"Shit," I sigh.

"I'll make biting orgasm number three."

My gut clenches. "What's one and two?"

"Mouth and hand stuff," he says, and he's definitely smirking.

I shiver in his hold.

"Well, I'm not busy right now." I aim for nonchalant and hit wobbly voiced nympho.

He rolls onto his back, cradling me, my arse tucked into his crotch. His arms loosen, his hands returning to splay on my stomach.

"It's not going to be that easy," he purrs in my ear.

"But don't you want to?"

He rolls his hips and even through two pairs of jeans, I feel him, hard and straining.

"Reiley, I want to fuck you until you can't think straight."

"I can't think straight right now," I whine. "Why wait?"

"Maybe I *am* punishing you a little." He slowly slides his hands up my ribs. "There I was, on my best behaviour, and you accused me of only trying to get in your pants."

His fingers brush the curve of my breasts, but go no further. I grind my teeth. His hands glide down to my waistband and pop the button on my jeans. All my blood pulses south. The sound of the zipper seems loud in the intimacy of our darkened room.

"While I do very much want to get in your pants—I fucking dream about it—I want something else first."

"What?" I sob.

His fingers spread my jeans and circle my hipbones.

"Trust."

"I trust you."

Did I say that too fast?

I happily wriggle out of my jeans to prove it, leaving me in only my pants. Vulnerable, open, and aching for him.

"Do you want me?" he says.

"Obviously."

His hand cups between my legs, the shock of it in the blackness bucking my hips. The touch disappears, and I make a frustrated noise.

"So wet, Reiley," he says, though his voice is thick.

"Kade, you're being a pain in the arse again."

"I know," he says.

I tilt my head, straining to see him behind me. His eyes are blacker than the room. I fist my hand in his hair. His breath brushes my cheek. I drag his mouth to mine and the contact sizzles to my toes. His lips are temptation, inflaming the ache rather than quenching it. Their softness teases me in the dark. And his tongue… *Fuck.* I'm breathless, arched and quivering on top of him. His hands stroke me—thighs, belly, ribs. I try to turn, and he pins me. I growl into his mouth, still kissing him.

"I'm keeping my clothes on tonight," he laughs. "I don't trust either of us."

He kisses me, exploring with his hands, until we're both trembling.

I've been horny before. Unsatisfied and between lovers. But I've never felt this *need.*

"Okay, I have to stop," Kade groans, his heart thundering between my shoulder blades. "I can't take any more."

He curls onto his side and spoons me against him, cradled in his body. Safe and warm. And throbbing. We pant quietly in the darkness. I track his heartbeat as it slows, matching mine.

I should get some sleep. Exhaustion stings my eyes. It's after midnight and Marianne wants to start fitness training at 8am. I suspect she's keeping me busy and tiring me out in the hope I'll spend less time with Kade.

Or I'm being ungracious and this is how training is for everyone.

Kade cuddles closer, tangling his hands in mine and tucking them both to my chest. He takes a deep breath and it tickles through my hair.

"Kade?"

"Hmm?"

"What did you do today?"

He nuzzles the top of my head. "Read a book. Watched a movie. Surfed on my phone. I have a Twitter account under another name. They're a big fan of yours."

I sigh. "You're @DemonLover69 aren't you?"

"Too obvious?"

"How many accounts do you have?"

"A few."

"And are they all my fans?"

He stretches, wiggling his hips, then slots his knees back into mine.

"Maybe."

"Just how long were you following me before we met, Kade?"

"Go to sleep, Reiley," he chuckles.

And, dammit, I do.

36

"Good dream?" Kade purrs in my ear.

I blink at the lightening sky through the open curtains, still cuddled in Kade's arms, the taste of his name in my mouth.

How loud did I shout?

"Oh, shut up, you smug arsehole," I say.

I wriggle until we're nose to nose in the narrow bed, the sheet covering us both. Kade gives me sleepy, half-lidded eyes and a slow smile, his hair tousled.

"Good morning to you, too."

"What time is it?"

He untangles his arm from the covers and peers at his watch. "Half six."

"Thirty more minutes," I mumble, burrowing closer to him.

He tucks my head under his chin, our legs tangled together, his jeans rough against my skin. Firm fingers draw swirly patterns on my bare back. I play with the toggle on his jumper, my other arm thrown over his side, my hand snuggled in the warmth under his hood.

I want to stay like this forever.

He shivers at my happy sigh, and I place a light kiss on his throat.

"I like your neck the most," I say.

He laughs. "My neck?"

"It's soft. And warm. And it smells nice."

I kiss him on each sentence and am rewarded with another shiver. I nuzzle my face into the scent and heat of Kade. His pulse flutters on my cheek.

Time for some tit for tat.

I roll him onto his back and pin his hands to the bed, my mouth on his throat. His pulse beats harder.

"God, I wish I could tie you up right now," I say between kisses. "Tease that tight little arse until you're swollen and close and beg me to let you come."

"Fuck, Reiley," he groans.

I grin and shove myself up. The sheet pools at my waist, cooler air caressing my bare upper body. I freeze, suddenly exposed, both of us painted in the orange and pink of sunrise.

Okay, so I didn't mean to give him *actual* tit.

I force myself not to cross my arms. Kade stares at my boobs like they're double Ds and not a paltry A. Midge bites, one of his floozies called them. Not that I care. At least they're natural.

"Shy, Reiley?" Kade says.

Crap, I'm hunching, my arms hugging my stomach.

He reaches for me, and I sit up straight.

"Hands on the bed. No touching."

He growls, but does what I say, delight sparking in his eyes. It changes to hunger when I arch my spine and run my palms up my ribs to cup my breasts.

"When did you last touch tits that weren't man-made?"

His gaze fixes on my hands. "It's been a while."

"Shame, since you're not touching these either."

I circle my hips, and the throb between my legs is a mixture of me and Kade, so solid through his jeans.

"Don't move."

I shimmy backwards, my arse in the air, and tease his jumper to the level of his ribs, baring his smooth stomach. Muscles slide as he breathes.

Christ, I've wanted to do this for ages.

My mouth explores each swell of silky muscle while Kade struggles not to move, his fingers clenching and unclenching on the covers. I lap at his bellybutton and he writhes, a sound suspiciously like a giggle catching in his throat.

"Lie still," I say.

He bites his lip, but stops wriggling.

I grin at him. "I love that you do what I say."

"It's hard not to when it always leads somewhere good."

"Well, this time you're going to lie there while I undress you and find all your tickly spots. Using just my mouth."

His throat bobs. "I'm not ticklish."

"Really?"

I stick my tongue in his bellybutton, and his shoulders jerk off the bed.

"Fuck," he sighs. "I knew this would be excruciating."

I smirk. "Kade, I'm just getting started."

* * *

I end up twenty minutes late to fitness training, though it's worth the scolding from Iona, who seems less forgiving than the other Diviners at my fascination with Kade. I left him half-dazed from my ministrations, dodging his hands as he tried to cuddle me back into bed. Remembering his reactions powers me through the first lap of the assault course.

The day is bright and warm, a light wind bringing the scent of water from Loch Fitty. Five other women, including Elsie, scramble up and over and through the many obstacles while Iona yells at us to go faster with threats of withholding lunch.

Peeling Kade out of his clothes was a test of my self-control, his flawless body spread before me. I finally got to explore the perfect dip of his spine, the swell of his shoulders. Turns out he's also ticklish on his neck, the bend of his elbows, and the arch of his feet.

So cute.

I tormented him by nibbling on his erection through his boxer shorts. Not ticklish, but definitely something going on there. He moaned my name, and I told him he was a bad, *bad* little demon.

My little demon.

The bottom of the rope ladder hooks my foot and I sprawl on my face, huffing into the dust. Iona barks like a proper drill sergeant. Elsie bounces past, barely out of breath.

"Come on, Reiley!" she chirps. "Only two more laps to go."

I groan into the dirt and heave myself upright, stumbling after the purple flash of her hair. Sweat soaks my t-shirt and borrowed shorts. I finish last. Iona, lady of no mercy, forces us to do burpies and sprints until I almost vomit, even though there's nothing left in my stomach. Elsie plops next to where I'm panting on the grass and staring at the unstreaked blue of the sky.

"Don't worry," she says. "It gets easier after a few weeks."

"A few *weeks?*"

"Yeah! I've done this training already, so I'm only doing it for fun."

I turn my head. She sits cross-legged on the grass, her hair perfect, her skin glowing with youth and vitality. My hair is tumbling out of its ponytail in damp strands and there's a very unsexy V of moisture darkening my t-shirt. I could wring out the cloth under my armpits.

"Elsie, you make me feel like I'm a hundred," I sigh.

"Don't be silly! You've only just started your training. By the end of it, you'll be running rings around the lot of us."

"I'm not a huge fan of running."

"Then you're not going to enjoy this afternoon," she laughs.

She coaxes me to my feet and we walk towards the house. A lone figure sits on the bank of Loch Fitty, contemplating the water.

"I'll catch you inside," I say to Elsie.

Her sparkle dims when she follows the direction of my gaze.

"Oh. Okay. We only have half-an-hour for lunch, then it's the wards tutorial."

"I'll be there."

Her subdued bounce spirits her into the kitchen from the rear porch. Kade tenses at my approaching footsteps, but the wariness dissolves into amusement at the state of me.

"I'm all sweaty," I say.

"I see that."

I flop onto my side and put my head in his lap. Gentle fingers smooth my wayward hair behind my ear.

I snuggle against his thigh. "What are you doing out here?"

"I got bored in the room. The old woman took my phone."

"Why?"

"Because, apparently, I must have every demon in existence on speed dial. She thinks I'm going to tell someone where we are. I only offered to order food. They all acted as if I'd spit in it."

I roll my head in his lap to look up at him. "This isn't exactly fun for you, is it?"

"The parts with you are." He quirks his mouth, though there's sadness in those expressive black eyes. "Getting treated like walking herpes, not so much. But at least it's peaceful here."

He raises his head to gaze over the loch, and I get a different view including the underside of his jaw and up his nostrils, which are just as cute as the rest of him. Dark lashes fan above sharp cheekbones.

"Is the city boy finally communing with nature?"

He slides me a grin. "I went for a walk in the woods. Didn't fall once. I like it when it's grass and ferns, not mud and spiny things."

"You're lucky you didn't trip a ward."

"Would just give them something else to hate me for. What happened to you?"

He swipes a finger down the damp centre of my t-shirt, the gesture innocent enough since I possess zero cleavage.

"As well as failing at knives, I'm unfit. Comes with being an author—it's a sedentary lifestyle."

"I could help you get fitter."

I narrow my eyes at him. "How?"

"Not like that," he chuckles, "though sex is great cardio. We could go for a run in the mornings."

"Running is not my favourite. I'd rather do what we did this morning."

His thumb brushes my cheek, his smile soft. "We can do that after."

"Fine," I huff, "but only if you run in front so I can look at your arse for motivation."

He smirks. "Deal."

We lapse into comfortable silence, watching the sunlight dance on the water. Kade pets my hair.

I should get up, grab a sandwich, find the classroom, but it's a lovely day and Kade playing his fingers through my ponytail is enough to turn my body semi-noodle. Such skilled hands.

Nope. Mustn't think about his hands.

"We can get you fit the other way, too," he says, and I startle, dozing in his lap.

"What way?"

"The way where I get you all to myself in my big bed. Every day."

"Every day?" I gulp.

"Multiple times," he says with a wicked grin. "I'll get you toned faster than—"

He sneezes and shakes his head, a wrinkle of confusion on his face.

"What the"—*sneeze*—"fuck"—*sneeze*—"is that?"

He scrambles out from under me, still sneezing.

"Goodness, it works." Annabel walks along the bank with another charm clenched in her fist. "I was beginning to doubt their efficacy, but I've never had a test subject before."

"I'm not your test subject," Kade growls. "Fuck's sake, my brain is itching."

He retreats a few steps, clutching his temples. Annabel shakes the pouch at him, and he skips back further.

"Annabel..." I say, a little growly myself.

"Sorry, Reiley, but I wanted to talk to you anyway." She perches on the bank vacated by Kade.

I climb to my feet, brushing grass from my shorts. Kade alternates between watching me approach and glaring at

Annabel. I cup his face.

"We have a cross-country run later, so I'm definitely going to need a massage"—I go on tip-toes to whisper—"all over," an inch from his mouth.

He bends his head and kisses me, his fingers curling around my hips. It's short and chaste by our standards, but it still spurts excitement to my belly.

"I look forward to it," he purrs.

He aims for the front of the house, avoiding the kitchen where several disapproving faces stare at us through the windows. I plonk down next to Annabel.

"That was mean. If you took a minute to get to know him, you'd discover that as well as being a demon, he's caring and funny and interesting."

Annabel holds out the charm, but I wave it away.

"I'm not wearing that."

"Can I ask you a personal question?" She fiddles with the cord of the leather pouch.

"I suppose."

"How can you have sex with him?"

I cock a brow at her. "You're kidding right?"

A blush pinks her high cheekbones. She ducks her head and rattles the contents of the charm, her ponytail slithering over her shoulder.

"I'll admit he looks wonderful, but he's a creature of lusts, Reiley. And that lust will always make him chase the next hot, young thing. I don't want you to get hurt."

"Did you just call me a hot, young thing?"

She covers her mouth with her hand. "Goodness, I did."

"It's nice that you worry about me, Annabel, but I…" I glance over my shoulder to confirm we're alone. "We haven't actually had sex. We're waiting. Until the demons are gone. And we can properly be alone."

I dig the toe of my shoe into the sandy soil surrounding the loch.

Annabel clears her throat. "But Elsie said she heard…"

"Well, I'm not saying we haven't done *stuff,* but that's me to him."

"Reiley, that's what I'm talking about. He only wants to satisfy his own selfish desires—"

"It was my choice. He's never forced me into anything, except maybe the first time, but that was an exceptional circumstance and actually turned into an amazing experience."

Annabel's turn to raise a perfect, blonde brow.

Okay, I'm not telling her I pegged Kade.

"Never mind," I say. "My point is, he's been on his best behaviour."

"Yes, but how long will that last? Until you're marked as a conquest and he dumps you for the next?"

I stand up, brushing more grass from my bum.

"Let me worry about that," I say.

She shakes her head, but leaves it alone, absently swinging the charm as we walk to the house.

I'm not worried about it. If Kade were only here for the sex, we would've done it already, probably in the shower right after I gave him what I hope was the best blowjob of his life.

Unless he's playing the long game, waiting for the Diviners to take care of his demon problem while he turns me into a puddle of lust. Craving him. Craving more. Becoming one of his women just like I was afraid of. Fighting for his attention.

Shit.

Maybe I *am* a little worried.

37

I've talked myself down by the time evening comes around. Kade has had multiple opportunities to press his advantage. If it were just sex, he wouldn't wait for it to be 'special' or care about us being alone. He'd shag me as many times as he could because he's an incubus and needs to feed. *Then* he would dump me when the demon problem was resolved and he got bored.

Which leads me to worrying about whether he's getting enough to eat. If he's not having sex or drinking blood, does he need more solid food? That's probably why I never saw him eat before. He had floozies, and energy, aplenty.

It's the first thing I ask him when I shut the door of our room.

He laughs. "Yes, Reiley, I'm eating. I scavenge, then leave before someone accuses me of stealing food from the mouths of starving Diviners."

I take out my phone and tap the screen.

"What are you doing?" he says.

"We're having a proper midnight snack."

He grins and pulls me into the circle of his arms. "I thought that was you."

He proceeds to kiss me boneless for the thirty minutes it

takes my phone to chirp. I stumble down to the front door, pay the bemused delivery driver, and sneak back to the room. Kade and I gorge ourselves on pizza. We feed each other ice cream and chocolate brownies until even he has a round little tummy. He stretches out on the floor beside me and we lie hand in hand, staring at the ceiling, too full to move.

"This is definitely not helping my fitness regimen," I say in the quiet of the room, the house hushed around us.

"You're going to hate me on our run tomorrow, then."

I slide him a look. "We're still doing that?"

"Of course. We're going to get hot and sweaty."

"Then shower together?"

"Aren't you cocky?" He rolls, and nuzzles my throat. "Do you think you can handle that, Reiley? Me, naked and wet. You, *totally* naked. No little panties to hide behind."

I swallow hard. "Maybe not."

"Still nervous?"

His lips curve against my neck. A fang grazes my skin. My breath catches, and heat sizzles to my belly. He trails his nose to the sensitive spot under my jaw.

"You fucked me, not the other way around," he murmurs. "Maybe I'm the one who's bewitched."

He braces a hand on the other side of me, trapping me in the arch of his body, and describes how he's going to return the favour. What he's going to do to me. How I'm finally going to scream his name.

Yes, he has noticed my restraint in that particular area.

My awareness narrows to the warmth of his breath, the brush of his mouth on my throat, his soft, husky voice. Goosebumps flare and prickle across my shoulders and down my arms. He barely touches me, just his face in my neck, but need tightens my stomach and throbs deeper. Lower. Kade raises his head, and my heart skips at the hunger in his black and bottomless eyes. The glimpse of fangs. The threat of pain. And pleasure. The risk of drowning in it until there's nothing but him.

How can I trust an incubus to spare my heart?

Damn Annabel, getting into my head.

"What are you thinking?" Kade says.

"You first."

He smirks at the wobble in my voice. His lips graze my cheekbone, the barest caress, but I wrestle with my eyelids not to flutter like some swooning damsel.

I remember the woman at Cabaret Voltaire. He kissed her palm and she melted into the couch, adoration stark on her face.

"No one else looks at me like you do," Kade says. "That's what I was thinking."

I snort. "A million women have looked at you that way and will continue to do so for as long as you strut about this Earth."

I wait for him to be mock-offended about the million women. Or the strutting. He gives me serious eyes.

"None of them have seen my real face, Reiley."

He kisses my other cheekbone and trails his lips to my temple. My eyelids win the flutter battle. He still doesn't touch me with anything but his gentle, wicked mouth. The toggles of his hoodie stroke my collarbones and the dip between. Tingles swoop south, hollowing out my stomach and filling it with heat.

"What were you thinking?" he murmurs.

His breath tickles my ear. His mouth explores delicate cartilage and sucks softly on the lobe. I'm glad I'm lying down.

My blood pulses, swelling my heart and jolting it against its cage of ribs, each beat full and heavy.

"Sex with you might be bad for my health," I say.

Kade stills.

Arse. I shouldn't have been truthful. Here he is, on his best behaviour—if getting me hornier than I've ever been in my life counts as behaving—and I don't trust him. The thought of having sex sends butterflies flitting in my stomach. I'm disappointed we haven't done it yet, and relieved. I ache for him. I fear him. I want him, but the intensity scares me. The conflicting emotions jumble together until I'm nothing but confusion and lust.

It's easy to convince myself when I'm alone. Convince myself he's just a guy. That sex with him is a physical act, not life threatening, no matter how spectacular. That I can be enough for him.

How can I be enough for him?

Fucking him, not the other way around, was supposed to protect me, but I've been bespelled ever since.

Kade sits up slowly, an arm braced on either side of me. A flop of hair obscures one eye.

"I'm not going to hurt you, Reiley," he says.

I should respond with something pithy, move the conversation on. No need to bare my soul.

"But what if you get bored?" I say to the corner of his mouth, unable to meet his gaze.

He cups my face. "I'm not going to get bored."

I'm sure he says that to all the women. The many model-perfect, big-titted, long-legged women.

He scoops me off the floor and holds me against his chest as if I weigh no more than a kitten. His legs bunch and he lifts me in his arms, crawling onto the bed and laying us down, me on top. The light clicks off. The steady thud beneath my ear soothes the tension in my shoulders.

"Maybe you'll hurt me," he says in the quiet of our room.

He cuddles me tighter and I bury my face in his neck, inhaling the scent of him. Deft fingers stroke my back. My muscles relax.

"I doubt I can," I say, though that's not entirely true. I hurt his feelings accusing him of only trying to get in my pants. He got snippy about being referred to as a friend. For all his arrogance and worldly wisdom, my little demon has a disarming vulnerability.

Warm fingers wrap around mine and place my palm on his chest.

"I may be a demon, but I still have a heart."

"And can a demon's heart be broken?"

Crap, why did I ask that? It's easy to whisper secrets and truths in the dark. Too many are dangerous.

"Mine can," he says.

A ridiculous ache flares between my ribs. To distract myself, I slip my hand under his hoodie and slide up silky heat to splay my fingers on firm muscle.

"Then I guess we'll have to be careful," I say.

Sure, because I'm the breaker of hearts in this scenario. Kade is the one with mystical sex powers and a body that's more addictive than crack. I'm a simple author and junior Diviner—how am I supposed to compete?

I sit upright and tease his jumper higher. His pale skin glows, the rest of him an indistinct shape except for his night-black eyes. He levers his torso off the bed and I peel his hoodie free, tossing it on the floor. My fingers explore the swell of his chest, the dip of his sternum, the perfect bunch of his abs to the waistband of his jeans. I pop the button. The rasp of the zip is such an intimate sound in the darkness. Kade's breathing speeds. I tuck myself back into his side, my head on his collarbone, and pet him—pecs, stomach, throat. I circle his hipbones and trace the waistband of his boxers with a fingertip. His fragile little heart trips along beneath my ear, jumping when I stroke the taut skin above his boxers and dip my fingers into his jeans to brush the top of his thigh. Two more lazy circuits, and he starts to wriggle.

"Reiley…" He swallows, loud in the hush. "At least kiss me if you're going to do that."

"No kissing. And my clothes stay on."

"So you're punishing *me* now?"

"Someone has to," I say.

He chuckles. "I can take it."

"Can you?" I whisper in his ear, and he shivers.

I'm not going to be one of his women. I won't be forgettable or disposable. He's going to crave me just as much as I crave him.

I count his ribs. Tease the tight bud of each nipple. Trace his half-parted lips. Tickle his bellybutton. His skin heats, scorching beneath my hand. A pulse deep in his belly throbs under my palm. Again, I dip into his jeans, following the sexy line of muscle that ends where I'm hoping he's solid and aching for me. I wrap my fingers around him and squeeze just to be sure. His air rushes out, his hips bucking off the bed.

"So hard, Kade," I say, and return to petting his soft and quivering stomach.

"Fuck," he growls. "I lied. I can't take it."

He captures my wandering hand, kissing my knuckles, and traps it against his chest. We lie in silence. His heart slows. His skin cools from scorching to hot. My own pulse, which was a bit excited, settles.

I love playing with him. Being in control. His reactions are just as glorious as when I pegged him.

God, I want to peg him again.

I snuggle closer, wide awake despite my energetic day. I listen to his breaths, his chest rising and falling beneath our linked hands. The heat and scent of him is like lying in long, summer grass, bees droning overhead, the rattle of grasshoppers between the stalks. Heady and full of promise.

Did Kade have idyllic summer days growing up—sunbathing, parties with friends, garden barbecues? I didn't, but some of the houses I lived in with my parents were rural. I could sneak away to lie in a meadow and daydream, no risk of bumping into anyone, human or demon.

"Kade?"

"Yeah?"

"Where were you born?"

He shifts on the mattress. "I don't remember, Reiley."

"I mean, what country?"

"Oh. Here—Scotland."

"Do you remember anything about your clan, except for the mountains and trees?" My next words rush out when he doesn't answer. "I'm asking for me, not the Diviners, but you don't have to talk if you don't want to."

He shrugs one shoulder. "I still don't remember much—being cold, in pain. Lonely. Young demons are like human children—dependent on those around them, reliant on solid food, susceptible to temperature extremes. But I was an outcast."

"Did you have to feed on sexual energy the whole time?" I say, trying not to shudder.

How would that work for a child—did they touch him? Did he have to watch others?

"Not until puberty." He squeezes my hand. "Then I did just fine on my own until I was legal."

"So how did your clan know you were an incubus if you were nine when you ran away?"

"I lacked the usual characteristics of a proper demon male. The fangs and the solid-coloured eyes marked me from the minute I was born."

"You had fangs when you were born?" I shiver. "You must have been a bitch to breast feed."

His laugh rolls from the darkness. "I don't think I was given the chance, Reiley."

The ache in my chest returns at the thought of an abused and abandoned Kade shivering in a corner, tousled blond hair, sad black eyes and dirt-streaked skin.

"You're lucky you survived," I say softly.

"Oh, they didn't want to kill me." His voice turns bitter. "An incubus has some uses after he hits puberty."

My breath freezes. "You mean…"

"Sexual healing. That's why I ran away. I was nine—I didn't know my sexuality, but I didn't want to spend my life being pimped out to injured males."

"The other demons can't heal themselves? I thought death energy was powerful."

"Healing is a rare skill. Rarer than an incubus. I've never heard of it in a male, only in females."

"What are female demons like?"

"Closeted. Raised for breeding. Some of them are like males, but the more human-looking ones are prized."

"How very double standard."

He snorts. "Tell me about it."

"So if you'd stayed in the clan…" I stroke his fingers in the dark and circle his palm. "I mean, how would that work? You can't heal if you don't… If you're not… excited."

His fingers flex in mine. "There's some energy in other acts, but direct sex is the most powerful. And an incubus that can't perform is worthless."

"So your choices would have been what—sex or death?"

"Pretty much, or so I've heard."

"Christ, Kade, that's awful."

"That's demons," he says.

I shove up on one elbow. He tilts his head to watch me, pale in the dark. I cup his cheek, and place a kiss on his lips.

His mouth curves. "I thought kissing wasn't allowed tonight."

"I'm making an exception."

He purrs low in his throat and kisses me back, gentle but insistent. My tongue meets his with an electric sizzle. Strong fingers grip my waist and pull me on top. He grinds me against his erection.

"I have more sad stories if that's all it takes," he says, the smirk clear in his voice.

I shake my head, my hair cascading around us. "I don't think I can stomach any more of your sad stories."

So I stretch out on top of him and tell him some of mine.

38

"What the fuck are Thaddeus and Myron waiting for?" Kade huffs and sits on the edge of our bed, elbows on his knees, his hands buried in his hair, which is still wet from the shower after our morning run. "It's been a bloody *week*."

I hook a finger under his chin. He tilts his head and the frustrated desire in his eyes dries the words in my mouth.

I manage a smirk. "My poor little demon. It seems your game has backfired."

It hasn't. The past week has been agony—excruciating, glorious agony. I used to go months without sex, for god's sake, now I can't last a week? My body is on fire and Kade is the only thing that can cool the heat.

Ironic, since he's a hotter-than-hell demon.

He growls, and suddenly I'm hoisted into the air. My thighs clamp around his waist. My spine hits the wall and Kade swallows my yelp of surprise, my hands pinned above my head. His mouth plunders mine with a merciless glide of tongue. I struggle to breathe. His hips flex, grinding his erection between my legs. Our moans tangle in the kiss. A sting barely registers—the taste of metal. It's all lost in the solidness of Kade and the throb of my pulse. He yanks his lips from mine, but my eyes refuse to open, my senses reeling.

"Shit-*fuck*," he pants. "Reiley. *Shit.* I'm sorry."

My response is part whimper, part hum of polite inquiry. My eyelids flutter. My heart ping-pongs between my ribs and the wall. Gentle fingers cup my cheek.

"Look at me, Reiley."

I crack open one lid. A flush pinks Kade's face. Colours sparkle in the depths of his eyes, and a blob of crimson smears his sexy bottom lip.

God, he's beautiful.

"Are you okay?" he says.

I lean forward, but one hand keeps me pinned, his lovely mouth out of reach. A whine curls in my throat.

"Reiley?"

I try to speak, but saliva floods my mouth. I swallow the metallic liquid. My tongue probes the inside of my lip. Sharp pain flares with the taste of pennies. My fingertips come away red.

"I'm sorry," Kade says, the sparkly light gone from his eyes. "I'll get you a tissue."

I tighten my legs around his hips and hold out my hand.

"Why let it go to waste?"

Wow, my voice is husky.

Kade goes very still. "Are you—"

I press my bloody fingers to his mouth. He hesitates for a second, then his lips part, wet tongue flicking out. He sucks my fingers between his fangs, and my breath catches. His tongue swirls around me. He takes my fingers deep, his dark, hungry gaze on mine. I sag against the wall, picturing that heat, that *look*, with his mouth pressed lower. Right where I ache.

It's almost too much.

A groan slips out. Kade smirks and gathers me close. Gentle kisses soothe my swollen lips, though there's no pain. I jerk free and prod at my mouth.

"You healed me," I gasp. "How?"

"Lust has power." He dips his head to whisper against my lips. "And you are a lusty, needful thing."

Christ, I'm kissing him again. Riding his body, begging noises in my throat. Bruising my mouth on his fangs. He rips himself away with a curse, head bowed, hands planted on either side of me, shoulders heaving.

"Please tell me this is hard for you, too," he says.

I lick my lips, tasting him and the lingering copperiness of blood. I'm trembling too much to make the obvious joke.

"This is torture," I whisper.

Delaying—*denying*—ourselves any gratification has left a constant ache. An ache for him. When I'm not with him, I'm thinking about him. Craving his touch, his voice. I love lying in the dark and listening to him talk, even if he's doing no more than holding my hand. I've never been this intimate with anyone, yet we haven't had sex.

Kade flashes me a grin, his damp hair flopping into his eyes.

"Thank fuck," he says.

We disentangle ourselves and I lower my shaking limbs to the floor, my back braced on the wall.

"So lust, huh? You've fed pretty well the last week. Seems like cheating."

He twirls a wet strand of my hair around his finger. Wet from separate showers. I'm still not that brave.

"Do you want me to starve, Reiley?"

My heart thumps despite his teasing tone. "Wait. Can you actually die without sex?"

"Of course. Just like you'd die without food."

"What the hell are you playing at, you idiot?" I gasp, and lunge for him.

My hands scrabble at his jeans—stonewashed grey today—fighting to reach the button. I get tangled in another of his cashmere jumpers, the silky-soft material the same colour as his eyes.

Is he malnourished? He doesn't look malnourished. He looks as gorgeous as ever—all high cheekbones, smirking mouth, and a body that should be illegal. Maybe it's not too late. How long can people survive without food—a week? More if they're not dehydrated?

Slim fingers trap mine against a warm chest. A chuckle rumbles beneath solid muscle.

"I'm fine, Reiley," Kade says. "I'm not going to keel over."

"But what if it takes another week? Two?"

He bends his head. His lips tickle my throat when he whispers, "Then I guess I'll have to feed on you."

Fangs scrape my skin. My kneecaps dissolve, but Kade catches me and I snuggle into him, my cheek pressed to the comforting thud of his heart. My palms slide around his waist and up the curve of his back to cup his shoulder blades. His breath sighs through my hair, his arms holding me close. I shut my eyes and melt into him.

My little demon gives good cuddles.

"You're going to be late," he murmurs.

I nuzzle his chest. "I'm always late. You're a bad influence."

He squeezes me tighter, then eases away. I take his hand and we walk to the kitchen. Voices spill from the open doorway. Marianne leans on the counter, sipping one of her herbal tea concoctions. Her gaze skips over Kade as if he doesn't exist.

"To answer your usual question, Reiley," she says with a smile, "no—the creatures have not yet appeared. In fact, that's why I've gathered everyone here."

Kade and I step through the doorway. The chatter of the Diviners stops, the tables nearly full. All women since Bryce volunteered to join the team watching my cottage. Kade sneezes hard enough to rip his hand from mine. He retreats into the corridor, his nose buried in his elbow, eyes narrowed. A pouch hangs around the neck of every Diviner except Marianne. Her bronze dress sweeps her sandals, a belt cinched at her waist. Annabel shoots me an apologetic look from the centre of the group, her fingers fluttering on the amulet at her throat.

I glare around the room. "Kade hasn't touched a single one of you since he used his powers to escape your torture dungeon. This is hardly fair."

"He makes them uncomfortable, Reiley," Marianne says patiently. "They are returning the favour."

"You hurt him. I think that deserves a little discomfort."

"He is a demon. We do what we must to keep ourselves safe."

I shake my head and grab two bowls, ladling in porridge and a scattering of nuts and blueberries. A drizzle of honey melts into the milky oats.

"I saved you a seat, Reiley." Elsie pats the chair next to her.

"Thanks, Elsie, but I think I'll go next door."

Marianne sips the last of her tea and sets the cup by the sink. "We have plans to discuss. I believe the demons must be watching your house, though we've seen no sign of them. They will be waiting for you to return."

"You're not using Reiley as bait," Kade growls over my

shoulder, his voice muffled in the crook of his elbow.

Marianne's gaze flicks to him. "Reiley can speak for herself, incubus. You have no say here."

I hand him a bowl and walk out of the kitchen. Marianne calls my name.

"If you want to talk to us, we'll be in the living room," I say. "And take off the demon repellent."

"Reiley, this is childish—"

We perch on the couch where Marianne threatened Kade when he was half-drugged. Rain scuttles on Loch Fitty in bursts of wind, the sky leaden.

The storm held off during our run, though the strengthening wind snatched my breaths away. Only Kade wiggling his arse in a pair of borrowed shorts had been enough to keep me plodding onward.

He shoves a spoonful of porridge in his mouth. "Thanks. That stuff feels like ants are crawling up my nose and chewing on the inside of my skull."

I swallow creamy oats. A blueberry squishes between my teeth in a bloom of sweetness.

"I thought they'd at least thaw towards you. It's not like you're antagonising them."

He chases a hazelnut around his bowl and avoids my eyes.

"Kade," I sigh.

"What? They treat me like I'm diseased. So I might be a bit aloof."

"More like smug and arrogant."

He grins. "It's what I do best."

A throat clearing draws our gaze to the living room doorway, but not before I watch Kade's playful expression fade to the mask he wears for everyone else. A challenge glints in his eyes, his face as cold and beautiful as a snowflake. Marianne ignores him, flanked by Elsie and Annabel minus their amulets.

"May we come in?" Marianne says.

Annabel holds up a cafetière. "I brought coffee."

I nod, and they range themselves on the seats opposite. Elsie sits cross-legged, her feet tucked under her bum. Annabel pours coffee for everyone but Marianne, who clasps her hands in her lap, her long hair tangling with the knife at her waist.

"I think we can all agree that our current situation is untenable." Marianne slides Kade a look. "The sooner we draw these creatures out, the sooner the incubus can leave."

"Trust me, old woman, I don't want to stay here any longer than I have to. Your hospitality is shite."

Annabel coughs and hides her face in her coffee mug.

I elbow Kade in the ribs. "What he means is how can we help?"

"I need you to return home," Marianne says. "Act like you've been on a trip and see if we can tempt the creatures out from wherever they're hiding."

"I'm going with her," Kade says.

Marianne's lip curls. "Absolutely not."

"You're not sending her alone."

"She will not be alone, incubus. We are her family now. I would not endanger one of my own. Bryce and his team are monitoring the cameras and streets. Iona's team will wait in the garden and surrounding grounds. As soon as the creatures appear, they will be dispatched before they can lay a finger on Reiley. Your presence would be a distraction, and an untrustworthy one at that."

Kade bristles. I lay a soothing hand on his thigh.

"They want Kade, too. Maybe more than me. They won't be able to resist if they can get us both."

I remember the greed in Myron's eyes. The violence. Promising to feed on my death and ruin Kade's face. I shiver. Kade covers my hand with his.

Marianne's eyes pinch, but her expression smooths when she focuses on me. "Are you comfortable with this, Reiley? I don't want to force you into anything. Elsie is about your height. She could take your place."

Elsie bounces in her chair. "Yeah! Those demons won't know what hit them. I'll get them for you, Reiley. Better than hiding in the garden."

"The creatures will not be allowed to enter the house, Elsie," Marianne says.

Elsie deflates before springing back. "Still—anything can happen on a hunt."

"I'll go," I say, and Kade's hand tightens on mine. "It makes more sense for Kade and me to be in the house and all your fighters to be on the streets. When do you want to do it?"

She glances at Kade. He gives her flat, black eyes.

"Today," Marianne says. "The sooner, the better."

39

A gold and orange sunset streaks the sky, the grey clouds from earlier little more than wisps, though the wind still whistles round the eaves of the Diviner compound. The light on the porch banishes the gathering shadows, ready to welcome us home if all goes to plan.

In a few hours, my demon problem could be over.

"Reiley?"

I jump at Kade's voice. He's standing in the driveway, hand held out, while I linger on the steps, my hair whipping my face.

Okay, *our* demon problem.

I take his hand and let him lead me towards the trees.

"Nervous?" he says.

I nod. "I know it's unlikely with a squadron of Diviners surrounding my house, but I really don't want to see Myron again."

I find myself rubbing my belly and force myself to stop.

"Thaddeus is worse." Kade stares off towards the darkening woods, his fingers stroking his chest.

"He was the one who tried to claw out your heart?"

Kade's turn to nod. A gust of wind skitters birch leaves across our path.

"Were they in your clan?"

"No, thankfully, or growing up would've been more of a nightmare. I might have run away when I was even younger, and died."

He almost died from exposure when he fled his clan at nine years old. He remembers being so hungry, it hurt. It gave him a phobia of running out of food. His cupboards and fridge are always stocked, though he wastes more than he eats.

Maybe that's also why he surrounds himself with women.

We enter the trees. The spindly shadows of silver birch stretch across the road. Darkness creeps between the trunks. The tiny hairs on my arms lift beneath my hoodie.

I hold up a hand. "We're close."

Kade halts. I kneel on the concrete and slide a piece of chalk from my pocket. The tip scrapes on the ground. I draw two symbols a couple of metres apart, both circles with careful lines connecting the words '*aperta*' in one and '*porta*' in the other. I cock my head, examining each ward with a critical eye. Loose chalk swirls in the wind. I stand, and dust my hands.

"That should be it."

Kade raises a brow. "Should?"

"Oh, demon of little faith." I grin at him. "I may be crap at knives and running, but wards are my thing."

Marianne was pleased with how quickly I understood the symbols and the meaning, my steady hand able to replicate all the basic wards and a few of the more advanced glyphs. She walked the boundary of the compound with me, pointing out each interlinked ward carved into the trees or painted on stones. As well as warning if a demon trips the barrier, the wards contain a gentle compulsion spell to keep people away. Non-Diviners find they take another route around the loch, their eyes guided beyond so they don't register what's happening in the compound. If they have a specific purpose for coming to the house—such as our pizza delivery guy and the postman—it overcomes the compulsion.

I step between my temporary symbols. A light wind tickles the hair on my arms, obvious now that I know what to search for. Kade approaches my chalk wards as if they're dogs preparing to bite his ankles. He darts through, shoulders hunched. The trees hiss and rattle their leaves.

"See?" I say, my smile smug.

Kade grins back. "Well, look at you. Reiley MacEwen—author and Diviner."

The toe of my shoe smudges the chalk, and the barrier closes with a snap deep in my inner ear. I shake my head to clear the strange sensation. We follow the road to the T-junction, and Kade's steps quicken. His Porsche waits exactly where I saw it over a week ago. He trails his fingers along the roof and buffs the driver's-side panel with his sleeve. I'm pretty sure he'd hug the sleek curves of the bonnet if I weren't here.

"Did the city boy miss his car?"

His fangs gleam in the darkness. "She gets lonely if I don't play with her."

"Don't we all," I mutter, and he smirks at me.

The lights flash as the doors unlock. I slide into the summer- and leather-scented interior. Kade adjusts the seat and pets the steering wheel, stroking his fingers over the gear paddles and buttons, reminding me of when I did the same. I clear my throat.

Stupid lumps.

"Are you okay, Reiley?"

I jump at his voice for the second time.

"I'm fine," I say quickly, but somehow keep talking. "It's just… when I came to get your stuff—the day you were tortured—I… had a little cry."

"You cried in my car?"

My cheeks flush and I stare at my hands in my lap, my fingertips chalky white. "Turns out seeing you like that—hurt and confused—hit me harder than I thought."

Fingers glide into my hair and cup the back of my head, turning me to face him. Soft lips find mine. The contact jolts to my stomach and sizzles outward, tingling in my toes. An eager noise shivers up my throat. I scramble into Kade's lap, ungainly in the tiny space despite my short legs. The handbrake jabs me in the thigh. I swallow Kade's laugh, still kissing him. It turns to a moan when I thrust my hips into his, our bodies pressed tight together. The solidness of him, the smell of him, drives me crazy. I need him to touch me.

I *need*.

On the other nights, the nights where we didn't just cuddle and whisper our secrets to the dark, we touched. Kissed. My hands explored until my fingertips knew his body better than my eyes—the dips and curves and hollows. The glorious planes of muscle and sculpted lines. Sometimes, we even left the light on.

He has a freckle on his shoulder blade shaped like a star.

The anticipation is immense. I yearn for release. Dream about it. The thought of Kade fucking me pushes me to the brink of climax.

I need him. Need him to fill the ache. I need to feel all of him—hands, teeth, the thunder of his heart, his dick deep inside me until we're one body, one heart, one breath, and the windows of his sexy little Porsche steam from our heat.

Goddamn, I want that.

"Kade," I whisper into his mouth, *"please."*

His hands squeeze my arse, grinding me against him. He rolls his hips and pleasure throbs deep, his erection straining through his jeans and mine.

"Tell me what you want, Reiley," he growls between kisses, his lips merciless.

I can't breathe. His taste overwhelms me. He is sex and heat and smoke.

"You," I pant. "I can't wait. Touch me, Kade. Fuck me. *Please."*

He groans low in his throat. I hook my fingers in his waistband and pop his button with one desperate flick of my thumbs. My addled brain can't figure out the logistics of how I'm going to get my jeans off while straddling him in the cramped space, but I get waylaid by the silky curve of his belly, the heave of his ribs. He kisses me like he wants to breathe the air from my lungs, and I'm ridiculously close to swooning in his arms. His scorching hands slip under my top and up my bare back. My fingers wrap around the head of his cock through his boxers. He's hot and throbbing in my palm, so hard I wonder if it hurts. The sound he makes pulses through my whole body.

Music blares from my pocket. It rips my mouth from Kade's, and my elbow rams the steering wheel, the blurting horn only slightly louder than the drumbeat trapped in my chest. All my blood has pooled south, so my mental faculties aren't operating at their best.

What the hell is that noise?

The song repeats, drowning Kade's ragged breathing.

Demons by Imagine Dragons.

"Phone, Reiley," Kade gasps. "Fucking hell."

His eyes are swirls of black and garnet that leave glowing afterimages when I blink. I collapse sideways into the passenger seat, my legs sprawled in Kade's lap. Shaking fingers hook the phone from my pocket.

"'Lo?" I grunt.

"Reiley, is everything okay?"

"Hi, uh… Marianne." My tongue refuses to cooperate, as swollen as the rest of me. "I'm—we're fine."

Wind crackles through the speakers. A siren wails in the background.

"Everyone is in position," Marianne says, her voice muffled as if she's cupped her hand around the phone. "What's your ETA?"

"We, uh… The wind messed with the wards, so that took a little longer. Say thirty minutes?"

A typical journey would take forty minutes, but I've seen how Kade drives. Fast and hard.

Heat flushes my already flushed skin.

"Don't forget to act normal when you get here," Marianne says, and hangs up.

What even is normal anymore?

Kade watches me through half-lidded eyes like banked coals, his head resting on the seat back. His jeans are undone, his boxers peeking in the exposed V, his cashmere jumper rucked up to flash a slab of skin. Rumpled and gorgeous.

A huge part of me—Christ, every part of me—wants to climb back into his lap.

"Marianne was right," I say, my voice still wobbly, "you *are* a distraction."

"Well, the old bat is wrong about the rest." He huffs out a breath. "I think I'm having a heart attack."

"Can demons get heart attacks?"

He cocks a brow at me and grabs my hand, placing it on his chest. His heart knocks against my palm.

I smirk at him. "Looks like you've met your match, little incubus."

He straightens his clothes and I rearrange myself in the passenger seat, my own pulse finally starting to slow. Slim fingers twist the key, and the Porsche roars. Kade revs the engine, his eyes on me, a spark of crimson in their depths.

"As soon as Thaddeus and Myron are gone, I'm taking you home," he says. "In a few hours, you're going to be naked and in my bed."

I gulp and Kade spins the wheel, tyres squealing. He guns the engine, and the car leaps down the road towards Edinburgh.

40

My house has that closed-up feeling, the air still and stale. I switch on all the lights to banish the shadows and any lurking demons, excluding the one behind me. I drop my bag of clothes in the living room, the first bag I packed for staying in the hotel and left in the boot of Kade's Porsche.

I tried to look like we were returning from a trip, but I walked the short distance from Kade's car to my front door as if expecting a blow. Shutting ourselves inside relieved the tension in my shoulders, though not the blip of guilt at hiding in the house while the Diviners risk themselves against Thaddeus and Myron.

I glance at the camera in the corner of the room and resist the urge to wave. "Do you think they'll come tonight?"

"If they've been watching your cottage this whole time, they will," Kade says. "They'll be furious."

I shiver and hug myself. Kade sprawls on the couch, his arms spread along the seat back. I pace in front of the fireplace, twirling my mobile between my fingers and glancing at it on every circuit.

Marianne promised to phone me as soon as it was over. Will we hear anything—shouts, scuffles, a disbelieving roar—or will they use wards to hide the battle from human ears and

263

eyes?

The screen stays dark.

"I'm making tea," I say.

Kade trails me into the kitchen and perches on a stool. I stare at the black panes of the window into the rear garden, seeing nothing but my pale reflection. In the opposite corner, my writing nook sits forlorn, the trees beyond tinted bronze by the streetlight on the road. The familiar act of brewing tea settles my nerves. Steam puffs from the kettle and it clicks off. My hands tremble, pouring the water into two mugs.

Are Elsie and Annabel watching me from the dark, crouched in my hydrangeas? The thought is comforting.

Kade and I take our tea and return to the living room. I force myself to sit beside him, my hands wrapped around the heat of the mug. The house creaks, and I jump.

"Just the wind, Reiley," Kade says.

My blood rushes in my ears. I count the seconds. The minutes. My tea cools, and I set it on the coffee table untouched.

"Maybe they've gone," I say with a hopeful lilt. "Maybe they don't care about us."

Kade places his empty cup beside my full one. "They care."

I check my phone. Still nothing.

"What if they're more than the Diviners can handle?"

Kade's black gaze meets mine. "Then we're screwed."

"You couldn't comfort me a little?"

"You want me to lie to you?"

"You have before."

He cocks a brow. "Have I?"

I open my mouth. Close it. Struggle to recall every conversation.

"You called my books trash."

"Actually, I said I don't read trash."

"Semantics," I grumble.

He grins. "Any other examples?"

"Your Twitter account," I say with relish. "And the takedown notice where you *lied* about copyright infringement."

"In real life, Reiley. Those don't count."

"The hell they don't."

"I was trying to protect you."

I cross my arms and wrack my brain. He's lied to me. He must have. Even a little fib.

"Having some trouble?" he smirks.

"Oh, shut up, you smug arsehole."

"You call me that a lot."

"If the cloven hoof fits…"

He captures my chin. His smile flashes fang. "I bet you called me worse in the beginning."

I glare at him in challenge. "You deserved it."

"And now?"

"You're still a smug arsehole."

He chuckles and leans close. His breath brushes my lips.

"You bet I am," he says.

My eyes flutter shut, my mouth half-parted. The kiss starts as a soft, teasing glide. My heart does a slow roll and drops into my stomach.

A distraction, but a good one. Snogging Kade will keep me from climbing the walls.

Is Bryce watching us on the monitor, his lip curled?

A crash thunders from the front of the house.

Kade leaps to his feet. I bark my shin on the coffee table. A wave of milky tea rolls across the glass and patters on the rug.

Two nightmare shapes darken the hallway between the front door and the living room. Leathery wings gouge the walls. Malevolence glints in jaundiced eyes.

"Pray, don't let us interrupt," the second figure says in a surprisingly mellifluous voice, "for this may be the last time you feed by choice, *incubus*."

I blink, my brain attempting to shield me from the horror of Thaddeus with blurred lines and blobs of colour. Something writhes on the border of his upper stomach. Bile squirts into my throat. Images penetrate the haze—red eyes, the slash of a pupil, four arms, two-inch talons. His skin is the shade of iron ore and dried blood, his only clothing a ragged pair of trousers.

"Your human is lucky," he continues. "She will feel my embrace only once. But you, incubus—you will go mad from it."

Thaddeus spreads his many arms, and laughs. The sound coats my muscles in frost and ices my joints. My breath locks in my chest. I blink, and it's a mistake. The wriggling blur sharpens to terrifying clarity. Wetness slicks my cheeks and, for a confusing second, I think my eyes are bleeding.

Tentacles squirm on the boundary between broad chest and abdominal muscle, marbled red and pink. Tiny mouths at each tip smack their swollen lips and reveal needle-like teeth.

Kade spins around and shoves me. "Run, Reiley!"

My legs seize. I topple onto the carpet in the space between the couch and the coffee table, my knife forgotten. My training forgotten.

A winged shape blasts overhead, and Kade disappears. A body smacks into something hard. A breath gusts out on a curse.

Writhing tentacles block my vision. The tiny mouths make sucking sounds and dance towards me. My skin attempts to crawl away. Thaddeus leans over, his smile pitying. He smells like the dark and forgotten depths of a cave.

"I will feed well from you," he says.

Doors slam. Yelling voices burst into the living room.

"Leave her alone, you overgrown octopus," Elsie chirps.

She leaps onto the couch and brandishes her knife, the blade swirling black, a shock of violet hair flopped across one eye. Thaddeus hisses, his teeth grey and irregular. He scuttles backwards, crouched low. His tentacles shiver in indignation.

I crane my head from my position on the floor. Kade and a semi-circle of Diviners surround Myron near the kitchen door. A shoulder plate and knee-length shorts are all the demon is wearing, his muscles thick and bulging in between. Kade's back is to me, but he doesn't seem to be hurt from his collision with the wall, though there's a divot in the plaster. Dust powders his black cashmere jumper. Myron sweeps his leathery wings, and bowls him and the Diviners over.

Elsie yelps, dragging my gaze to her. Thaddeus hoists her aloft. Her trainers kick air. The talons of his four, grasping hands shred her sleeves and pin her knife to her side. He pulls her in against his chest almost gently. Tentacles nuzzle exposed flesh.

"Elsie!"

My cry echoes above the grunt and roar of battle. Kade's head whips around, and he rolls to his feet. Next to him, Bryce sways onto his knees, his knuckles white on his knife, his normally warm brown eyes flat and hard and on Kade instead of the winged demon in front of him. Annabel and Marianne chase Myron into the kitchen. Bryce follows after a second's hesitation. Kade and the remaining Diviners advance on Thaddeus, hampered by the furniture.

I finally drag my arse off the floor and yank my knife free, nicking the heel of my hand in my haste. Blood stains the cuff of my hoodie. Elsie struggles in the nightmare grip of Thaddeus, whimpering low in her throat. I slash at the pulsating tentacles. Flesh crinkles in a wisp of smoke. Purple blood spurts from dark veins. Thaddeus bellows and hurls Elsie, her body colliding with mine and sending us both to the carpet in a tangle of limbs. My breath huffs out. The back of her skull thuds into my cheekbone, and coloured lights flare behind my eyes. Her weight disappears. I blink at the ceiling. The light silhouettes a head and shoulders—slimmer than Thaddeus, no wriggling appendages.

"Did he scratch you?" Kade says in a rush. "Did he bite you?"

His hands flutter over me, careful of the knife still clenched in my fist.

"I don't… I don't think so."

I sheath the blade, and he helps me sit up. My cut stings, blood streaking the creases of my palm. Elsie is sprawled on the couch as if tossed there. Her pale face makes her cobalt eyes huge and glittering. Circular welts ring her neck and weep red fluid. The living room is empty except for Iona hovering protectively over the sofa back.

"Are you all right, Elsie?" she says, and glares at Kade.

Elsie nods, her head bobbing rapidly while she holds the rest of her body still. Blood oozes through the rips in her sleeves. Her chest hitches on each breath.

"She's not all right," Kade says.

Iona sneers. "Don't pretend to care. You were spawned from the same ilk as those beasts."

Kade tenses, but I put my hand on his arm and he focuses on me instead. His lip is swollen.

I smile softly. "Can't you get through one fight without being smacked in the mouth?"

"They like to punch me in the face." He licks the blood from his lip. "They're just jealous."

Iona's scoff is interrupted by Annabel and Marianne trooping into the living room from the kitchen doorway. Annabel glides to Elsie, her voice a soothing murmur. Marianne frowns at where I'm cuddled into Kade on the floor.

"The creatures have fled. I've sent the others in pursuit, but I doubt they'll be successful." Her frown deepens. "Did you know they could glamour themselves invisible?"

"Shit," Kade sighs.

Marianne cocks a brow. "And you did not think that information would be useful? Whose side are you on, demon?"

"You're the expert, old woman. You tell me."

"You compromised the entire mission—"

"I knew, too," I blurt. "I saw Myron after he attacked us—the wavering hid his whole body. I didn't even consider what it would mean for tonight. I'm sorry."

Marianne barely spares me a glance. "You are a novice, Reiley. That's to be expected. But *him*—he kept that knowledge in order to sabotage our trap."

"The hell I did," Kade growls.

Marianne gives him a tight smile. "How apt you mention hell. I should have sent you there the minute I found you."

She reaches for the knife at her belt. Kade and I jump to our feet in complete synchrony. Annabel whistles long and loud, and we all freeze.

"I don't think I'm all right," Elsie whispers, and vomits blood on my carpet.

<h1 style="text-align:center">41</h1>

Swollen wounds circle Elsie's neck and the backs of her hands, oozing yellow pus. The smell catches in my throat in her small bedroom, cramped from the press of nearly every Diviner in the compound. She lies on her bed, the sheets damp and twisted. I brush a lock of limp hair off her forehead. Her skin is hotter than Kade's.

Marianne banished him from the room before we stripped off Elsie's shirt to examine her injuries, the journey back to Loch Fitty made in a speeding convoy. Kade travelled alone in his Porsche, my bag returned to the boot, while I cradled Elsie's head in my lap in the Volvo SUV with Marianne and Annabel.

Ragged bites stipple Elsie's torso where the tiny mouths mauled her through her clothes, chewing the material along with her flesh. Her bra is the same colour as her hair, bright against her pale and clammy skin. Inflamed claw marks stripe her arms.

They remind me of that stormy April night, Kade at my door, wounded and shaking.

"His talons are poisonous," I say through numb lips, the chill in my body at odds with Elsie's burning frame. "Thaddeus. It's how Kade came to me—clawed half to death. Sick. He would have died without help."

Marianne snaps her fingers. "Get the incubus in here. It's time for him to earn his keep."

Her words have barely penetrated when Kade is herded through the door muttering, "Make up your mind, old woman."

The gathered Diviners part to let him pass, jerking away from his proximity. A bruise borders his swollen lip. The sleeves of his cashmere jumper are rolled up, showing delicate forearms. Marianne points a finger at him, then gestures to Elsie writhing on the bed in only her bra and trousers.

"Heal her," she barks.

Kade's gaze flies to me. Something lost and stricken flits across his face before it's smothered by his usual arrogant expression.

"You want me to have sex with her?" he drawls.

I smother a flare of jealousy at the thought of him touching anyone else, even to help Elsie. I want to be the only one he touches. My monogamous incubus.

I'm such an idiot.

Revulsion shivers over Marianne's face. The other Diviners act like a dog has just crapped on the floor. Kade's fists clench at his sides.

"I want you to save her life," Marianne says through her teeth. "Reiley told me you suffered similar injuries and almost died."

Kade slides me a look.

I really should stop telling Marianne everything about him.

"She'll probably die without help," he says reluctantly.

Marianne curls her lip. "So do the only thing you're good for, and heal her."

Kade's shoulders stiffen. A muscle tics in his jaw.

"No," he says.

An angry murmur ripples through the room. My stomach drops into my shoes.

"As if I needed more proof that you are a malevolent force, you would let a young girl die when you can save her." Marianne gives a sharp smile. "You fuck everything that moves—am I to believe you're suddenly prudish?"

The angry murmuring swells. Fingers grip knives. Marianne scans the faces of her Diviners and finishes on me, her expression close to pity.

"And what of Reiley? Do you think she'll accept Elsie's death if you could have stopped it? Tell him, Reiley—tell him to heal her or your relationship is over."

Kade turns guarded, black eyes to me. My heart swells into my throat.

"I can't," I choke, and Marianne goggles at me. "I can't force him to have sex. This is exactly what he was trying to avoid when he fled his clan."

"No sex," Elsie croaks, dragging our attention to her.

"You're dying, Elsie," Marianne says patiently. "You'll die without his help, loath as I am to ask for it."

Okay, she's really not helping the situation.

"I won't—have sex—with it."

Elsie convulses on the bed, her hands fisted in the sheets. Agony shuttles across her face.

He doesn't have to have sex. He could masturbate over her like he did for me when my intestines were exposed to the world, transferring the energy with nothing more than a chaste touch.

I bite my lip to keep from blurting it out.

It has to be his choice. I love Elsie—she's like a sister to me. But I can't shame Kade into saving her, or threaten him with an ultimatum. Though if he watches her die and does nothing, I'm not sure how I'll feel about that. Feel about him.

Anxiety and indecision war in my stomach.

"Get the worthless incubus out of my sight," Marianne growls. "We will heal her ourselves."

Bryce pops from the crowd and draws his knife. Kade backs up, his hands raised. His gaze flicks to me, full of uncertainty and too much I can't read.

But still he says nothing.

* * *

An hour later, exhaustion grits my eyes. It's three in the morning and Elsie is getting worse. Her cheeks are flushed, but her skin is cold. Redness streaks from her wounds. Brown pus leaks through the poultices Annabel applied. Complicated wards drawn in Elsie's black eyebrow pencil border each inflamed bite and scratch mark. My spine still aches from bending over her, a headache pulsing between my temples. I had to redo several of the painstaking lines when my tears smudged the careful symmetry.

Disappointment and grief expand in my chest.

Kade could heal her. How can he do nothing? Does he care so little that he won't even do it for me?

Marianne, Annabel, and Bryce sit opposite me on the other side of the bed. Marianne ordered everyone else away to get some sleep. Silence fills the room, punctuated by Elsie's ragged breaths. Her eyes move rapidly beneath her closed lids.

"Do you believe me now, Reiley?" Marianne says, her voice tired. "An incubus will only do what's best for himself. He is sex and lies."

"Filthy, useless fucking demon." Bryce crumples his woollen hat between his hands, his black hair mussed and sticking up in all directions.

Annabel sighs. "Even I thought... for a second... he would help. That he was on our side."

"His manipulation worked well." Marianne tucks the sheet around Elsie where she's kicked it free. "I'm starting to believe the way he first offered himself to protect Reiley from harm was also a ploy. It got him exactly what he wanted—I sheathed my blade and allowed him to stay."

The door slams open against the wall. The three Diviners shoot to their feet while I'm still struggling out of my chair.

"Funny how you talk of ploys and manipulation, old woman, when you're trying to force me to heal."

Kade stands framed by the doorway, a harsh yet gorgeous figure in his black cashmere and stonewashed jeans. A triangle of hair falls across one eye.

Marianne cocks a brow. "Should I have asked you to do it out of the goodness of your heart?"

"Wouldn't have hurt," he smirks.

Bryce bristles with leashed violence. "Get out, *demon,* you're not welcome."

Kade stares until Bryce blushes, and Kade gives him a smug smile.

"Which is why making you three help me heal her is going to be all the sweeter."

Marianne wrinkles her nose. "You're going to rape us?"

"I do not rape," Kade snarls.

Some might say, "Semantics," but I keep my mouth shut. My stomach flutters nervously.

What exactly is he planning—an orgy on top of Elsie? I wanted him to volunteer, but there's no way I could watch that. Or join in.

Kade takes a deep breath, and his anger melts to arrogance. He hasn't looked at me the entire time he's been in the room.

"In fact," he says, calm again, "I don't even have to touch you."

Stars spill across his eyes. A prickling warmth swells through the small space. Only the edge of it brushes me, but it's enough to shock my pulse. Bryce jolts, the longing on his face quickly masked by panic.

"Not me," he gasps. "Nope, not again."

He hustles for the door, sliding his back along the wall to give Kade a wide berth.

"Who's useless now, *Diviner?*" Kade says.

Bryce scuttles away.

No wonder Kade doesn't have any friends. He's not exactly gracious in victory.

He turns his sparkly gaze to Marianne and Annabel. Annabel flinches, but raises her chin.

"If it will save Elsie, then do what you must, Kade."

Kade starts. It's the first time any of the Diviners have used his name without prompting.

Marianne gives him steely eyes. "Do your worst, incubus."

"Oh, it won't be my worst." He grins, flashing fang. "But you may feel different about me later, old woman."

Marianne's throat bobs. Elsie gasps a breath, and it rattles in her chest. Kade's gloating expression disappears.

"Sit down, both of you. This has to be fast."

Marianne opens her mouth as if to argue, and Kade barks, "Sit or fall—it makes no fucking difference."

Their bums hit the chairs. Power flexes outward, stoppering my breath, the air thick and heavy. Marianne's eyes widen before she tosses her head back, her spine bowed. Annabel writhes on the seat. I frown at Elsie when hands wander to places not touched in polite company, but I can't do anything about the noises they're making, except put my fingers in my ears. My cheeks flame at the loud groans, the pleading, the enthusiastic agreement.

Why am I excluded? Not that I'm jealous. Kade wanted three people. Surely I should've been subbed in for Bryce?

Kade leans over the bed and places a hand on Elsie's bare shoulder. The cries of Marianne and Annabel reach a crescendo. A shudder runs through Kade and into Elsie.

For a heartbeat, nothing happens. Then the red streaks in her skin start to shrink, sucked back towards the wounds. Her breathing eases. Her sickly flush calms. She blinks open dazed, cobalt-blue eyes. Her brow wrinkles at the sight of Marianne and Annabel panting next to her bed, boneless in their seats.

Kade slumps in the chair I vacated. "That's the best I can do without more."

I pluck a poultice from Elsie's hand. The wound is still raw and slightly red, but there's no sign of infection.

"Goodness," Annabel gasps. "That was—that was amazing."

"Annabel!" Marianne's shocked scold is somewhat subdued since she's having trouble focusing from half-lidded eyes. Her long skirt is rucked up to her knees.

"What the hell is going on?" Elsie says.

Relief weakens my legs, and I collapse into Kade's lap. His

breath huffs out in surprise. Or I'm really that heavy. I grab him in a tight hug and bury my face in his shoulder.

"Thank you," I sob into his neck. *"Thank you."*

42

An alarm wails and startles me awake. Am I late for work? Do I still work at The Spark House? No, it's dark. I must have set it for 5am. Time to write.

I slap at the bedside cabinet and knock my phone onto the floor, the screen blank. The alarm continues to wail. Something warm shifts against my back and groans in my ear.

"What the fuck is that noise?"

I join my phone on the carpet. A click, and light floods the room. I blink at Kade peering down at me from the bed.

"Why are you always on the floor?" he says.

Doors slam out in the corridor. Voices and footsteps rush away.

I gape at Kade. "The wards have been breached."

We hustle into our clothes from the day before, the cuff of my hoodie still bloodstained. Kade, somehow, is perfect and unruffled.

I stayed up and watched over Elsie until way past dawn, even though she insisted she was fine. When she finally fell asleep, Marianne, Annabel, and I planned how we could take a second crack at Thaddeus and Myron. I went to bed early evening, too exhausted to do anything but cuddle into Kade.

It feels like I only shut my eyes for a second.

Night cloaks the lawn through our bedroom window, stretching empty to the birch trees. No winged or tentacled figures.

Are Thaddeus and Myron invisible and flying towards the house? How did they find us?

I scan the sky, but can't see a wavering shape in the darkness.

We join the flow of Diviners into the wood-panelled hall. Marianne stands in a circle of worried faces, her own pale and pinched.

"Is it Thaddeus and Myron?" I say.

She shakes her head. "Wards have been tripped all over the compound."

"What does that mean?"

She sends Kade a pointed look. "It means we're surrounded by demons."

"They don't like me, either," he says. "Maybe you should form a club."

Marianne sucks a long breath in through her nose and turns to the waiting Diviners. "Everyone outside. Defensive positions just like we've practised."

"What about me?"

Elsie sways at the top of the stairs, dressed in boots, leather trousers, and a fitted shirt like most of the others. Bandages circle her throat and hands.

"Get back to bed, young lady," Marianne says. "Bryce, Reiley—go with her."

Elsie pouts, but shadows ring her eyes, and she braces a hand on the banister. Marianne, Annabel, and the rest of the Diviners spill out of the front door and into the night, a knife in every hand. Bryce hops up the stairs to Elsie's side and steers her towards her bedroom.

"Come on, Elsie. You need to lie down."

Kade and I troop along after their departing figures.

I'd feel guilty about yet again being in the house while the Diviners risk their lives, but last time the fight came to us. Thaddeus and Myron won't give up easily. And they've brought friends.

Elsie sits on the edge of her bed, coaxed by Bryce, then springs to her feet and peers out the glass. I strain my ears, but everything is strangely silent. Bryce hovers beside her.

"What's happening?" I say.

"They're facing off. There's a lot of them." She bounces on the balls of her feet. "I should be out there."

"You need to rest," Bryce says. "You're injured."

She presses her nose to the glass, and her breath fogs on the surface. "I see the octopus monster."

"Get away from the window, Elsie," I say quickly.

She takes a step towards the bed, pivots on her heel, and walks right up to Kade, her head tilted back to meet his gaze since she's shorter than me. He stares down at her, his expression carefully neutral.

"Thank you for healing me, Kade," she says.

His eyes widen and flick to me, then back to Elsie.

"You're welcome," he says.

Bryce screws up his face and glares at his feet. A roar rattles the window, and I jump. My hand finds Kade's. His fingers tangle in mine, squeezing tight.

"You were right," I say.

He cocks a brow. "About what?"

"Thaddeus is worse."

The night beyond the room erupts with sound—screaming,

thuds, yells. Orange light flickers.

Elsie pumps her fist. "They've killed one already."

Glass shatters. A huge, writhing shape drags itself through the window and crunches onto the carpet. Four arms spread wide as if in welcome, black talons flexing. The scent of wet stone and rot clogs my nostrils.

Thaddeus grins at Elsie, baring his irregular teeth. "You smell like fear, human."

Bryce sweeps Elsie behind him, shielding her with his body, his knife held straight out. "You won't touch her, demon filth."

Thaddeus chuckles. "You can keep the little pixie. I crave other flesh tonight."

His red gaze fixes on me, and the same terror that froze me during the battle in my cottage threatens to ice my limbs. My knees wobble, but I stay on my feet, my knife in my hand.

"I will taste you, like he has." Thaddeus glances at Kade, and his tentacles smack their lips. "Though my kiss will be a little different."

Kade plants himself in front of me. "You'll have to go through me first."

"Gladly," Thaddeus sneers.

Kade launches at the tentacled horror, and my heart leaps with him. The beautiful, brave idiot. I'm the one with the weapon.

A dusky arm snaps out, catching Kade in the ribs. He grunts and flies sideways, thudding into the wall and dropping onto his hands and knees, his head bowed.

"He is a lover, not a fighter," Thaddeus tuts. "We will break him quickly."

Four arms and a multitude of tentacles reach for me. In the centre of the mass, two appendages hang limp, black wounds gaping wide. I slash my knife in a wild arc. A scalding hand traps my wrist and crushes the delicate bones together. Teeth tug at my hoodie. Rubbery flesh nuzzles my breasts.

Kade jumps onto Thaddeus's back and buries his fangs in his throat. Thaddeus bellows, releasing me to claw at Kade. Kade shoves clear of the poisonous talons. Thaddeus stalks him across the room, growling deep and low. Garnet blood pumps from his neck and splatters the carpet. Bryce lunges, his knife stabbing down, and Thaddeus slaps him away without looking. Elsie attempts to catch the reeling Bryce and they end in a tangle on the floor, blood a stark crimson on Bryce's mouth.

"You taste like shit," Kade says to the advancing demon, wind from the broken window ruffling his hair.

Thaddeus snarls. "I will rip off your limbs until you're nothing but a torso for fucking."

I grip my knife in two hands and hack at the demon's back. His burning flesh smells like cooked mushrooms. A roar batters my ears. Thaddeus spins and I fall to my knees to avoid his flailing arms, my face level with his tentacles and all the tiny, suckling mouths. Something wriggles through my hair and strokes my cheek. I scream, and my knife punches out, sinking into flesh. I throw myself backwards, ripping the blade free. A liquid patter follows me as I scrabble away until my spine hits the wall. Thaddeus stares at me, his jaw slack. He takes a step, and his leg collapses. Blood spurts from a wound in his groin.

"Grab him!" Kade shouts, springing across the room to pin two of Thaddeus's arms to the floor.

Bryce and Elsie trap an arm each. I pant at them through a flop of hair.

"Stab him in the heart, Reiley," Kade says, his teeth gritted with effort. "He won't die from this."

"*You* will die for this, incubus slut," Thaddeus snaps.

He wrenches his arms, lifting Kade clear off the floor. Panic flits across Kade's face.

"*Now*, Reiley!"

I crawl on the squelching carpet, avoiding Thaddeus's legs and tentacles. His broad chest heaves. My blade slips easily between his ribs and stops at the hilt. Smoke tickles my nose. Red eyes widen, the slash of a pupil dilated and disbelieving. The demon's large frame convulses. Bryce and Elsie scuttle away. Slim, strong arms hoist me to my feet while I gape at the body.

My first demon kill.

Skin, once the colour of iron ore and blood, pales to grey. A sickly green flame licks from the knife wound in the demon's chest.

"I'll get the fire extinguisher," Elsie chirps.

She skips into the corridor, apparently rejuvenated by the death of her attacker.

"Reiley!" Kade yelps.

I whip my head around, expecting to see Myron swooping through the window like a huge bat. Bryce and Kade are locked together, Kade struggling to hold Bryce's knife away. Bryce drives him backwards, and Kade trips on his own feet.

His name lodges in my throat.

A blade swirls black and deadly, and aims for his chest.

43

Bryce slams Kade onto his back and straddles him. Biceps strain. Kade's cashmere jumper rucks up to flash a band of flat stomach. Curtains billow in the wind through broken glass. The stench of burning carpet fills Elsie's bedroom as Thaddeus smoulders. Desperate fingers grip Bryce's wrists, stopping the downward slash of the knife. Bryce puts his whole weight behind the weapon.

"You fucking tortured me, arsehole," Kade says, his voice strained. "You got off lightly."

"Stop making me want you," Bryce growls.

"That's all you! I'm not doing anything."

Bryce grunts and pushes harder. I grab his hands and bend his fingers the wrong way, yanking the knife free.

I step out of reach. "Get off him, Bryce."

His shoulders slump. He lies half-sprawled on Kade, his upper body lifted away by Kade's hold on his wrists. Bryce jerks his arms sideways and the sudden movement spread-eagles Kade on the carpet and brings them chest to chest. Kade's eyes widen. I reach for Bryce's collar, but I'm too far to stop him before he headbutts Kade or goes full animal and chews on his face.

Kade licks his lips. "Bryce, wait—"

Whatever Kade was going to say is swallowed by Bryce's mouth. Kade freezes in the act of bucking him off. Bryce kisses like he's drinking Kade down—his jaw working, little whimpers of pleasure shivering from his throat and muffling Kade's protest. His hips grind against the pinioned incubus demon.

My little demon.

I clear my throat. "Um, Bryce…"

Bryce pulls away, breathing hard and sitting up, his fingers splayed on Kade's chest.

"Fucking hell," Kade gasps.

Stubble burn stipples his cheek. He looks even more gorgeous when he's shocked and rumpled.

"God, I hate you," Bryce says, and punches him in the mouth.

Bryce sprints from the room and barrels past Elsie in the doorway, who hugs the fire extinguisher and gapes at him. Smoke puffs to the ceiling. A fire alarm shrieks. Elsie twitches out of her stupor and covers the conflagration on her carpet in a cloud of white. I kneel beside Kade and help him sit up, his hair mussed and flopping in his eyes.

"I probably deserved that," he groans, "but did he have to hit the same side as Myron?"

Fresh garnet blooms on his lip, the skin already swelling under the violet bruise from Myron's fist. Kade massages his jaw, wincing under the probe of his fingers.

"The poor guy probably needs some therapy after you," I say.

"We all will," Elsie says, attacking the last of the sickly green flames.

Dirty foam bubbles on the ash of Thaddeus, the carpet singed in a circle around his remains. The clash of battle filters through the broken window.

I squeeze the knife in my fist. "Does Bryce have another Dyrn-thingy?"

The fire extinguisher clunks at Elsie's feet. She frowns at the weapon in my hand.

"No, just the one."

"Crap. We need to find him in case he joins the fight."

"Great," Kade mutters. "Let's give him a chance to punch the other half of my face."

Bryce's bedroom on the second floor is messy, but empty. We thunder down the stairs as the front door ricochets off the wall and splinters on the charging form of a demon covered in lumps and spines. Garnet blood slicks broad muscle. Annabel leaps through the shattered entrance, her ponytail in a blonde trail behind her, and drags her blade across the demon's throat from behind. Thick liquid explodes onto the pretty paintings of Loch Fitty through the seasons. The demon tangles in a coat rack and thuds onto the polished floor. Annabel jams her knife between his ribs.

"Goodness, he was a quick one," she pants. "I chased him half-way around the compound."

"Have you seen Bryce?" I say.

"Was he not with you?"

I glance at Kade. "He, ah, left. He dropped his knife."

"Oh, dear. I haven't seen him." Her gaze falls to the smouldering demon at her feet. "Elsie, would you—"

"On it!"

Elsie bounds towards the kitchen. Crisp, night air licks through the broken front door, bringing a hint of smoke and metal.

"Can you watch Elsie?" I say. "Kade and I will find Bryce."

Annabel bites her lip. "I'm not sure you should go out there. You're not trained—"

"It's our fault he lost his weapon. And we want to help. We killed Thaddeus."

"The hideous tentacled one? Impressive." Annabel peeks over her shoulder, as if someone might be listening. "Okay, but be careful. Find Bryce, then come straight back. And don't tell Marianne I let you go."

I mime sealing my lips. We trot out the door, and I hear Elsie whine, "But how come they get to fight?" before the chaos on the lawn drowns her voice.

Flames dance on the grass. Diviners and demons run everywhere, screaming, roaring, grappling. Heavy clouds obscure the sky, the air damp with the promise of rain. Five Diviners stand in a line on the road leading to the house, firing arrows and protected by a cluster of other Diviners with knives to keep them from being overwhelmed. Demons howl and writhe on the ground, shafts bristling from chests and throats. Marianne attacks two demons in the centre of the melee, her sandalled foot catching one in the chest and driving it back while she drops into a crouch and slashes at the thigh of the other.

"Huh," Kade says. "The old woman can move."

A blur of white leaps onto the demon Marianne kicked in the chest. The creature stumbles and falls, Atka's teeth in its neck. Marianne dispatches both demons and disappears into the throng, her long hair twirling like a cloak, her dog at her side. I scan the clumps of wrestling people.

"No sign of Bryce."

Kade nods to the east near the boundary of the tree line. "Myron."

A dark shape flaps above the birches. Kade's eyes drop to my hand rubbing my stomach from the ghostly pain of slashes.

"We don't have to—"

A male scream comes from the direction of Myron.

"Shit," I say, and start running.

Kade's trainers pound on the grass in tandem to mine, though he soon pulls ahead. Out of habit, I sneak a peek at his arse. He skids to a stop, and I nearly collide with his back.

Myron dangles Bryce in mid-air, curved claws hooked in his jumper. Bryce has lost his woolly hat, and each beat of Myron's leathery wings stirs his hair. He scrabbles at the corded muscle of Myron's forearm. Myron fixes us with a jaundiced eye.

"I hope you've saved your energy, incubus, for many of us need healing. Perhaps I will let you keep your human so you can perform." He bares his yellow teeth in a grin. "And the rest of us can watch."

"Watching is the closest you'll ever get, you ugly fucker," Kade says.

Myron hisses. "For that, I will eat your friend while you do nothing. Then I will have a piece of your female."

Myron flaps harder, gaining height. The archers are at the opposite side of the lawn—too far to help us. Myron's mouth stretches wide, and drool glistens between his teeth. Bryce tugs frantically at the demon's hand. I grip Bryce's knife, tell myself not to think, and lob the weapon like Iona taught me. The blade slices through the air. Bryce screams. My knife sinks into Myron's bicep instead of zipping miles past the target like all my other attempts.

No one needs to know I aimed for his throat.

Myron roars and drops Bryce, who hits the ground feet-first. His legs collapse, and he slams onto his face. Myron rips the knife from his arm and tosses it deep into the trees. I draw my weapon from my sleeve.

"I will gut you with that, human," Myron snarls. "But first…"

He stoops for Bryce. Kade dives and tackles the Diviner as he's struggling to his hands and knees, rolling them both clear of the demon. Myron's taloned feet gouge clumps of dirt and grass. Powerful muscles bunch. He springs for me, wings spread, his wicked claws extended. Kade yells my name. I throw myself backwards and slash at Myron as he swipes at empty air and flies over me. With a sharp jerk, my knife disappears from my hand. I pant at the sky, my fingers stinging. Raindrops speckle my face.

Something mewls.

I scramble to my feet. Kade and Bryce slither to a stop beside me. Wings slap at the damp ground. Claws sink into the grass. Myron shivers on the lawn, split open from chest to groin, his intestines tangled in his legs.

I swallow hard. "Jesus Christ."

Bryce gags and clamps a hand to his mouth, mumbling, "Put the damn thing out of its misery."

"Karma's a bitch." Kade shudders.

I take a step closer to the stricken demon, searching for my knife. His whimper turns to a growl so deep, it rumbles in my gut. Wings thrash and hold me at bay. I notice the sudden hush a second before Marianne says, "Step aside, Reiley."

The leader of the Diviners strides forward and javelins the spear from the research department into Myron's chest.

44

Myron dies in a wash of flame as jaundiced as his eyes. Marianne yanks the spear from his chest, and his ribs crumble to ash. I scoop my knife from the wet grass, the swirly blackness slicked garnet. A crowd of dishevelled and panting Diviners surrounds us, their faces glowing beneath the soot and blood.

"Did you kill them all?" I say, a little awed.

Marianne passes the spear to the Diviner from the lab and brushes grass from her hands.

"We have defeated the demon scourge, yes." Her shrewd, hazel eyes slide to Kade. "All but one."

Kade throws his hands up. "Seriously, old woman, you're starting to piss me off."

Bryce shuffles forward and clears his throat. His gaze bounces from Kade to Marianne, then settles on the scuffed toes of his shoes.

"Actually, Marianne, he saved—"

"Marianne!" Annabel hustles across the lawn, Elsie in tow. "The house is on fire."

We turn as one to the white beacon perched on the edge of Loch Fitty. Orange and yellow light flickers in several windows on the ground floor. Marianne barks orders and the

291

Diviners scatter, leaving me, Kade, Marianne, Annabel, and Elsie on the gently smoking grass.

Bryce mutters, "Now we're square, demon," before scuttling off to join the others.

Kade smirks. "I think he likes me."

"Tell me, incubus," Marianne says, her expression grim, "how did the creatures manage to find us?"

"How the hell should I know?"

"It's a little coincidental that they escaped our trap only to appear a day later with an army."

"You took my goddamn phone," Kade growls. "How am I supposed to have contacted them—bloody smoke signal?"

"How else would they have found us so quickly?"

"They could have followed us from Reiley's cottage."

Marianne crosses her arms, the bodice of her long dress splashed with dark fluid. "It is impossible to trust anything you say or do."

"For fuck's sake—I healed your Diviner, didn't I?" He gestures at Elsie, who avoids his eyes and drills her toe into the mud.

"Ah, yes, but you had to be cajoled. You waited until the eleventh hour to help her, so excuse me if I don't treat you like a white knight."

"Come on, Marianne," I say. "That's hardly fair."

She shakes her head. "I tried, Reiley. I'm sorry."

"Sorry about what?"

I ease in front of Kade in case 'I'm sorry' means 'I'm sorry I'm about to ram my knife into your demon's chest.'

Annabel and Elsie watch our exchange with identical expressions of discomfort. Marianne gives me a pained smile.

"As long as you are under his influence, you can never fully be trusted, either," she says, her voice gentle but firm. "You must make a choice. Will it be the incubus—a creature of casual lusts—or will it be us—your family?"

Tears grip my throat at the soft regret in her words.

"What are you saying?" I choke. "If I stay with Kade, I can't be a Diviner?"

"Goodness, Marianne, you can't—"

"Yes, Reiley," Marianne says over Annabel's quiet reproach, "that's exactly what I'm saying. You're a talented, intelligent woman. Your ward skills surpass anyone else at your level. Don't toss all that away for a demon, no matter how pretty he is on the outside."

My breath hitches. Something like grief hollows my stomach.

The Diviners are everything I've ever wanted—family, acceptance, love. Badass sisters—and one brother—I can fight demons with. No more feeling like a freak.

But Kade...

I've never been so close to anyone, so intimate, even without the sex. He's complicated, vulnerable, cute. Sexy as hell. My skin buzzes with the need to touch him and inhale his summer scent. He's protected me, saved me. How can I cast him aside?

Elsie widens her shimmering, cobalt eyes, and swallows a sob. "Reiley, please stay."

Tears burn my cheeks. I send Marianne a pleading look.

"Marianne… I can't—"

"You just couldn't let it go, could you, old woman?" Kade says behind me, his voice harsh and low. "No piece of ass is worth this shit."

My body swivels to face Kade. I cock my head. Blink a few times.

"What?" I say.

Black eyes, as hard and empty as obsidian, meet mine. His mouth twists in a sneer. The prickle of his gaze sweeps me from top to toe.

"I mean, she's not even my type—short legs and no tits."

"Nice try, Kade," I say, though my voice wobbles. "You said you wouldn't hurt me and you only lie to protect me, so…"

"And you believed that? Christ, you're gullible."

The arrogance on his face is almost painful. No, wait—it's my breathing that's painful.

Annabel and Elsie seem to have frozen. Marianne's look of sympathy nearly cuts me at the knees before she returns to glaring at Kade.

"Thanks for getting rid of my demon problem, old woman. You can keep your pet author." Kade slices me a cruel smile. "I haven't fucked her yet, but I'm already bored."

"Stop it," I wheeze. "I know what you're doing."

"You have no idea what I can do, little human," he snarls.

A flare of heat gives a second of warning. Then—*desire*. Arousal. I'm drowning in it. Oh god, I'm hot, wet, throbbing. Touch me. I need someone to touch me and fill the ache. I yank at my clothes, stick my arse in the air, and make begging noises in my throat. Take me hard, fast. I want to hear the slap of our bodies. I want to feel you so deep, it hurts. I want—

I suck in a breath of cold air, and cough on the ash of Myron. Dew dampens my clothes. My pants are soaked, but not from rolling on the ground. A soft groan jerks my head around, my cheek on the chilled grass. Marianne humps the lawn, stops, blinks, then curses long and loud. Annabel is curled in a ball, Elsie crumpled next to her, their eyes squeezed shut. Worried shouts echo from the direction of the house, and the thunder of footsteps shudders into my ear. I prop myself on my elbows, my hair tangled across my cheeks, my pulse still swollen and confused. The grass stretches to the tree line, black and burnt and empty.

Kade is gone.

<h1 style="text-align:center">45</h1>

It takes two days to clean and secure the compound after the demon attack, though the repairs will continue for weeks. Marianne and I refresh the wards, the energy dissipated by the alarm spell, some damaged by the slash of claws. Bryce and Iona are searching for new headquarters since the location on Loch Fitty has been compromised.

One demon escaped.

Marianne has been extra gracious in my company, coddling me, making sure I have everything I need—coffee, a sympathetic ear, comfort food. She hasn't once said, "I told you so," but if she flashes me another understanding smile, I may scream. At least twice a day, she asks for Kade's full name and address, promising to take care of him, quick and quiet. I won't even have to know what happens. When I refuse to share, she gives me a patient look and says she'll listen when I'm ready. Annabel and Elsie are strangely silent on the matter, intent on trying to make me laugh instead. Sitting with them on the porch and watching the loch sparkle has helped soothe the ache in the centre of my chest.

I called the number for my little demon. A polite, robotic voice said it was no longer in service but I haven't deleted it from my phone. My Twitter account lost a few followers, including @DemonLover69, who blocked me.

Tidying the fire-damaged house keeps me busy during the day but it's harder to be strong at night, alone in my room. Alone in the single bed that seems too big and cold. I let myself cry for ten minutes then force myself to write until the words blur, and I fall into an exhausted sleep.

Reiley MacEwen—author and Diviner.

And nothing else.

* * *

"You're going to see him, aren't you?" Annabel steers the Volvo into my driveway. "Do you think that's wise?"

She switches the engine off and turns in her seat. The night settles in the car, her face in shadow. I fiddle with my seatbelt and avoid her gaze.

"Probably not."

I told Marianne I needed a couple of days back in my cottage, surrounded by the memories of my aunt, who had her own grief to deal with. She said to take all the time I need, but to call if I want to talk. And to not do anything rash.

I open the door, and Annabel stops me with a hand on my arm.

"Be careful, Reiley."

"He won't be there," I say. "He'll have flitted off to some exotic location."

"But you're hoping he hasn't," she says softly.

I stare at the ground, one foot on my flagstones, the other still in the car. "I'm trying not to think about it."

"Hope is wonderful, but it can also make the reality more painful." She squeezes my arm and lets go. "Phone me after?"

"You won't tell Marianne?"

"Of course not. Elsie and I just want you to be happy. What are sisters for?"

I wrap her in a hug. She smells like lavender and thyme. I wave as she reverses smoothly out of the driveway and zooms off down Old Church Lane. My bag of clothes hangs heavy in my hand.

My other bag is still in the Porsche of a certain contrary demon who may or may not be getting a kick in the nuts.

I scrub Elsie's dried vomit from my carpet and rearrange the furniture knocked askew in the fight. My fingers stroke the divot in the wall. I shower and dress with care—patterned silk skirt that hugs my hips and ends mid-thigh, tight top and heels. My hair spills over my shoulders, my make-up subtle.

If Kade is going to break his promise, and my heart, for real and not just for show, I'm going to look fantastic while he's doing it. Then I'm going to grind my shoe into his testicles.

The taxi drops me at his apartment complex. The bush that ate my bike in December bristles with tiny, yellow flowers. The 'Sold' sign is gone. I check my outfit again—quite different to my wine-soaked leggings or my dusky-gold hoodie and jeans. The last time, Kade carried me out, mauled and bleeding and unconscious.

I may feel like two of those things after our confrontation, but he'll be the latter.

If he's even here.

The label on the top button still reads 'McKade'. I buzz every flat except his. No one lets me in. Damn security-conscious rich folk. I linger around the corner, out of sight of the vestibule. Goosebumps prickle my bare arms in the cool night air. In the distance, cars rumble over cobblestoned streets, and sleepy gulls squabble on the roofs. After thirty minutes, a young couple approaches the flats, arms around each other, a takeaway bag clutched in the guy's hand. My heels clack rapid-fire on the pavement, and my fingertips catch the entrance an inch from closing.

I smooth my hair in the mirrored lift, swipe a finger under one eye, and reapply my lip gloss.

"You can do this," I tell my reflection. "Be calm, be confident. Don't take any of his shite."

I find myself wringing my hands, and force myself to stop. The doors slide open into Kade's private hallway. I suck in a breath and tip-toe across the polished floor. No sounds come from the flat, but my heart is thumping quite loud. I cover the peephole with a finger. My knuckles hesitate on wood.

All the hurtful things he said flash through my mind. He knew exactly where to land a solid punch. What if he's still as cruel and sneery as he was on the lawn? What if he has a gaggle of women in the house with him and they all mock me, like before?

Then I knee him in the balls, return to the Diviners to lick my wounds, and spend the rest of my life writing books and fighting demons alongside my new family.

It could be a lot worse.

My fist bangs on the door. I hold my breath and count my heartbeats—ten, twenty, thirty.

Oh god, he's gone. The bastard really meant it. The manipulative little wankstain deserves a fucking Oscar. I'll—

A lock clicks. My pulse rockets into my mouth.

Is there still time to make a run for it?

The door swings wide and bangs the wall. The knot in my gut loosens. I try to turn my sag of relief into a sexy pose against the door frame.

"Wow," I say, "you *can* look like shit."

Kade's blond hair is tousled and hanging over his forehead, his eyes human and red-rimmed, though the whites have a grey tinge, as if he's struggling to control his glamour. Stubble roughens his jaw. There are stains on his pale-blue t-shirt and, judging from the smell coming off him and the rum bottle gripped in his fist, they're mostly booze.

"What…" He licks his lips and tries again, his voice slurred. "What're you doing here, Reiley?"

"You and I are going to talk, truthfully this time and without any of your incubus arse-baggery."

His mouth twitches, but his face crumples into a frown. He spins on his heel, wobbles, then stomps away on bare feet, his spine rigid.

"I've nothing… nothing else to say. Shut the door on your out—*way* out."

I shut the door, but follow him into his living room. He flinches at the click of my heels. Plywood covers the pane of glass Myron jumped through, but the rest of the space is still a warzone—shattered coffee table, bloodstained floor, canted sofas. The dining table displays a scatter of takeaway containers. I listen for female twittering, but the only sound is a liquid sloshing as Kade takes a swig of rum, his back to me.

"Have some dignity, and go," he growls at the window. "I don't want you here."

"Look at me and tell me that, Kade."

He makes a frustrated noise. I step closer, and his shoulders tense.

"Just leave me alone, Reiley," he says a little desperately.

"You know, if you *were* that evil, you would've encouraged me to leave the Diviners for you, shagged me, then dumped me before I could put my knickers back on."

"Is that what you want—pity sex?" His laugh cracks. "Need to be *way* more drunk for that."

"Look at me, Kade," I say softly.

He gulps from the bottle. "No."

Stubborn demon.

"Well, you're obviously drowning your sorrows and if you say it's not because of me, I will kick your gorgeous arse out that window."

He bows his head. The rum dangles from limp fingers. A shudder runs down his spine.

"You're a Diviner," he says in an agonised whisper. "You can't be one if you're with me. You love it there."

"I do. I love the compound. Annabel. Elsie." My breath wobbles in and out. "But they're not the only things I love."

He frowns over his shoulder. One eye is almost completely black, the human blue submerged in ink.

"The old woman won't stop you writing about demons," he says bitterly, "but god forbid you touch one."

Another swig of rum. I step closer. He jerks around, nearly overbalancing, and grabs onto the couch. Liquid sloshes against glass.

"Not writing, Kade," I say. "What else is there—in this place, right now—that I could possibly love?"

He blinks. "I'm too fucking drunk for puzzles, Reiley."

I corner him against the sofa and cup his cheek, my heels giving me a couple of extra inches of height. Dark circles ring dazed black eyes.

"You," I say. "I love *you*."

The bottle clunks to the floor, spraying rum on my legs and pattering on his jeans. A flush pinks his cheekbones.

"What?" he says.

My thumb traces his bottom lip, still scabbed and bruised at the corner. His breathing is ragged and tickles hot across my fingers.

"You're my little demon," I say, "and I love you."

He whimpers low in his throat. His mouth collides with mine. Arms yank me against the familiar solidness of him— the chest and stomach and hips I've traced in the dark. We topple over the back of the couch and I land on top of him, legs tangled, lips frantic. Heat sizzles to my belly. He tastes of smoke and rum. Smells like summer and sweat. I shove up on my elbows, panting hard.

Even pished, he can kiss me breathless.

"When did you last shower?"

His forehead wrinkles. "What day is it?"

"Sunday."

"Maybe Thursday. Friday?"

I shake my head. "You silly, sexy little demon. What the hell were you thinking?"

"I was trying to make it easy for you."

I pinch his ribs, and he squirms. "What part of that was easy?"

"I was being the good guy," he says, his eyes half-lidded. "It's not worth abandoning your new family just for sex."

I snort. "We haven't even had sex and I'm in love with you."

He manages to open one eye, then the other, both black and vulnerable. He hauls himself upright until I'm straddling his lap. His nose bumps mine.

God, he's cute when he's sozzled and graceless.

"Say it again," he whispers.

I do. Again and again.

He buries his face in my neck. Trembling arms curl around me.

"I love you, too, Reiley," he murmurs.

I stroke his back. "You're quite soft-hearted, for a demon."

His chuckle warms my throat and teases my pulse.

"Don't tell anyone," he says.

46

Kade's soft breaths fill the room. A shaft of daylight stripes the bed and highlights gold streaks in his hair.

He likes to leave a gap in the curtains so he's woken by the sun on his face.

I watch him sleep, curled on my side, my palm on his chest over the steady beat of his heart. Cool silk caresses my bare legs.

Last night, after I coaxed a drowsy Kade into the shower, I called Annabel to update her. She seemed happy for me despite the consequences of Marianne's ultimatum. I thought about sneaking around behind Marianne's back—having my demon and eating it, too, if you will—but dismissed the idea.

My aunt kept her demon a secret and look how that ended.

Kade mumbles, and I wriggle closer. The warmth of him slides through my borrowed t-shirt. It smells like him—a long, lazy nap in hot grass. A triangle of hair has flopped across his forehead, and I brush it back. His eyelids flutter to half-moons of black.

He gives me a sleepy smile. "Hey."

An ache swells in my chest. I stroke the smooth line of his jaw and the roughness of a cut where he nicked himself shaving half-sozzled in the shower. A blue bruise fans from the corner of his mouth to the bottom of his cheek.

"Hey," I say, my voice husky.

He captures my hand and kisses the knuckles. My stomach swoops.

"You're in my bed." His smile widens to a wicked, fang-flashing grin. "And we're all alone."

Hello, squiggles.

Kade rolls on top of me and chuckles at my yelp. My breath catches at the weight of him, the press of his hips. All the days of denial, the hours of exquisite torture without release—the teasing, the touching—flare beneath my skin like a banked coal suddenly exposed to a lick of wind.

Kade shudders. "Fucking hell, Reiley."

My pulse clogs my throat. I can't do anything but blink at him. Garnet swirls in his dark, hungry eyes.

He smirks. "You're going to scream my name so fucking loud."

"Aren't you hungover?" I squeak.

He bends his head and nuzzles my neck. A sharp tooth scrapes skin. My pulse ping-pongs into my mouth.

"I have a great metabolism," he says.

I should brush my teeth. Morning breath isn't sexy. Maybe I should shower first, too.

What if I'm a disappointment after all this anticipation?

Kade props himself up. "Still worried I'll break your heart?"

"You're more likely to break you own trying to be the good guy," I say. "But you make me nervous."

Before I fell asleep, wrapped in his arms in his orgy-sized bed, he told me what happened after he'd walked away, leaving me writhing on the grass in a fog of arousal. He almost crashed his car. He made it to the motorway before he was forced to stop, hunched over the steering wheel, shaking. He said it felt like Thaddeus had his claws in his chest all over again—sinking deep, tearing at him. Aiming for his heart. Ten minutes of berating himself got him moving to a twenty-four-hour off-licence and a clinking bag of booze, the clerk eyeing him warily due to his monosyllabic grunts and sunglasses despite the middle-of-the-night hour. Then back to his fancy penthouse to drink himself unconscious.

My poor little selfless idiot of a demon.

Kade's smile is shy. "But it's good nerves, right?"

A million tiny wings flutter in my stomach.

"Oh, yeah," I say.

He teases my mouth with gentle kisses. The dip of his tongue curls heat in my belly. His hands slip under my t-shirt and scorch up my ribs.

"Incubus demons get nervous, too," he whispers over my choppy breaths.

My t-shirt disappears somewhere in the expanse of the bed until I'm sprawled beneath him in nothing but red, lacy underwear. Fingertips trace the scars on my chest with the same reverence he showed in our tiny bed at the compound on Loch Fitty. This time, though, he bends his head and his hot mouth captures a nipple.

"I didn't mean the tits and legs thing," he mumbles around me. "I happen to like your tits."

"Glad to hear it," I gasp, my spine bowed.

His lips curve against my breast. Two more minutes of his clever mouth send my pulse thudding deep, the ache of need stretching my skin and hollowing my gut. Kade scoops me upright, our legs entwined, and snogs the last of my breath away. My hands creep under his t-shirt to silken muscle and the swell of ribs. I hook my fingers in the waistband of his boxers and brush his erection. The sound low in his throat has me squirming against him. He crushes me closer, grinding himself into me, and the friction is enough to start that slow, glorious burn. He eases away, and it draws a whimper from my lips.

"Christ, Reiley," he groans. "You're making it hard to keep my promise."

"Screw five orgasms," I say. "Just fuck me, Kade. *Please.*"

He spins me around, jerking me onto my knees, one arm around my middle, his erection pressing into my arse.

"And you think I'm the one with powers," he growls.

He cups between my legs over my underwear. Pleasure swells outward. My head flops back onto his shoulder, my heart in my mouth and as swollen as the rest of me. His fingers tickle along the waistband of my pants.

"I finally get to touch you properly after *weeks* of wanting," he whispers in my ear. "I have to punish you a little."

My moan is half-protest, half-greedy abandon. I'm so horny, I may just climax from one swirl of his hand.

His finger circles my clit and glides lower, sliding inside me. Kade swallows my sob of his name, his mouth merciless on mine. My hips buck against his hand, two fingers stroking inside me. A warm heaviness builds and throbs, trembling on the edge of bursting. I hold my breath. My heart thunders. Kade steals his glorious hand away.

"God, I can feel how close you are," he says, his voice rough. "You taste so good."

He fixes his teeth in my shoulder, and growls. The vibration tingles to my belly.

"Kade, please," I whine.

He shudders against my back. "Tell me what you want, Reiley."

"Let me come. *Please.*"

He chuckles. "I'm just getting started."

The magical fingers return, stroking deep inside while the heel of his hand pumps against my clit. Heat washes through me, and I spasm in his arms. He cuddles me in the dazed afterglow, my smile decidedly goofy, waves of pleasure lapping to my toes. He lays me down, covers me with his body, and kisses me back to life.

And, since the damn guy is made of crack, I want more.

"Take off your clothes," I say.

He smirks. "You first."

He scoots backwards, trailing his mouth down my body—collarbone, the swell of my breast, the curve of my stomach, hipbone, thigh. He slides my pants off, exposing me completely, and his dark eyes drink me in. His grin holds the promise of pleasure and pain. My lashes flutter, unable to meet the intensity. Strong hands spread my legs. Slim fingers massage upwards. His mouth brands the inside of my thigh, and I gasp.

"I liked biting you here," he says.

A rush of arousal leaves me tingling and woozy.

"Do it."

"Not yet."

He purrs at my whimper. His black gaze pins me, swirling garnet mixed with specks of violet and gold. Beautiful. He places a soft kiss between my legs, and I lose a couple of minutes. When I finally refocus on him, his tender smile sends my gut all a-squiggle.

"What else am I great at, Reiley?"

"Everything," I sigh.

He laughs. "True, but more specific."

His tongue circles my clit, hot and wet and amazing. My whole body convulses on the bed, my hands fisted in silk.

"Oral," I moan. "You're great at oral."

I remember him offering to avoid his first pegging. How quickly his uncertainty was overwhelmed by sensation. His glorious noises as he surrendered.

"Look at me, Reiley," he says. "Watch while I make you come."

"Oh god, Kade, I can't."

Despite my words, I manage to prop myself on my elbows, dazed by the expression on his face. The effort quivers in my stomach muscles. He sucks until I feel the solid press of fangs on delicate flesh. I cry out, boneless and shaking, and he stops until I'm able to blink at him again, his smile wicked.

"God, I want to fuck you so bad right now," he says.

Somewhere in the garbled sounds from my mouth there's a desperate, "Please, Kade."

He dips his tongue inside me, lapping from my opening to my clit, over and over and over. Watching him is unbearably erotic—his mouth between my legs, those black eyes on me and framed by a cage of hair, fingers clenched on my thighs. The pleasure crests in a stunning wave, and I shout his name so loud, it echoes.

He hums in appreciation. "That was worth the wait."

He crawls up my limp body. He tastes like heat and smoke and sex. I tug at his t-shirt, hampered by my trembling muscles. He pulls it over his head and flings it away. My fingers caress hard muscle and soft skin. I aim for his boxers, but his mouth on my throat freezes all motor function. My pulse hammers beneath his lips.

"Bite me," I whisper.

A smile curves against vulnerable flesh. "I love you, Reiley."

Fangs prick my neck—a tiny stab of pain, then… Oh, holy hell. He wasn't lying when he said he didn't use any incubus voodoo crap the last time he bit me.

But he uses it now.

A throbbing line forms from his mouth to thud in my stomach and flare between my legs with each beat of my heart. His jaw works, the suction overwhelming, but instead of draining me, pleasure fills my skin, stretching me tight. I'm vaguely aware of Kade sprawled across me, his bare chest scorching, the glorious suck of his mouth and the lap of his tongue on my throat. The orgasm detonates from my core, and I scatter into a thousand fluttering pieces. His lips find mine—copper and heat.

"Say something if you're all right, Reiley."

I get the impression he's been asking for a while.

"What?" I croak.

"Good enough," he says.

He shifts. A packet crinkles. Fingers tangle in mine and stretch my arms above my head, pinning my hands to the bed. It teases my eyes open, though I have some trouble focusing on Kade as he holds himself off me. No bruises mar his face. His gentle smile and shaking arms don't help the burn of emotion in my chest.

"You are perfect," he says.

"You're just saying that because I'm naked."

His mouth twitches. "Naked and mine."

"Naked and yours," I whisper.

He sheaths himself inside me, and our identical sighs float

to the ceiling. I tilt my hips, taking him deeper. He groans in my ear and grips my hands tight. The long, slow glide of his body punishes my heartbeat. My muscles weep, gloriously abused. Tingles and pressure build where he's speared me. On each thrust, he does something with his hips that rubs his cock against a wonderful, aching part inside me. I pant his name. His rhythm falters.

"Ah, fuck," he moans.

"Are you okay?"

"Give me a minute. I need to think about Thaddeus. Or starving children."

I laugh at the consternation on his face. The movement clenches my muscles around him, and panic flits through his lovely eyes.

"Is my little demon struggling to last?" I purr, and arch my spine.

"Reiley, wait," he says, frantic.

I push against his hands, using the leverage to drive myself onto him, flexing my hips and stroking him inside me. My name catches in his throat, and his loss of control throws me over the edge. We fall together, slick and quivering, but before I have even a second to recover, heat builds where our bodies are joined—hands, hips—and the second orgasm sends me writhing underneath him, sobbing his name as fast as I can draw breath.

"Five," he gasps, and collapses on top of me. "That's fucking *five.*"

47

"Are you absolutely certain this is what you want, Reiley?" Marianne says, her voice a little tinny through my phone speaker. "You're choosing the incubus over your own people?"

I twirl myself in Kade's office chair, my toes on the thick carpet. The setting sun slants orange light through the windowed wall of his study.

I hunch at the reproach in her tone. "I'm sorry, Marianne, but you forced this on me. Kade is no threat to you or the Diviners. He loves me."

"Lust is not love, Reiley," she scoffs. "Just how skilled in bed is he?"

My heels hit the floor, and I stare at my phone on the desk. If Kade were here, no doubt his response would be, "More skilled than you'll ever know, old woman," but he's in the hot tub on the roof, enjoying the last warmth of the day and reading my final draft of book eight, *Demon Mate.*

Before I can splutter a reply, Marianne huffs a breath that crackles through the speaker. "My apologies, Reiley—that was inappropriate. I'm just very disappointed with your decision."

"A decision I didn't want to make in the first place," I say softly, a catch in my throat.

It's been two weeks since I confronted Kade and ended his

martyrdom. I convinced Marianne I needed more alone time to grieve. In reality, I couldn't drag myself away from Kade, especially not for a conversation I wanted to avoid. The day of five orgasms became eight only a few short hours later and it's been like that ever since. He wasn't lying when he said he'd get me fit. I have more muscle definition from the sex than from running at Loch Fitty, for god's sake.

The guy really is made of crack.

I freaking love it.

"I'm sorry, Reiley," Marianne says, sounding like she means it. "I wish it didn't have to be this way, but I must do everything in my power to protect my Diviners. A demon can never be trusted."

I don't bother arguing. I thought the same.

"I understand, but you have to promise me you won't hunt Kade," I say firmly. "Leave him alone and he'll leave you alone."

He was terrible at that with me, but I'm glad he was such a pain in the arse. He was trying to protect me.

She tuts. "Be reasonable, Reiley."

"If it wasn't for your mistrust and the slaughter of her demon, my aunt would still be alive."

"That's hardly the case—"

"*Marianne.* Promise me."

She heaves another heavy sigh. "Then, under duress, I promise, but the incubus is your responsibility. Should the creature return to preying on women, I will not hesitate to track him down."

Why does she still refuse to call him Kade? Maybe she thinks saying his name will make him appear, like a sexy Beetlejuice.

"He's not going to prey on other women," I say.

I don't tell Marianne he can strut down Princes Street and

feed on the lust he creates like he's licking an ice cream cone.

"When he inevitably loses interest, come find us," she says as if I haven't spoken. "There will always be a place for you here."

There should be a place for me there right now!

I bite my lip on the burst of furious words.

"Thank you, Marianne," I say in a mild voice, "but he's not going to get bored of me."

She wisely keeps silent, and we hang up less than a minute later. I text Annabel and Elsie and two pings come back, one message measured, the other an abbreviated and emoticon-heavy teen-speak I struggle to decipher. Although it's not been explicitly stated by Marianne, the implication is that all contact with me should cease. Annabel and Elsie both agreed that was ridiculous. We arrange a coffee date at my house for next week.

I get to keep the best part of being a Diviner—family. Who wants to fight demons anyway? I'd rather stay at home and snuggle with mine.

I smile and run my fingers over Kade's fancy Macbook, tucked to the side of his desk. I wonder how he's finding *Demon Mate*. Similar to the plot in *Demon Lover*, the protagonist falls for the very creature she's hunting, but she resists, scarred from the first betrayal. The demon has to work for her trust. Prove his loyalty. Just like Kade. As soon as it's published, the book will join the seven on his shelf, freshly creased.

I tuck the chair beneath his desk and skip up the two flights of stairs to the roof. A pleasant breeze blows the scent of mown grass from The Meadows below. Kade sits with his back to me, droplets of water gracing the sweep of his shoulders, his hair dark and wet and slicked to the side. My hand aches to cup the vulnerable nape of his neck. The purr of the hot tub and the burble of water are soothing on the private terrace, no risk of being spied on even through the glass of the balcony. A tumbler of wine rests on the tile at Kade's elbow, the liquid deep garnet in the glow of sunset. He flicks a finger across his tablet, turning the page, careful to hold the device clear of the bubbles.

I've slept at his house every night for the last two weeks. After seven days of marathon sex, we settled into a routine. Each morning, he drops me at my cottage to write and get on with the business of maintaining my author career now that I'm killing it. Mrs Dounray scuttles over at the first rumble of his Porsche in the driveway, practically throttling her puff of a chihuahua in her haste to coo at Kade. The first time she saw him, she flushed as pink as her fluorescent leggings. He'll swing back round at lunch, bringing food and coffee, and hang out, amusing himself while I do some marketing or we'll watch an afternoon movie, cuddled on the couch, or go for a walk.

If he's been good—which, let's be honest, he always is—I'll peg his sweet arse, but only after he begs me for it. I tie him to the bed or a chair or bend him over my writing desk and tease him until he's squirming and making the most delightful noises. I give him what he wants until he's limp and trembling, and I can barely stand. He loves when I scold him for being a messy little demon.

We'll clean up—often fooling around in the shower—and head out for dinner or eat at his house, then more sex, and bed.

Who knew life could be so perfect?

I unzip my hoodie. Kade, an incubus demon well-versed in

the sounds of a woman disrobing, glances over his shoulder, and grins.

"This may be your best yet," he says. "Part of me wants to keep reading, even though you're getting naked."

"Who says I'm getting naked?"

I strip down to my underwear while he smirks at me, tenderness sparking violet and gold and emerald in the black of his eyes. I gasp at the heat of the tub and nestle into the front of his body, his hands on my stomach pulling me closer, my blood pulsing deep at the feel of slick skin and hard muscle against my back. He tucks my hair behind my ear and trails his lips down my throat, teasing my bra strap off my shoulder with his mouth.

"How'd it go?" he mumbles on my flushed skin, little nips of his fangs making me shiver.

"Exactly as predicted." My words hitch as his fingers dip into my bra.

His hands pause in their skilful ministrations. "I'm sorry you had to choose."

I crane my neck to look at him, sliding my fingers into his hair. He gives me a gentle smile, and lowers his head.

"I'm not," I whisper against his lips.

Because in the end, the choice was easy.

Free Bonus Scene

Thank you for reading my book! For a bonus scene from Kade's point of view, exclusive only to members of my mailing list, join at nadinelittle.com/bonus-scene by scanning the QR code below:

Wasn't Kade just the best soft-hearted and misunderstood little demon? Leave me a review and let me know. Every review will bring new readers and give them the joy of Kade getting his pegging comeuppance. It needs to be shared with the world!

Can't wait to hear from you :)

Order the Next Book in the Series:
Give the Devil Her Due

Seraphina: angelic name, for a demon. She escaped the lies of her clan for a better life. She has her coffee shop and her best friend. What more is there?

Jace: a Diviner with hidden scars. He's trained his whole life to kill demons. Can he see Seraphina for who she truly is before it's too late?

About the Author

Nadine Little lives in Scotland and is an ecologist who loves botany. She should probably stop writing a different biography for every book series, but it's kinda fun.

Working four days a week, she spends her Fridays having brunch adventures and sunny walks. Weekends are for writing. When she's not scribbling away, you can find her in her hammock or out sniffing the flowers.

For more on her books and a peek behind the scenes, sign up to her mailing list and follow her on social media.

You can connect with me on:

🌐 https://nadinelittle.com

🐦 https://twitter.com/Nadine_Little_

📘 https://www.facebook.com/nadinelittleauthor

Subscribe to my newsletter:

✉️ https://nadinelittle.com/bonus-scene